MIST OVER THE WATER

On Ely Island, the Normans are proclaiming their authority with a magnificent cathedral. Its construction means the Saxon chapel dedicated to St Etheldreda must be destroyed and, to those who revere her memory, this amounts to sacrilege. When Morcar, fishing for eels, is attacked and left for dead, his cousin Lassair is sent to nurse him. He tells a frightening tale of assassins in the dark and a brief vision of horror. Then the killers strike again... Lassair realizes more is involved than random violence against the eel catchers. The secret hidden within the walls of Ely Abbey claims more victims and, as she comes face to face with the brutality of the past, Lassair is forced to face a challenge that she fears is far beyond her.

Alys Clare titles available from
Severn House Large Print

The Hawkenlye Series

THE PATHS OF THE AIR
THE JOYS OF MY LIFE

The Aelf Fen Norman Series

OUT OF THE DAWN LIGHT

Mist Over The Water

Alys Clare

Severn House Large Print
London & New York

This first large print edition published 2011
in Great Britain and the USA by
SEVERN HOUSE PUBLISHERS LTD of
9-15 High Street, Sutton, Surrey, SM1 1DF.
First world regular print edition published 2009 by
Severn House Publishers Ltd., London and New York.

British Library Cataloguing in Publication Data

Clare, Alys.
  Mist over the water.
  1. Normans--England--East Anglia--Fiction. 2. Eel
  fishing--Fiction. 3. Fishers--Crimes against--Fiction.
  4. Detective and mystery stories. 5. Large type books.
  I. Title
  823.9'2-dc22

ISBN-13: 978-0-7278-7921-9

Severn House Publishers support The Forest Stewardship Council
[FSC], the leading international forest certification organisation. All
our titles that are printed on Greenpeace-approved FSC-certified paper
carry the FSC logo.

Printed and bound in Great Britain by the
MPG Books Group, Bodmin, Cornwall.

*In memory of the long line of my
East Anglian and Fenland ancestors,
with affection and admiration*

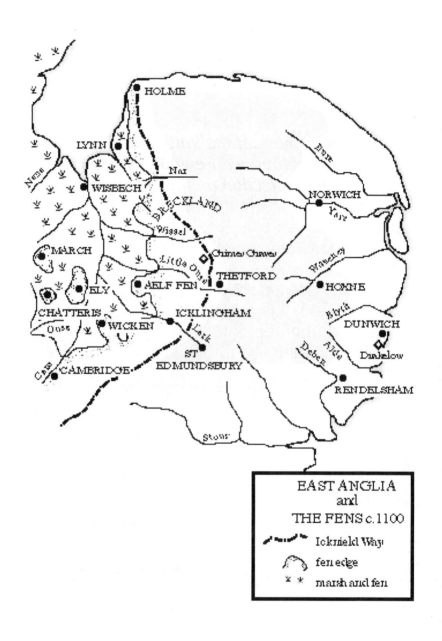

EAST ANGLIA
and
THE FENS c.1100

━ ⌒ Icknield Way

⌒ fen edge

✕ ✳ marsh and fen

ONE

It was raining. It had been raining all day and most of the day before. Now the temperature was dropping as light faded on the short, late October day and the incessant raindrops were turning into hard, spiteful little pellets of ice.

The man stared wistfully up the muddy, puddly track along which the last of his companions had lately disappeared. He wished more than anything that he could down tools and follow. The lodgings might be bare, basic, chilly and mean, but anything was better than standing hopelessly out in the cold rain. He sighed and once again hefted the long pole, noticing how the light of a flare up on the abbey wall caught the vicious, hooked barbs of the trident on its end. Then, for what felt like the thousandth time that day, he stood right on the edge of the steep bank above the stream and, focusing his mind, tried to seek out the dark, secret place where the eels lay burrowed deep in the black mud.

He waited. He lunged, thrusting the gleeve – the locals had taught him the new word – down into the slow-moving water. He felt the cruel points go down, down into the sludge of the stream bed. He muttered a swift prayer.

He drew the gleeve out of the water. The three

points dripped diamond-bright droplets back into the stream. They were empty; for the thousandth time he had failed.

He knew he was asking too much of himself, for this was a new skill and even the experienced eel men had remarked that conditions were tough today, as the drop in temperature had sent the eels deep down into the mud where they were undoubtedly going to remain. Nevertheless, all the other men had caught something; only he would return empty handed. It was a depressing thought.

His name was Morcar, he was about twenty-five or twenty-six – he was not sure – and he was a flint knapper. He lived in the Breckland with his widowed mother, Alvela, and such was his skill at his work that normally the two of them wanted for little. He could strike the flint by instinct and from his quick hands the flat-faced, glittering black stones fell in neat, regular shapes, all ready for building or facing walls. He was reliable and he was honest. By the standards of their particular stratum of society, he and his mother were considered quite comfortably off. But times were hard and everybody from lord to serf had to make economies. Nobody was building anything new; few men sought out the services of a flint knapper – even a very good one – when they were struggling to put bread on the table.

In this the third year of his reign, King William was proving to be an exacting monarch. He had held England safe from the attempt made two years ago by his brother, Duke Robert of Normandy, to seize it from him, which his dubious people were informed was something to be celebrated. However, Duke Robert's aim had been to unite England and Normandy under one ruler, as had been the case in the time of the brothers' great father, William the Conqueror – an aim both brothers shared. Duke Robert had failed to win England. Now it was King William's turn to make his attempt on Normandy.

The campaign had got off to a good start and Robert, alarmed at the speed with which his dukedom seemed to be slipping away from him, had desperately appealed to his overlord, King Philip of France, for help, who obliged with an ostentatious show of force. The wily William, however, had swiftly sent his French counterpart a huge bribe, which had sent Philip's army scuttling back to his own realm.

The bribe had to be paid for, just as did every single man, horse, weapon, wagon and its contents in King William's army, and the payment came from the taxes extracted from the people of England. It would have been hard enough in times of plenty, but the last two years had seen an unprecedented succession of natural disasters. It had rained in spring, summer, autumn and winter. In late summer a year ago, there had been a terrifying earthquake that had had the priests moaning and tearing their hair, crying out that God was furious with his sinful people and the only way to appease his wrath was for every man to give as much as he could and more to the church. The earthquake had seemed to be the natural expression of a climate gone mad; it had been so cold that the crops hadn't ripened until well into the autumn, and the meagre harvest had continued into November.

And all the time there was the constant, on-going worry of taxation. *The king is waging this campaign against his brother on the people's behalf,* the men of power said. *Pay up, it'll be worth it in the end!*

As if there were any choice.

People paid up. Then they scrimped and saved and tried to replace what they'd just had to stump up, only to have a further demand.

It was no wonder nobody had much use for a flint knapper.

Morcar had heard of the wonderful new cathedral that the Normans had commanded to be built on the Island of the Eels. The new rulers of England were building, even if nobody else was; they were busy stamping the land with their big, brash constructions that shouted out for all to hear that the old ways were gone for ever and a harsher order now held sway.

There had been a monastery on the Isle of Ely for more than 400 years, since the time of the beloved St Etheldreda who, despite being twice married, had maintained her maiden state and had finally been allowed to flee to the island, the gift of her second husband. There she had founded a double community for monks and nuns, becoming its first abbess. She died of a tumour on the throat and her grieving community had buried her in the monastery grounds, later moving her body into the little monastery church. The removal revealed a miracle: despite having been under the earth for sixteen years, St Etheldreda's body was sweetly fragrant and perfectly preserved, the tumour magically healed.

For 200 years, Etheldreda's community flourished around the sacred burial place of its beloved founder. Then the Vikings came. In the wake of destruction came resurrection; a Benedictine community settled on the island and the focus of their love and devotion was St Etheldreda's shrine.

It seemed to those who cherished and honoured the old ways that the Norman newcomers must be blind and deaf, totally insensitive to the precious, fragile atmosphere of Etheldreda's little church, where not only her bones but those of other worthy figures were safely interred. Showing scant respect, the Normans were knocking it down, and now a new, grand, showy cathedral was slowly rising up where once it had stood.

Cathedrals were built from flint, Morcar had thought when first he had learned about what was going on at Ely; from flint and stone. There was no work at all back at home so he had carefully wrapped his tools, shouldered his pack, kissed his mother goodbye and headed off, out across the heathland and then down into the Fens and over the water to the island. There, however, he had met with stunning, bitter disappointment; the new cathedral was being built not of flint but solely of stone, purchased from Peterborough Abbey and ferried from the quarry

11

to Ely on barges that wound their way through the inland waterways.

The masons, hard at work on the magnificent new building, had no use at all for a flint knapper. However, there was work to be had on the island for any man willing to do it, for the monks of Ely were paying their brethren at Peterborough for the stone in eels. Thousands of eels: some said more than 8,000 per year. The rich waters around the island offered a constant, generous supply of eels, and it was the obvious thing to do. Morcar had heard tell that in one year, an incredible 52,000 eels had been caught, but this fact had been related to him by a loose-mouthed drunkard, and he was quite sure it was an exaggeration.

Morcar had to earn money, for his own well-being and that of his mother depended on it. The poor and the hungry could not afford to be proud, so he bowed his head, stowed the tools of his trade safely away in his lodgings and offered himself as an eel catcher. It looked easy and as he watched and listened to the other men, his confidence rose. The eel were caught in a variety of ways, they told him, depending on the season. When the water was warm in spring and summer traps were set, but in autumn and winter the eels retreated down into the deep mud of the stream bed, where they could only be caught with the long eel gleeves. 'Them eels are made out of that mud, see,' an older man had informed Morcar. 'They disappear deep down there as the year fails, then in springtime out pop a whole lot more of them, fresh-made out of the guts of the very earth.'

Morcar, lacking the knowledge to agree or dispute, had merely grunted. Then he had taken his gleeve and set off to catch some of the huge population of eels that the dark fen waters provided in such abundance. Or so he had hoped; in five days, his total was eight, and he had only caught those because a kindly and more experienced man had helped him. In despair, he was on the point of giving up.

Morcar was nothing if not determined, however. Taciturn, slow to lower his habitual guard sufficiently to make friends, he was by nature a solitary man and, other than to his mother, rarely spoke more than a handful of words to anyone. Silence concealed not weakness but stubborn strength; now he ground his teeth till his jaw ached as he made up his mind. *I will try once more*, he decided, *and then I will call it a day*.

Perhaps his luck would change if he moved upstream a few paces ... Eager now, filled with a sudden, unreasoned hope, he hurried up the track, away from the abbey and the confusion of the building site, at last quiet as evening approached. Once again he took up his pose on the very edge of the high bank. Then he stared down into the water.

He waited.

What was that? Movement? Did his eyes play tricks, or was there really a dark, sinuous shape moving silkily through the water?

There was no time to think. Raising his gleeve, staring fixedly at the faint ripple just beneath the surface, he drew back his right arm. Using his left arm as a pointer, he sighted along it and then with all his strength hurled the gleeve into the water.

He knew immediately that at last he had done it; the heavy weight on the end of the gleeve told him so. Hurriedly, hand over hand, he drew the pole back to the bank, laughing aloud as he saw what was wriggling and struggling on the barbs. Quickly he reached for the eel – it was a large one, almost the length of his arm, black and shiny in the faint light – and, releasing it from the barbs, he dispatched it swiftly as he had been taught and flung it down on the ground.

In his jubilation he forgot to be cautious. Eager to collect his gear, his eel and at last head for his lodgings, he forgot the perils of the steep bank and the narrow track that ran along the top of it, slippery from the incessant rain and the many feet that had trudged up and down it. He turned too fast, missed his footing and tumbled down towards the water.

If he fell in he would probably die. Nobody was there to hear him cry out, he could not swim, the water was deep and the sides of the stream so steep that he would not be able to climb them unaided. Acting instinctively – there was no time for thought – he thrust his gleeve into the bank.

It stuck securely into the earth and brought him to a shuddering, trembling halt. It undoubtedly saved his life. Unfortunately, in his panic he had managed to drive its sharp points through his right foot.

He lay there shaking with shock. The pain had

not started yet – he knew it was only a matter of time – and before it did he edged himself up over the lip of the bank so that his shoulders and chest were safe on the track. Then he gritted his teeth and worked away at the gleeve until, with a nauseating squelching sound and a horrible grating as the metal spikes ground against bone, it ripped free of his foot. Before the agony really took hold, he gathered the last of his strength and swung his legs up on to the track.

He risked a quick look at his right foot. The leather of his boot bore two long, tattered tears – it seemed he had only speared himself with two of the three points – and he could see his pale flesh already dark with blood. A wave of dizziness washed through him, and he put his head on the wet ground.

I can't stay here, he told himself. *I must find shelter. Help. Clean water and cleansing herbs.*

With a huge effort he stood up. Using the gleeve as a staff, he picked up his eel and his pack and began to hobble back along the track.

Morcar pulled the hood of his new cloak forward in a futile effort to shield his head from the biting cold. The cloak was quite short, its hem reaching scarcely to his hips, and it did not keep the wet out nearly as efficiently as the merchant who had sold it had promised. Moreover, it stank of whatever animal fat had been rubbed into it. The rain had at long last eased and now was no more than a misty dampness in the chilly air. Tendrils of white mist were swirling up from the sodden ground, twirling around his feet and ankles.

15

He hunched his shoulders and pressed on. He was close to the abbey walls now, and the flares set high up to light the track illuminated the puddles. He was still beside water, but now it was a stinking, dirty ditch, all but stagnant, and he doubted there would be anything living beneath the scummy surface.

Something caught his eye. An eel? Surely not. But if it were, he ought to have a try at spearing it, for he had suffered so much that day and two eels instead of one would be a more cheering result for all the hardship. His foot was throbbing, each throb so painful that he all but swooned. Forcing himself to ignore both the agony and the sensible voice in his head urging him to get back to his lodgings immediately and stop being such a fool, he put down his pack and the dead eel and once more raised his pole.

Whatever was down there under the water did not seem to be moving very much. The light from the flares caught it now and then; Morcar waited a moment and then took aim. The points of the gleeve struck, there was a clatter, as if metal had hit metal, and then something huge seemed to roll over in the dark water, sending up great bubbles of gas that burst as they surfaced, emitting a stench so foul that Morcar gagged.

Dear God in heaven, what was it?

Morcar stepped closer.

Beneath his horrified eyes, bobbing gently in the foul water, lay what had once been a man. A warrior, for the remnants of his rusting armour still clung to the skeletal remains. Morcar, his heart beating fast from the shock, wrenched his

16

gaze away from the macabre apparition and turned his face to the sanctuary of the walls.

Then the lights went out.

He cried out in terror for, in the instant before the darkness came, he saw – or thought he saw – a pale shape rising up out of the mist, which now lay like a soft, slowly billowing blanket across the ground. His eyes wide, he stared, quite incapable of looking away, and the horror of the image that still seemed to burn into his eyes brought a long, low moan of dread from his parted lips. Then he saw more figures – a group of them, shadowy, vague – and he heard a sharp cry, quickly suppressed.

He sought frantically for a rational explanation, but panic gripped him and sense had flown.

From some resource deep within him he found the strength to pull himself out of his horrified trance. His wound hurt so much that he all but retched as he hurried up the track, heading almost blindly for the bulk of the abbey walls rising up before him. *I must find the gate*, he thought, fighting the abject fear that threatened to turn his bowels and his bones to water. *I must find the gate, for within the walls there is light and company and safety.*

Running – trying to run – had screwed tight the pain in his foot until it was all but intolerable, making him weak and faint. Leaning heavily on his gleeve, he forced his legs to move. One step. Two steps. Three. Four.

They came at him out of the impenetrable darkness of the shadows beneath the walls, and he had no warning of their presence. One of

them took his gleeve out of his hand, and without its support he fell heavily, into the arms of
the other one. He tried to wriggle free, tried to
leap away, but his foot would not let him – and,
anyway, they were too strong. One went on
holding him and the other backed off. But only
for an instant; then something hit Morcar with
the force of a charging bull and suddenly he was
in the air, flying in a smooth arc out over the
bank. Then he fell into the filthy ditch and foul,
black water closed over his head.

TWO

When I started work this morning, I had not the tiniest inkling that today was going to be the start of something so extraordinary. So much for the skill at reading the future on which I pride myself. I can do piddling little things like saying when it's going to rain (easy when someone's taught you how), when a ewe is going to deliver her lambs (again, relatively easy, and pretty much a matter of observation and experience) and reading the sex of an unborn baby (quite tricky, that one, but then I don't always get it right). But if something really big is looming, I'm as blissfully oblivious as everyone else.

I live with my aunt Edild, who is a herbalist and a healer. I've been living with her since my sixteenth birthday back in the summer, mainly because I'm now officially her assistant and there's so much work to do that it would waste time having to go home to my parents' house late at night and then return early in the morning. Living with Edild means I get a little extra time in my bed in the morning, and that's reason enough for me. In fact I love sharing the house with her, anyway, and it's certainly not because I was unhappy under my parents' roof. Far from it; I love my family dearly and, once my elder sister Goda had married and left home three years ago, I have nothing but happy memories of life with my clever and efficient mother Essa, my dreamy, precious father Wymond, my stammering brother Haward, my mischievous younger brother Squeak, my baby brother Leir and my Granny Cordeilla, who is a bard and the most wonderful story teller. I love my sister Elfritha, too, although like Goda and me she no longer lives at home. Ever since she was a small child she has wanted to be a nun and last year she got her wish. Now she's a novice with the Benedictine nuns at Chatteris and, as far as any of us can tell from the few short visits any of us have made, she's as blissfully happy as if she were already in heaven. The last time I saw her was just after I'd moved in permanently with Edild and we shared a big, silent and slightly self-congratulatory hug because both of us were living the life we wanted.

I can't imagine what it's like to be a nun. It is a hard road, I know. I have looked into my sister's face, pale, thin and tense inside the unfamiliar white wimple that covers her throat and her bright hair, framing her forehead, temples and chin. I have seen the haunted look in her wide eyes and taken in the dark grey circles around them. I have seen her bite her lip and mutter as she strives to commit to memory the words of new and unfamiliar prayers. I am in no doubt that learning to be a nun is not easy. I had expected all that, and when first I saw my sister in her new life I tried not to let it dismay me. What I had not expected was the laughter.

Despite the rigours of the life, despite the huge challenge of living up to vows of poverty, chastity and obedience and of spending all your waking hours either praying or working as hard as the lowliest slave, Chatteris rang with laughter. Whatever else they may be, I have had to accept that, in the main, nuns have a light-heartedness and an endearing jollity that make them laugh like children.

I don't think anyone at home misses me. If they do, I'm only a short walk away. I go back to see them all at least once every week but already they seem to have expanded to fill up the space I left. It makes me sad if I think about it so I try not to.

Life with Edild is hard work but I enjoy it very much. Well, most of the time I do, although it's only fair to say that there are moments of extreme discomfort. The worst thing is when I have to perform intimate examinations; when, in order to determine what's wrong with a patient, I have to inspect bits of the human body – male as well as female – that decent folk normally keep well hidden. Edild is relentless, however, and deaf to my protests.

'There is nothing to be ashamed of in a human body,' she tells me sternly, 'and you will never be a healer until you can control yourself sufficiently to look without embarrassment or false modesty at the most secret and private of its parts.'

So I am compelled to take my turn with my aunt when someone comes creeping in, red in the face and trying to pretend they are anywhere

21

but in a healer's house. In fact it is the shame and the distress of the patient that usually helps me get over my diffidence. *This poor soul is in pain,* I tell myself, *and the nature of the complaint means they probably haven't had even the small comfort of talking it over with someone else.* Then the compassion takes over and I just want to help them feel better.

When I managed to tell Edild this, blushing and stammering as badly as my poor brother Haward, she looked at me coolly and said, 'You may have the makings of a healer after all, Lassair.'

Edild is not one to overly praise her apprentice.

The other uncomfortable moments are when my aunt takes me down the strange, dark pathways that lead to the mysteries that lie at the heart of our calling. Only a little way down, for I am still fearful and she respects the fact that I'm doing my best. She builds up a good fire in the circle of hearth stones in the middle of her floor, and we sit cross-legged either side of the leaping flames. She mutters her incantations, inviting the guardian spirits to be present, and I listen intently, forming the words in my mind and trying to commit them to memory, for one day when Edild has gone to the ancestors I shall have to do this alone. Then she puts certain herbs on the fire – I'm only beginning to understand why she uses this herb or that for the immediate purpose – and we sit and breathe in the new aromas that twist and spiral up into the air. Sometimes she asks for guidance; when, for example, she is uncertain how best to help a patient. Sometimes she asks for strength, for herself or for me, if we have been drained by a difficult case. Sometimes she just wants to say thank you, for we both know full well that we could not do our work without help.

'We are but instruments, Lassair,' she tells me often. 'The healing gift is bestowed by the spirits and they use us to do their work.'

If I were ever inclined to get swollen-headed because I'm a healer, Edild is very good at knocking me down to size.

The scariest times are when Hrype comes to sit around the fire with us. Hrype is my friend Sibert's uncle, and he lives with Sibert and Sibert's mother Froya, who was married to Hrype's dead brother, Edmer. Sibert is a little older than me, and usually we are good friends. Two years ago I saved his life and he saved mine. It has forged a bond between us. Sometimes we like each other, sometimes not. We are not and, I think, could never be indifferent to each other.

Sibert is a little odd; Hrype is *very* odd. He has dark blond hair that he wears rather long and his silvery eyes sometimes look as if they're lit from within. He has high cheekbones and he looks like a king. When the three of us sit around the fire I look from him to Edild and when the light from the flames turns her red-blonde hair to liquid gold, she, too, seems to be alight. I feel very ordinary by comparison. I don't think even the fiercest firelight could make me glow like that. People say I resemble my aunt. I wish I could believe them.

Hrype is a sorcerer. I realized that some time ago but I only began to understand what it really meant once he started joining Edild and me around the magical fire. He has frightened me several times but, despite the way my heart thumps in terror and the fact that for several nights after he's done something really spectacular I'm suddenly scared of the dark, I keep coming back for more. If for nothing else, I can never pass up the opportunity to watch him cast the runes. He keeps them in a small leather pouch that always hangs at his waist. It's smooth and soft as if it is very old – as indeed it probably is, for Hrype comes from a long line of cunning men. Before he even opens the bag he closes his eyes and descends into a trance. It's so strange – you can almost see him withdrawing. He goes on sitting there, still as a stone and hardly breathing, but you just know that the essence of him has gone somewhere else. He opens the bag and takes from it a square of linen, its hems neatly sewn. He spreads it on the ground before him, carefully smoothing it out. It is always immaculately clean. Then he picks up the leather bag and holds it in both hands, his long fingers wrapping protectively around it but with a touch so light that it might be full of quail's eggs. He chants for a very long time and then – and it always makes me jump – suddenly he casts the rune stones on to the cloth.

The stones are beautiful. I have no jewels, nor am I ever likely to have any, but even if someone offered me any I would prefer to have rune stones like Hrype's. They are pale, translucent green, and he tells me they are made of jade, brought to this land from far, far away by one of his ancestors who voyaged east to find the rising sun. Into each stone had been carved a strange shape whose lines glitter like gold, and Hrype reads their mystic messages as easily as a scholar reads words from a parchment.

Once, unable to help myself, I stretched out a finger to touch the nearest stone. Quick as a snake Hrype's hand was wrapped round my wrist, holding me in a grip that hurt. I gave a little bleat of pain and he eased the pressure. Then, staring deep into my eyes so that I felt quite unable to look away, he said softly, 'They are not for you, Lassair. Their power would un-make you.'

Despite my fear of Hrype and having to deal with embarrassing ailments, I am happy. I want to be like my aunt, for as well as being fasci-nated by her craft I love her independence. She is the only grown woman I know who lives on her own – well, apart from me and I don't really count – and I envy her that so much. Most of my contemporaries are already settling for this boy or that and quite a few are married with babies. They often look at me pityingly, believing that my thin, boyish body is unattractive beside their curves and that no man would ever want me to warm his bed and bear his children. I don't want their pity, even when it is kindly meant and not prompted by spite. Any fool of a woman can conceive a child – even I could, for although I am still flat-chested and my hips are as slender as Sibert's, my courses started some time ago and I know that I am fully mature – but not many are called to be a healer. No; I want to stay here with my aunt until she has taught me all the things I want so much to know.

This morning Edild and I were working on a basket of comfrey root that we had harvested the previous day. Comfrey is such a generous plant; in spring and summer we use its fresh green leaves for healing wounds and knitting broken bones, and mixed in wine it makes a remedy for an abnormal blood flow in women. Today we made sure to set aside some of the root we had collected for drying, so that we would have supplies through the winter, but the majority we intended to use straight away. Like almost all preparations, the potency is greatest with fresh ingredients. Edild was making a decoction. She had boiled pieces of comfrey root in fresh water and now was carefully placing the vessel at the edge of the fire so that it would simmer steadily until reduced by a third. She planned to take some to an elderly man in the village who was suffering from burning in his stomach; Edild had diagnosed ulcers. The remainder of her brew would be made into a syrup and set aside for the first of the winter's crop of coughs. We could be sure that, living as we did so close to the Fens and their perpetual damp air, almost everyone in Aelf Fen would succumb to the phlegm sooner or later.

I was busy with Edild's mortar and pestle, crushing the comfrey root and steadily adding little dribbles of water to make a paste. This paste is good for slow-bleeding wounds that are reluctant to heal and I planned to use some in the afternoon on my mother's cousin's haemorrhoids.

Edild and I were so absorbed in our tasks that neither of us heard our visitor till she rapped on the door. Edild shot a significant glance at me – as the apprentice, one of my jobs is to answer the door – and, trying not to let my reluctance show, I laid down the pestle, wiped my hands on my apron and, making sure my hair was neat under its white cap, went to see who had come calling.

I opened the door to my aunt Alvela, youngest sister in the brood that includes my father and my aunt Edild. She is actually Edild's twin, and I suppose they are quite alike to look at even though they are very different in temperament. Edild is level and cool; Alvela tends to lose her head and fall nose-first into panic at the least provocation.

She was in a real state this morning. Before I had got further than, 'Good morning, Alvela, what can we—?' she had elbowed me out of the way and, eyes frantically searching, cried, 'Where's Edild? I need her! Oh, don't say she's not here, she must be here, she *must*!'

'I am,' said Edild coolly, rising gracefully to her feet from her crouching pose beside the hearth. 'What's the matter, Alvela?'

Alvela's face crumpled and tears overflowed from her red-rimmed eyes. It was obviously not the first time she had succumbed to weeping this morning. She threw herself into Edild's arms

27

and said, 'It's Morcar, it's my boy, my precious boy!' Morcar was in his mid twenties and therefore hardly a boy, I thought, to anyone but his mother. 'Oh, Edild, what am I to do?' she wailed. 'What is to become of me?'

'Calm yourself,' Edild said, somehow managing to give her twin sister a comforting hug and a bracing shake at the same time. 'Come and sit down' – she led Alvela to the bench on the far side of the hearth – 'and Lassair will make you a soothing drink.' She shot me a glance, nodding towards the pot in which we keep the mildly sedative herbal mix that we prescribe to those whose fears and anxieties threaten to make them ill. I hastened to obey, reaching down a clean mug and checking to see that there was water almost on the boil in the pot suspended over the fire.

'Now,' said Edild as Alvela collapsed on to the bench, 'tell me what has happened.'

Alvela stared at her for a few moments, her mouth working although no words came out. Then she gulped, blew her nose on a soaked piece of cloth, dabbed at her streaming eyes and said, 'He went to Ely to work on the new cathedral.' She sobbed again. 'He's had an accident, a terrible accident,' she managed through the tears, 'and he's all but drowned!'

'But *not* drowned?' Edild demanded.

Alvela raised her head to stare at her sister. 'Not quite,' she acknowledged.

Edild gave her another little shake. 'Well then!' she said encouragingly. 'He'll probably—'

But Alvela was not ready to be comforted. 'He's stabbed through the foot like Our Lord on the cross!' she cried out, agony in her voice.

What? They'd *crucified* him? Surely not...

Edild, similarly perplexed, glanced at me, her frustration evident in her eyes. 'Explain,' she commanded, her arm around her sister's waist.

The infusion was ready. I blew on it to cool it and handed it to Alvela, who took it with barely a nod and then stared at it as if wondering how it came to be in her hand. 'It's very hot so you must sip it,' I said gently. 'It'll do you good, Aunt.'

She gave me a weak smile and did as she was told. She sipped once, twice. Then, haunted eyes back on Edild's face, she said, 'He stuck an eel spear in his foot. Then he fell in a ditch. Someone found him – thank *God*, some monk was hurrying back to the abbey before they locked the gates for the night and heard my poor boy spluttering and gasping.'

'This monk managed to haul him out of the water?' Edild asked.

'Yes, yes, then he went for help and they carried him – Morcar – back to his lodgings on a hurdle.'

'Then—' Edild began.

'Oh, will you stop *interrupting*!' Alvela shouted with sudden, impatient fury. Edild folded her lips on whatever retort she had been about to make. 'Sorry,' Alvela muttered. She took a mouthful of her infusion, then another. It seemed to be doing her good. She looked up, first at her sister and then at me, eyes narrowed as if she were assessing our relative strengths. Then she said, 'A peddler brought word this morning. Morcar lies abed wracked with pain and nearly out of his mind with fever, and if you don't help him he'll die.'

THREE

I think I probably made the herbal infusion too strong, for quite soon Alvela started yawning, and then her body went all sort of floppy, and I had to help Edild get her over to my bed, where we laid her down and covered her with my woollen blanket.

Then Edild shooed me out of the way as she began methodically assembling the potions and medicaments that she required.

'He'll need something immediately to bring down the fever,' she said, reaching for balm mint, cinquefoil, wood sorrel, 'something to expel the poisons' – her busy hands found the dandelion, or piss-the-bed as it was known – 'something to help him sleep' – dill – 'and something to clean the wounds in his foot.' She drew a huge bag of dried lavender from its place on the shelf. 'Put water on to boil, Lassair,' she said over her shoulder, 'and I'll tell you what you must do.'

I hurried to obey, flying around the small room as my aunt thought up more ingredients that might or might not come in useful and telling me what to do with them. I thought at first that there were so many potions and remedies to prepare that I was going to have to do my full share of the work. She kept saying *you* and not *we*, so I amended this and thought instead that I would be doing all the preparation while she went away to think quietly how best to treat her sick nephew.

I must have been very stupid that morning. I didn't realize that I was going to Ely on my own until my aunt told me so.

'*I can't!*' I hissed in a sort of muted scream, anxious not to wake the slumbering Alvela. 'Morcar's got a fever and a spear wound in his foot! I can't deal with all that!'

'Yes you can,' Edild said calmly. 'You have treated many fevers and there's nothing to tending a wound, even a deep one, except cleaning it carefully, inserting a stitch or two if necessary and binding it up with a bit of comfrey ointment to knit the skin together, all of which you have been doing without my supervision for many months.'

Her cool tone and her obvious confidence in me were affecting me, as no doubt she knew they would. 'But he's *really* ill,' I said, my voice a good deal closer to its usual tone. 'Suppose he dies?'

'If he does, then it will not be because you failed in your care but because you got to him too late, which would not be your fault,' Edild said in that same voice of reason. 'Otherwise, you know how to care for a man coming back from the brink of death. Keep him resting, help him sleep if necessary, keep him warm, make sure he drinks and, as soon as he's ready, start him on a light diet.'

Yes, she was right. I did know all that, for with her help I had nursed more than one villager recovering from a serious or lengthy sickness.

I had one last objection. 'What about Alvela?' I whispered, as if the sound of her own name would wake her up. 'Won't she be cross if you send me instead of doing what she said and going yourself?'

Edild glanced at her sleeping twin. 'Probably,' she agreed. 'But I am not on this earth to do my sister's bidding. I am fully occupied here in my accustomed place, and I neither wish nor am prepared to desert those who depend on me.'

She was right, as she usually is. There are several people in the village who, for one reason or another, Edild has reserved to care for by herself, without any help or interference from me. One is a frightened and very young woman about to bear her first child; my aunt and I both know that it will take all Edild's skill to bring both mother and baby safely through the labour. There is a skinny old man with an ague so severe that the shakes are almost making his bones fall apart; I could treat him, but for some reason he has taken against me and will not let me near. There's also a younger man who finds it a torment to discuss whatever serious condition ails him with my aunt, never mind a girl like me, as well as a crop of severe coughs, colds and putrid throats among the village children that are driving them and their families close to despair. And a small boy with an angel's face has the quinsy, his poor little throat so constricted with swellings that it takes all Edild's skill and patience to get as much as a drop of the soothing medicine into him.

No. If I stopped to think about it, I could see that now was no time for the village healer to absent herself on a mission to help one man. Not when she had an apprentice to send in her place.

I squared my shoulders, met my aunt's eyes and said calmly, 'Tell me very carefully what I must do.'

It was October, wet, the roads and the tracks were ankle-deep in mud and probably impassable in places, and there were reputedly robbers and bandits about. I was not allowed to go on my journey without an escort. Hearing what I was planning to do, my father at first said I couldn't but then relented – thanks to my mother and Edild – and said he would go with me. It was a lovely thought – I get on so well with my father, and the idea of several days in his company was just wonderful – but we all knew that Lord Gilbert would be reluctant to spare a hard-working man unnecessarily. Then Edild suggested Sibert and, even as she spoke his name, I felt glad. Not quite as glad as I would have been if my father were to be my escort, but not far off. As I said, most of the time Sibert and I like each other.

I had to go up to Lakehall, Lord Gilbert's manor house, to explain my mission and seek permission to leave the village. I was expecting to see his reeve, Bermund, who usually heads the lower orders off at the gates and takes messages inside to Lord Gilbert – as if Bermund alone out of all of us is deemed fit for the lord's presence. That is probably quite true in Bermund's estimation, if in nobody else's. Bermund is not a bad man – we all know we could do a lot worse – but he is humourless, meticulous to the point of being fussy, solitary and withdrawn. He treats us with scrupulous fairness – again, we know that is more than can be said of many men in his position – but there is no true humanity in him. He is not a family man and has never once been seen in the company of a woman. It is said that on the few occasions he allows himself a tiny spell of relaxation he heads for neighbouring villages where he is not well known and seeks out youths in the scruffiest taverns. That, however, is gossip, and nobody should listen to gossip.

Today it was not Bermund to whom I had to address my request but Lord Gilbert himself, sitting on a bench by the fire in his great hall in the midst of his family: red-faced, bulging paunch pushing against the rich crimson cloth of his tunic, mouth stretched in a happy smile. After the usual courtesies – he struggled to remember who I was, and then immediately asked after my father, who supplies him with the finest eels – he told me to state my business, and I did so.

At first I thought he was going to refuse; to his credit, he seemed well aware that quite a few were sick in Aelf Fen just then. Happily for me, his wife, Lady Emma, sat beside him, her little boy playing with a wooden sheep at her feet and her baby girl in her arms. Lady Emma smiled at me in a conspiratorial way and then, turning to her husband, said softly, 'My dear, we are blessed in that we have not one but two healers here in our village. The younger, Lassair here' – her dimples deepened as she smiled at me again – 'is already skilled, but she has much to learn.' How right she was. 'To me it would appear that it can only serve to increase both her experience and her confidence to go on this pilgrimage of mercy to aid her kinsman, and the consequential augmentation of her skills can only be of benefit to all of us here in the manor. Do you not agree, my love?' She has a dainty way of putting things, even if it does take a few moments to understand exactly what she is saying.

Lord Gilbert had been staring at me indecisively but, at his wife's appeal, his face cleared and he said, 'Yes, yes, quite right, my dear wife, quite right!' Wise man to agree, especially when it was so very clear that she was far more intelligent than he was. Still, that applied to most people. 'Off you go, er—'

'Lassair,' supplied his wife.

'Lassair, yes, yes, Lassair!' Lord Gilbert beamed at me. 'You and the young man—?' He looked hopefully at his wife and she supplied the name. 'Sibert, yes. You and Sibert have my permission. Go safely, treat your brother-in-law—'

'Cousin,' said his wife.

'—Your cousin, and come back to us when you can,' he finished. Then, with a wave of his fleshy hand, he dismissed me.

* * *

I was ready, or as ready as I was going to be. I don't know how I appeared to others, but inside I was nervous and fearful, my confidence and my courage right down in my boots. Morcar was my cousin, my kinsman, and, although I did not know him very well, he was of my blood. His mother, my aunt, thought the sun rose and set in him. The weight of responsibility sat so heavily on my shoulders that it was all I could do to keep upright.

The heavy, leather bag of remedies that Edild and I had prepared stood, its straps neatly fastened, by the door. Sibert was going to carry it. Now I was fussing over my own small pack, stowing clean underlinen, a washcloth, the bone comb my brother Haward had made for me, the beautiful shawl Elfritha had given me, a spare hood...

I sensed Edild's presence behind me and turned.

'Lassair, step outside for a moment, please,' she said in a low voice.

My eyes flashed to Alvela, who was now sitting propped against the wall, her head on my pillow. She looked dazed, but she was awake. Sort of. I stood up and followed Edild outside into the sunshine of early afternoon.

'You will have to leave very soon,' Edild said, 'for you must reach Ely before dusk or the gates will be locked. But there is something I must say to you before you go.' She paused, gathering her thoughts, and I guessed she was going to impart some final advice as to how I should treat my patient.

I certainly did not expect what she actually said.

'My mother – your Granny Cordeilla – tells the tale of our ancestress Aelfbeort the Shining One, who spoke with the spirits and learned from them. You remember?'

'Yes!' I said, almost indignantly. I remember all Granny's marvellous tales, but I couldn't help wondering why Edild was speaking of them just now, in this crisis where speed was so vital.

'Good. You will recall, too, then that Aelfbeort bore a daughter, Aelfburga, who—'

'She found Aelf Fen and led the people here,' I interrupted eagerly. 'It was a time of terrible peril and the people needed a safe refuge. Aelf-burga's mother Aelfbeort was beloved by the spirits and they taught her much concerning the deep, dark matters beyond the understanding of mortal kind. Because of that love they helped her daughter by showing her how to find the secret, hidden safe ways to Aelf Fen, where with their aid she constructed an artificial island in the black waters of the mere and—'

'They showed her how to find the safe ways,' Edild repeated softly, cutting off my river of words. I looked at her blankly. She gave a small tut of impatience. 'Come on, Lassair, it's not like you to be so slow.'

That hurt. *Think*, I commanded myself. Safe ways. The island of the eels. Helpful spirits. My ancestress. 'You think the spirits will show me how to get to Ely?' I demanded, my voice high with terrified excitement.

Edild smiled. 'They might, but I don't imagine

their aid will be necessary since there are plenty of boatmen to row you over. No, Lassair. That is not what is in my mind.' She looked at me gravely.

'What is it?' I whispered.

'We already know that you are a dowser, able to find both water and also hidden objects through the medium of the willow wand,' she said. She was right. It is a strange gift and, although I have used it from time to time, once in a matter of very great danger, I do not yet understand much about it. If I'm truthful, it scares me a little and I try not to think about it. 'I have long wondered,' Edild was saying, 'if you may also have inherited the gift that the aelven folk gave to Aelfburga.' She waited, her eyes alight.

'You mean I might be able to find the safe ways across the fens?' I demanded. She nodded. 'Oh, Edild, but that secret is only known to a handful of the Ely monks, and they only reveal it when they have no choice!' We had all heard the tale of William the Conqueror's furious frustration when he could not get his great army across the treacherous marshes to put down the revolt that Hereward had led from Ely. The king had tried to build a causeway but it had collapsed, taking vast numbers of William's men fully armed to their watery graves. One of his knights then managed to slip across, and he bribed the monks to tell him the secret way. The more generous version said that the monks were not unanimously in favour of the rebel Hereward in their midst and revealed their precious secret in order to get rid of him. Either way, the Conqueror finally stormed across and took Ely, although Hereward got away.

Edild was regarding me steadily, and again I sensed that she was waiting for me to work it out for myself. 'You want me to test out your theory.' I hesitated. It seemed so extraordinary, but then my aunt Edild is an extraordinary woman. I smiled, for suddenly I knew what she was thinking as clearly as if she had spoken aloud. 'You do, don't you?' She returned my smile. 'You've been itching for an opportunity for me to test myself and now, when pure chance has sum-moned me to the very place, the moment has arrived.' Another thought struck me. 'But why didn't you suggest that I have a go around here? There's plenty of dangerous marsh and fenland all around the village – no need to go to Ely to look for safe routes over perilous ground!'

Her expression turned enigmatic. 'Too easy, Lassair,' she murmured. 'You've lived here all your life, and I would wager a silver penny that you could skip over the tussocks all around Aelf Fen without even getting your toes wet.'

'I'm sure I couldn't!' I protested. 'I—'

Edild held up her hand. 'Enough,' she said, but she was still smiling. 'Do not take unnecessary risks, Lassair, but keep your eyes wide open for the chance that will present itself. You will not fail.'

It sounded horribly like a prediction. 'But—'

I was talking to empty air. My aunt had spun gracefully around and was gliding back inside her little house.

I stood out there in the sunshine for a few moments, waiting until I felt calm enough to face Alvela. Edild has always pressed on me the importance of a serene demeanour when dealing with the sick and the disturbed; even in the face of the highest fever and the deepest wound, she says, the healer must give the impression that this is all in a day's work. People can be killed by shock, she tells me, and someone already gravely ill could suffer a seizure if the person who has come to heal them were to throw up her hands in horror and go *aaaagh, I can't deal with that!*

I breathed in deeply and slowly let the air out, repeating the process several times. I was admittedly quite thrilled at what Edild had just said, and part of me was just longing to test myself to see if I could do it. The more sensible part, however, was moaning that too much was being asked of me. As if it were not enough to be sent alone to deal with a gravely ill man suffering from a high fever and a deep wound in his foot, now somehow I must also find the time to slip away and try out my skill at marsh-hopping. I felt my stiff shoulders relax. *If* the opportunity arose – and it was only *if*, I reminded myself, even Edild had said *if* – then I would cope with it. For now, there were other things to perplex and worry me.

Primarily this: Morcar had suffered his accident on the Isle of Ely, where the Normans were building a huge and showy new cathedral. That cathedral was a part of a Benedictine abbey, no doubt full of learned monks who read the ancient tracts and studied the knowledge that had been handed down to them out of the past. Quite a lot of that knowledge would be concerned with the healing arts, and not a few of the monks would undoubtedly be skilled and renowned healers.

So why on earth had whoever was caring for Morcar sent the message to his mother to bring help for her son? Why had they not taken him straight to the abbey's infirmary, where he could be tucked up beneath clean, linen sheets with bland-faced, psalm-chanting monks gliding around him and swiftly and efficiently answering his every need?

Why, in the dear Lord's name, was *I* going to Ely?

For the first time, I felt a deep shiver of unease.

FOUR

Sibert and I set out in the early afternoon. As the crow flew it was probably only eight miles or so from Aelf Fen to Ely, but Sibert and I were not blessed with wings and would have to trudge along many extra loops and detours as the track edged it way round numerous watery obstacles. In addition, although it was fine today it had been raining hard for the past few days, and the water level everywhere had risen quite dramatically.

It really was no time for a would-be marsh walker to test her probably non-existent skills.

We were basically good friends, Sibert and I, but it was some months since we had done more than nod a greeting to each other as we passed in our daily round in the village. Consequently, it took a mile or two before we even *began* to be easy together. Sibert asked a few polite but stiff questions: are you well? Are you enjoying working with your aunt? How's your sister, Goda? Still as awful as ever? To the last I was able to answer honestly that, yes, Goda was pretty much her usual self. She bore her first child – my beautiful little niece, Gelges – two summers ago, and the baby's safe arrival did, for a precious few months, turn Goda into a nicer person.

43

Unfortunately, the improvement hasn't really lasted, although I have to admit she's not quite as waspish as she was before. In the spring she had another baby, a boy who was rather unimaginatively named Cerdic, after his father. He is large, blank-faced and, compared to his sister, a little dull, although it's hardly his fault, and it's not fair to judge a child who is still so young.

I gave Sibert an edited account of all that and then we fell silent. I knew that I ought to ask him about his family in return, yet I hesitated. Hrype scares me and as for Froya, on the few occasions she emerges from her cottage she always seems so fearful and anxious that I feared to enquire after her in case the report was bad. Still, we had many miles to go yet, and we could hardly pace along without saying a word.

I drew a breath and said, 'How's your mother?'

Briefly, Sibert raised his head and gazed up into the clear sky, an expression of pain crossing his face. Oh dear. 'I'm sorry I asked,' I muttered, feeling myself blush.

He turned to me and gave me a very nice smile. 'There is no need to apologize,' he said. 'In fact I'm grateful for the chance to speak to you about her.'

'To me?' I said stupidly.

He smiled again, and this time there was an edge of humour on his face. 'You're a healer, Lassair,' he said patiently.

Belatedly, I understood. 'Sorry,' I repeated.

Sensibly, he ignored that. 'She's not exactly sick,' he said, 'or anyway we – Hrype and I – don't think so, otherwise we'd have made her see Edild or you.'

'You can't make people see a healer,' I protested. 'Well, not unless they are beyond seeking help for themselves.'

'Perhaps she is,' he muttered.

Sibert's mother has experienced much tragedy in her life. She nursed her dying husband and somehow managed to get him away from those who were after his blood following the Ely rebellion, bringing him to Aelf Fen where he died while his child, Sibert, was still in her womb. She was supported by Hrype, and the help of such a man was surely invaluable. Nevertheless, the one she had loved and married was no longer on this earth, and sometimes it seemed that Froya would never get over her loss. If, indeed, it was grief that ailed her.

It was time for me to be the healer I was meant to be. 'She grieves still for your father, do you think?' I asked gently.

'I don't ... Yes. I suppose so.' He seemed uncertain.

'Describe to me how she seems to you,' I prompted. 'Does she not eat? Does she not sleep? Does she speak to you and Hrype of her worries?' That Froya had worries was no feat of diagnosis. You could tell that just by studying the poor woman, with the perpetual deep frown that creases her smooth, white brow and the constant droop of her shoulders, as if she carries a heavy load.

Sibert was clearly thinking, eyes narrowed as if he were conjuring up an image of his mother. 'She prepares food for Hrype and me – good, tasty food, for she's always been a good cook and is able to make something substantial and appealing out of little – but she doesn't eat much herself. She picks at it, but I never see her finish a decent meal.' He frowned. 'I don't know if she sleeps. I fall into deep sleep as soon as I'm in bed, and I don't wake till either she or Hrype wake me.'

'And her anxieties? What troubles her, do you think?'

'*I don't know!*' The words were almost a howl. Then, more calmly, he went on, 'Once I came home and heard her weeping as I approached the house. I hurried on inside and she was in Hrype's arms, beating her fists against his chest and crying out something about punishment, and he was soothing her, telling her in a quiet, steady voice that she was good and kind and full of courage. Then he looked up and spotted me and that was that.'

'You didn't ask him what the matter was?'

'No, Lassair, I didn't,' he said testily.

I should have paused to think. Instead I said, 'Why not?'

'Oh, come on!' he cried. 'You know what Hrype's like. He gently pushed my mother away from him, and she hurried away to see to the meal. Then he just fixed me with those odd eyes of his, and it was as if I could hear his voice in my mind telling me – no, *commanding* me – not to ask my mother anything.'

I could well imagine the tense little scene. I was silent for some moments, thinking. Then I said, 'She spoke of punishment. Do you think

46

she fears earthly or heavenly punishment? I mean,' I added, 'has she broken the law or has she sinned?'

He smiled grimly. 'I can't imagine her doing either.'

He was right. I couldn't, any more than he could. 'Punishment,' I murmured. It sounded rather as if Froya had a guilty conscience. Why? She seemed to have led an exemplary life, as far as I knew, tending her wounded husband devotedly and doing everything in her power to save his life. If she could not get over losing her Edmer, the man she had loved, it was surely nothing to feel guilty about. Poor Froya, stuck in Aelf Fen in the constant company of Edmer's son and Edmer's brother, the two people who more than anyone else on earth must daily remind her of the man she had lost...

'Do either you or Hrype resemble your father?' I asked.

Sibert looked surprised. 'I am told not,' he replied. 'My father was broad and heavily built where Hrype is tall and slender, and my mother once referred to his dark eyes. I look like my mother.'

He did a little, being lightly built and quite tall, with fair hair and a naturally pale complexion, although a child can have attributes of both parents, and, for all I knew, Sibert might have his father's mouth or his laugh. Not that I imagined there was much laughter in that particular home. 'Oh.'

'Why do you ask?' Briefly, I explained my theory. 'Hmm. It's possible, I suppose, although

47

my very existence must remind her of my father, irrespective of whether I look like him.' His frown deepened, and all at once he looked very sad.

'Sibert, that's a *good* thing!' I said quickly. 'Just imagine how much worse it would be for your mother if she didn't have you!' Vividly, I saw an image of Froya's face two summers back, when it had looked as if Sibert would be hanged. Hastily, I pushed the memory away. The intensity of Froya's expression, with the terrible hunger of her love and the black despair turning her living face to a skull, had been frightening.

Sibert looked a little encouraged. 'Do you really think so?'

'I know so,' I said unhesitatingly.

Then I realized something I ought to have worked out before. Sibert's father had died as a result of the wound he had received at Ely. Now, because of me, Sibert was being forced to go to the very place. 'I'm sorry that you're going there,' I said quietly.

I'm not sure he understood. 'What? To Ely, you mean?'

'Yes. I realize it must hold bad memories for you.'

'How can it?' he said roughly. 'I never knew my father, either at Aelf Fen or Ely. Going to the place where he received his fatal wound is hardly going to bring back memories of any sort, bad or otherwise.'

'No, I can see that.' Typically, I hadn't really thought it through, and I accepted the implied rebuke.

'Besides,' he began. Then he stopped.

'What?'

'Oh ... I don't know. I probably shouldn't bother you with it.'

'Well, you've mentioned it now, whatever it is, so you'd better go on or I'll drive myself silly imagining things.'

He smiled faintly. 'Very well. It's just that I've always wanted to go to the island.'

I nodded. I could understand that. 'As a sort of pilgrimage, I suppose.'

'No,' he said, 'nothing like that.' Again he paused. Then he said in a rush, 'There's something strange about the story of what happened to my father, something that I can't really get straight in my mind. I'm saying no more than that' – I had opened my mouth to ask at least four questions – 'but, believe me, Lassair, I'd have gone to Ely sooner or later so it may as well be now.'

We walked on. After a while he said, 'What should I do about my mother?'

I did not know. I'm all right with cuts, sprains and everyday maladies – or for Morcar's sake I hoped so – but whatever was wrong with Froya was beyond me. 'Let her know you love her,' I said. No harm in that, whatever Froya's problem was. 'Encourage her to get out of the house,' I went on. 'You and Hrype are out all day so she must spend a lot of time on her own, and that probably gives her too much occasion to brood over what she had lost instead of be glad for what she has.'

'Ye–es,' he said slowly. 'Yes, I do see the sense

of that.'

'She needs grandchildren,' I plunged on thoughtlessly. 'Unlike yours, it wasn't as if *my* mother was sad to begin with, but having Gelges, and now little Cerdic too, has brought her so much joy, and she's always busy with something concerning them, either making a little garment for them, or going over to help Goda with some minor difficulty, or—'

Sibert was laughing. Far too late I remembered that he was an only child and that any grandchildren Froya might have would be engendered by him. The nearest thing to a girl on whom he might be sweet enough to wish to marry was walking right beside him.

The flush began on my cheeks and spread up over my forehead and right down my throat. Anything I could possibly think of to say would only make matters worse. I folded my lips together and strode on down the track.

We made our slow but steady way in a wide semicircle around the south-east and south of the Fens, stopping at the edge of the hard ground opposite Ely in the late afternoon. The sun was low in the sky as we stood looking out towards the isle of the eels, rising in a low, dark hump before us like some huge creature from the deeps. I did not know how it would be normally, when the island was not experiencing such a vast and important new build, but just then the shoreline was crowded and busy, with craft of all sorts and sizes lined up along the quay. We were on the bank of a wide river, no doubt made wider by the recent rains; stretching away into the distance, I could make out the rough line of the waterway. The great expanse of marshy, sodden ground on either side looked as if it could bear the weight of nothing heavier than a duck. Here and there stands of alder and willow rose up, the trunks of the trees knee-high in the dark water.

Beyond us were drawn up a number of barges laden with huge slabs of stone. Beyond them was a line of similar barges, only these were empty. Presumably, this was a holding place for the transportation of the stone for the new cathedral; the empty barges would no doubt set off in the morning for another load.

Work seemed to be winding down for the day, but it was still light and we had no problem in finding a boatman to take us across. He helped me down into his small craft and Sibert jumped in after me. We settled ourselves as comfortably as we could, and the boatman pushed off from the quay and then dipped his oars in the black water.

He was probably after a tip because quite soon he began to entertain us with a lively description of the horrors that lay beneath us.

'Water's high,' he said, glancing from me to Sibert and back again. 'There are deep, dark dikes and ditches down below, and you'd be able to see in them if it hadn't been so wet lately. Not as how you'd want to,' he added, leering at me. 'Full of dead things, they are,' he hissed. 'Horrible, foul, rotten things. Things as would give you nightmares if you ever caught so much as a glimpse of them.' His eyes seemed to bore into me and it was quite clear he was enjoying himself. 'Bits of bodies, skeletons in rusty armour, black, empty eye sockets staring up at you, bony hands reaching out for help—'

I wasn't going to put up with someone trying to scare me out of my wits. 'I suppose it must have been near here that the Conqueror built his causeway,' I interrupted, trying to make my tone nonchalant.

The boatman looked surprised that I should know that but quickly he rallied. 'This here were Hereward's stronghold, see,' he said proudly, 'the place he chose to set up his standard when he came home to find his lands forfeited and his own brother's head on a spike over the door.' I had heard the tale many times but it was still shocking. I imagined returning to my own home and finding my dear Haward's head on a pole. Quickly, I turned my attention back to the boatman.

'The Conqueror made many attempts to get over the fen but each time he was thwarted,' the man was saying, puffing slightly as he pulled on the oars, 'and finally he gave orders for a fleet of wooden rafts to be built and formed up into a causeway. Right here.' He nodded at the water beneath the keel. 'Not content with that, he got hold of a local witch and set her up in a high tower, from where she hurled down terrible curses on everyone on the island. Seemingly, he thought she'd undermine our resolve, but she fell and broke her neck and that was the end of that.' He cackled, coughed, then leaned over the side and spat. I had noted *our resolve*. Intentionally or not, the boatman had just told us plainly on which side his loyalties lay. It was as well for him that Sibert and I were not Norman spies.

'What happened then?' Sibert's eyes were wide.

The boatman looked gratified at having such an absorbed listener. 'Well, Hereward knew all about the Conqueror's causeway, see, and according to some he disguised himself and went out to lend a hand in the building of it. Then when the army was halfway across, too late to order them back, at last the Conqueror realized what Hereward had done.' He chuckled again. 'He'd set traps, see,' he explained before we could ask. 'He'd made weak spots at intervals all along that long causeway, and when the moment was right he made the planks collapse under the weight, then he set fire to what was left. Most of the soldiers drowned,' he added in a matter-of-fact tone, 'and those who didn't ran away for fear of the deadly, sucking stickiness of the black marsh and what lay hidden beneath.' He leered again, rolling his eyes for added effect.

'I understand that the monks revealed the secret ways across,' I said calmly. I guessed this must have been the next chapter in the boatman's story, for he looked quite cross. 'Some of them were not wholly behind Hereward's revolt, or so I am told.'

'You're told right then, lass,' the boatman agreed sullenly. 'Not that it did them much good in the end, either their disapproval of Hereward or their treachery, because, far from being grateful that they'd told him what he wanted to know,

the Conqueror was angry with them for not telling him sooner. There's kings for you,' he added
softly, almost to himself, with a world-weary
inflection, as if he had known dozens of kings
and was all too familiar with their little foibles.

'What did the Conqueror do?' Sibert asked.

The boatman smiled grimly. 'He made the Ely
monks travel halfway across England to seek
him out, and then he told them coldly what he
wanted from them, to make it up to him.' Again,
his eyes flicked from me to Sibert. 'Only a
thousand pounds!' he hissed.

Sibert and I both gasped. It was an unheard-of
sum. 'How did they possibly manage that?' I
whispered.

'Sold or melted down every bit of gold and
silver they possessed,' the boatman said, not
without a certain air of satisfaction. It appeared
he had little more time for monks than for kings.
'Crosses, altar pieces, chalices, basins, goblets
and all, as well as jewels aplenty and a beautiful
statue of the Virgin and the Holy Child.' He
sighed. 'Now that – that was a hard loss.'

We were approaching the island now and,
abruptly, the boatman fell silent, his attention on
the other craft now bobbing about all around us.
I turned away and stared over the side at the
water hurrying past. It was so dark, so sinister,
and I was overcome with a sense of the unnam-
ed, unnumbered dead down there. I shivered,
neither from the cold nor from the boatman's
macabre story.

It was the place itself that frightened me, and
my visit was only just beginning.

FIVE

Sibert and I set off from the waterside, jostled by people hurrying to complete the day's business before the light faded into night. One or two boats were still setting off across the water but it was clear that ferrying operations were winding down. We passed one of the barges, half of its cargo of stone already unloaded. A gang of men were quitting work for the day, laughing and calling out to each other as they set off for their own hearths. Their garments were coated so thickly with stone dust that they looked like moving statues.

We could see the abbey walls, rising sheer and uncompromising ahead of us. I increased my pace, grabbing hold of Sibert's sleeve and dragging him with me. The monks must surely be on the point of shutting the gates for the night, if they hadn't done so already, and if Morcar were inside then I had to get to him before I was shut out. I heard Edild's voice in my head: *if he dies, it will be because you got to him too late*. The sensible inner core of me told me that wasn't exactly what she had said but, all the same, it was the last thing I wanted to think about just then.

Sibert had moved ahead of me, thrusting a way

through the hurrying crowds and, with me a few paces behind, we reached a gatehouse. The gates were still open, but a frowning monk was waiting, tapping a foot in impatience, while an old woman and an even older man shuffled out of the abbey. He had a bunch of huge keys in his hand and he was jangling them against his leg.

I pushed past Sibert and said, 'Please, brother, may I speak with you?'

The monk's eyes swivelled round to look at me. He did not seem to like what he saw. His face went vinegary and he sniffed, drawing back. 'No women, not without permission,' he snapped.

I could have pointed out that the person hobbling along next to the very old man was a woman but I thought better of it. 'I understand,' I said meekly, bowing my head so that I was not staring at him. I have been told (by Edild; who else?) that some men in holy orders take exception to women purely because of their sex, taking the view that the forbidden stirrings they feel in their groins at the sight of a woman are all the woman's fault simply for existing and nothing to do with their own lustful urges. Surreptitiously, I drew my hood forward, hoping to conceal most of my face. 'I have come to aid a sick kinsman,' I went on quickly – the keys were making even more noise now and I knew the monk was just itching to boot Sibert and me out of his gateway and lock up – 'and I was hoping that you might be able to give me news of him?'

I risked a glance at the monk. His expression had thawed imperceptibly. Perhaps the fact that

56

I had come on a mission of mercy and wasn't just a flighty little piece of nonsense after his virtue had affected him. 'What's his name?' he snapped out.

'Morcar,' I said eagerly. 'Morcar of the Breckland. He's a flint knapper,' I added, 'but—'

'We've no use for flint knappers here,' the monk said dismissively. *'Our* abbey's new cathedral's being built of Barnack stone, best that money can buy.'

'He was injured,' I hurried on, 'and he has a deep wound in his foot. He also has a high fever. I have brought medicaments and I—' Too late I realized my mistake. This monk, so proud of his abbey, so obviously viewing himself and his brethren as rarefied beings several levels above the rest of us, would not be happy at the implication that some slip of a girl thought she was a better healer than the Ely infirmarer.

The monk was shaking his head. 'I know nobody of that name,' he said baldly. 'There are no cases of high fever in our care at present.' He might as well have added *and that's the way we want to keep it*, for it was plainly written on his sour, disapproving face.

Anger rose up in me, but I managed to hold it in. My mission had only just begun, and it would be foolish to make an enemy so soon. I bowed again and said, 'Thank you, brother. I will pursue my search elsewhere. Good evening.'

I pulled Sibert away, the monk's faintly surprised dismissal and perfunctory blessing echoing in my ears. 'Why were you sucking up to him?' Sibert hissed. 'He couldn't have been

57

less helpful if he tried!'

'I know,' I hissed back. 'But he might come in useful later.'

Sibert frowned, clearly trying to work out what I meant. But I had other things to worry about. We had reached the end of the abbey wall and it turned away abruptly to the south. Ahead of us lay the town, and I wondered where in its sprawl of narrow streets and huddled dwellings I was to find my cousin. *Think*, I commanded myself. *Think*.

There must have been hundreds of workers there on the island, all of them connected in some way with the new cathedral build, all of them housed in temporary lodgings. Was there, then, a specific area where they were putting up? It seemed likely. I looked swiftly around me. Spotting a plump and cheerful woman of about my mother's age, holding the hand of a small child, I approached her.

'Good evening,' I said, and she returned the greeting with a smile. 'I'm looking for the workmen's quarters – my cousin is wounded, and I've come to help him.'

Her smile widened and I could have sworn she winked. 'Have you now!' she said. I realized, suddenly, what sort of a girl she thought I was, and I felt the hot flush spread across my face.

'Yes,' I said simply.

She studied me and her salacious grin slowly faded. 'Oh.' Then, shortly, 'Sorry. My mistake. The workmen lodge down there.' She nodded down the alley that ran along the abbey wall. 'Cross the marketplace then take any one of the

58

streets leading off it to the south. There's a huddle of lodgings down there towards the water, set up in the shelter of the abbey wall.'

She was gone before I had finished thanking her; it was her turn to blush.

Sibert grinned hugely. 'She thought you were a—'

'Yes, thank you, Sibert, I know what she thought I was.' I didn't want to dwell on that so I set off down the alley, and I heard his footsteps as he fell in behind me. We strode across the marketplace – empty now – and hurried down the first of the alleys leading off it. Presently, the more solid, permanent houses petered out, and we found ourselves in the workmen's quarter.

You couldn't really call the dwellings houses. Some were not too bad, although the walls looked flimsy and the roofs must surely let in the rain. Some were no more than lean-tos, and although we tried not to it was all but impossible not to catch glimpses of men huddling round small, inadequate hearths, with cloaks, blankets or even sacks wrapped round their shoulders to keep out the all-pervasive damp. Down towards the water, the plump woman had said, and now I realized what she meant. Space was in short supply on the island of the eels, and the only place to house the suddenly expanded workforce was down on the low ground where nobody else – nobody in their right mind – would want to live.

A man pushed past us, presumably making for his lodgings, then quickly apologized. 'Didn't see you there,' he muttered.

I stopped him. 'I'm looking for my cousin,' I said for the third time. 'His name's Morcar and he's injured. I'm a healer,' I added, in case this man thought, like the plump woman, that it was other comforts I was offering.

The man spun round, and I thought I saw relief in his face. 'Oh, you are, are you?' he demanded.

'Do you know where he is?' I snapped out.

'Oh, yes, I certainly do,' the man replied angrily. 'He lodges next door to me, and his moans and groans have kept me awake these past nights!' Then his better nature got the better of him. 'I'm right glad to see you, girl, and so will he be,' he said. 'Come on, I'll show you the way.'

He set off at a trot along an alley that led off to our right, and we passed several dwellings that gave the impression they were leaning on each other for support. Their walls were made of hazel hurdles on which daub had been haphazardly slapped, and not one of them had a properly fitting door. The man stopped at the one that was almost at the end of the row, and pushing open the door – I noticed that he did not bother to knock – he jerked his head towards a long shape lying on the floor and said, 'There he is.'

He was about to leave – I could sense how much he wanted to be away from the foetid, stinking little space – but, again, he must have listened to the voice of his conscience. He leaned close to me and said softly, 'If you need anything, my door's next one down.'

There were two things I needed immediately. 'I must have water and I need to mend the fire,'

I whispered. There was a hearth in the middle of the floor – my cousin lay curled around it – but the circle of stones enclosed little more than faintly glowing embers.

The man nodded. 'Firewood's behind the house. Water you'll need to send your man to fetch' – I realized who he meant, and I almost laughed as Sibert's faint snort of protest indicated that he did too – 'from the end of the track. You'll find a bucket and pots in the corner there.' He indicated to where the vague shapes of cooking pots and other utensils lay in a heap.

'Thank you,' I said. 'You've been very kind.' I realized he was swaying with exhaustion. 'Go and get some rest.'

He bowed briefly and hurried away.

Sibert had struck his flint and was putting a light to a tallow lamp on the floor beside the insensate Morcar. I smelt the fat and registered it as one more unpleasant aroma in the midst of all the others. Then I gathered my courage and looked around me.

The room was filthy. There were the remnants of very old straw on the beaten earth floor, and from the stench I knew it must be sodden with urine and worse. Morcar lay on a thin piece of sacking, and that, too, was soaking. I could see suspicious stains spreading out from his backside. It looked as if he had tried to wrap himself in his cloak, but then the heat of his fever must have made him push it off, for now he was naked except for a linen shift, torn open to the waist, and his hose.

His face was deadly pale. He was soaked with

sweat and shivering like a wet dog. I made myself look at his wounded foot and then wished I hadn't, for it was caked with black blood, oozing yellow pus and it stank of rot.

I glanced at Sibert. He was staring fixedly down at Morcar, his expression a mixture of revulsion and compassion. Before revulsion could win the upper hand, it was time to get him busy.

'Sibert, please would you build a good fire?' I said, gratified to note that my voice sounded calm. 'As quickly as you can, for the first thing to do is to prepare hot water and lots of it.'

Sibert turned his eyes to me. He looked as if he were about to be sick, and I could not blame him. Through my work with Edild I was starting to get used to the various stenches of disease, but all the same I could feel my mouth filling with water as I desperately quelled the heaves that rose up from my stomach.

'We're going to clean up?' he said hopefully.

'Yes,' I said firmly. 'We're going to make this little room smell as good as Edild's house, and we'll wash poor Morcar till he's fresh as a newly baptized baby.'

Sibert put aside his squeamishness and worked tirelessly, splitting wood, building up the fire steadily until he could put on larger logs. Then he took the bucket down to wherever this community drew their water, following my instructions and first filling the vessels in which I would make the infusions, suspending them on a tripod above the heat. Next he filled a larger pot

62

for washing water. While he was busy with this I rolled Morcar off his sacking and on to the cleanest of the straw, which I had heaped up ready. Then I swept out not only the space where he had been lying but also the rest of the floor area, what there was of it, right down to the bare, beaten earth. In his foraging Sibert had located the clean straw supply, and he dragged in a bale, cutting the twine around it and strewing it on the clean floor. We padded it up as best we could, and then I took a sheet from my pack and laid it on the makeshift palliasse. Sibert took Morcar's blanket outside and gave it a good shake – it was not soiled because, like his cloak, he must have pushed it off as he burned with fever – and folded it up out of the way until we needed it.

Then I turned my attention to my cousin.

It was fortunate that I did not know him very well for the tasks I had to do for him now were of the most intimate nature. He was my patient before he was my kinsman, and I found it easy to find the necessary detachment, focusing only on caring for him. Sibert helped me strip off his foul garments, taking them outside the house. I would see to them later. Then I dipped a length of linen in the hot water and began to bathe the stinking, sweaty, soiled body. It took two changes of water until I was satisfied. I had thrown a handful of dried lavender flowers into the water as it simmered and now at last the sweet, sharp smell was overcoming Morcar's stench.

The water in the smaller vessels had come to the boil, and I paused in my washing task to make the febrifuge, making up a brew of white willow bark. As soon as it was sufficiently cool, I tried to feed a little to Morcar. Sibert propped up his head, and I put some drops on his cracked lips. As I had hoped, he licked them off with his poor, dry tongue, so I dripped some more. *Slowly*, I warned myself. *Slowly, for probably he has not drunk for a long time, and too much all at once will only make his stomach clench so that he vomits.*

Then at last I looked at his foot.

I had not yet even washed it, merely covering it with linen while I attended to the rest of him; I was afraid that the wound would start to bleed as soon as I touched it, and I wanted to be sure that both he and the room were as clean as I could make them before that happened. I was ready now. I nodded to Sibert, and he came to kneel beside me at Morcar's feet, holding the lamp so that its light shone down on the wounds.

I removed the piece of linen. I dipped my washing cloth in the lavender-scented water and, taking a steadying breath, began to bathe Morcar's right foot. As the crust of blood and pus came away I saw that there were not one but two wounds, one deeper than the other and torn around its edges. As gently as I could, hoping that my cousin was too deep in his unconsciousness to feel the pain I must be causing, I delved into the bloody holes in his flesh.

I had almost forgotten about Sibert when he spoke. 'Looks as if he speared himself with a pitchfork,' he whispered.

I only remembered then that he didn't know

the details of Morcar's accident. 'Almost right,' I whispered back, 'but it wasn't a pitchfork, it was an eel gleeve.'

'Er—'

I smiled. 'It's what they call the three-pronged thing they catch eels with.'

'You would know,' Sibert remarked. As I've said, my father is an eel catcher, but he invariably uses willow traps rather than a spear. It was not really the moment to mention it though so I just nodded.

I concentrated on the wounds, trying to bring to mind everything Edild had ever told me about deep cuts. *Stop the bleeding.* Well, it had stopped now, or at least it had till I'd started poking at the holes, and now the blood was only welling up slowly as if in token protest. *Clean out pus and dirt.* Yes, done that. *Check for damaged bones.* Hmm. Trickier; if I eased open the wider wound I could see pale bone, but judging whether or not there was any break was beyond my skill. I would just have to hope there wasn't. *Stitch if necessary.* Oh, Edild, must I stitch the bigger wound? *If there is play in the edges of the cut, then yes.* I don't think I can! I've only ever practised on a pig's bladder! *You must. Do it now.*

I was used to obeying my aunt and even now, when the authoritative voice only existed inside my head, I did so. I asked Sibert to fetch my pack and rummaged in it for my bone needle and the thread made of gut. Then, working from the middle outwards, I put five stitches in Morcar's foot.

I sat back on my heels looking down at what I

65

had just done. Then suddenly, the tension and the fear caught up with me and my head swam. *Don't you dare faint!* said Edild in my head. *You haven't finished yet.*

But it was not my aunt but Sibert who brought me back to myself. He was staring at Morcar's foot, then looking up at me, slowly shaking his head.

'What is it?' I demanded urgently. Had he spotted something I'd missed?

He smiled, then a soft laugh broke out of him. 'Lassair, you just sewed up someone's foot,' he said, still smiling. 'You really are a healer, aren't you?'

I was absurdly pleased, so much so that I could have hugged him. I didn't. Instead I repeated his words silently to myself, my confidence rising with each repetition. Then, before I could get carried away with my own importance, I reminded myself that there was still a long way to go.

'He's not better yet,' I said quietly. I rested a hand on Morcar's leg. 'He's aflame with fever. I'm going to dress these wounds' – I reached for comfrey to make a poultice – 'and then we'll try to get some more of the willow bark infusion into him.'

It was a very long night.

Once Morcar was clean and bandaged, Sibert and I laid him on the clean sheet and wrapped him up in his blanket. He was burning up and shivering at the same time, and I did not know whether to cover him to keep him warm or to

66

remove the bedding to cool him. I compromised by tucking him up but removing the blanket frequently to sponge him down. All the time I kept dribbling more and more of the febrifuge into his parched mouth; soon he was actually drawing the liquid in, which I hoped was a good sign.

When, amid the sponging and the administering of the medicine, I occasionally had a moment's rest, I closed my eyes and prayed as hard as I could to the friendly guardian spirits who help healers in their work, begging them to guide my hands and make me do what was right. Recalling that we were cheek by jowl with a great Christian abbey – the second-largest in all of England, men said – I also appealed to the good Lord as well. I muttered Edild's favourite incantation, over and over again. Whenever I felt my eyelids droop, I made myself get up and feed some more of the infusion into my cousin.

Sibert was fast asleep, curled up in a ball on the far side of the hearth. I did not blame him; he had worked as hard as a man could work, and I was enormously grateful. Besides, Morcar was my patient; it was up to me to sit vigil by him.

I think I dozed for a while for suddenly the little room seemed brighter. Not exactly light; just not quite so dark. I guessed dawn must be close. Feeling guilty that I had slept, I rolled closer to Morcar and stared down at him. The tallow lamp had gone out, its fuel exhausted, but there was enough light from the glowing fire for me to see him well enough.

I studied the rise and fall of his chest. He was

breathing more deeply now, and that frightening gasp, pause, gasp as he struggled for air had eased. His face was not so deathly pale and his brow no longer had the sheen of sweat. Tentatively, hardly daring to hope, I stretched out my hand and put it on his forehead. He was still hot, still full of fever, but no longer burning up.

Perhaps it was time to hope that he just might live.

I sat down cross-legged beside his head and prayed.

Some time later Morcar opened his eyes. He looked at me, and it was instantly apparent that he had no idea who I was. Well, he hadn't seen me for quite some time so that was not necessarily significant. I smiled. 'Hello, Morcar,' I said softly. No need to wake Sibert yet.

'Hello,' he responded. He stared around him, frowning.

'You are in your lodgings on the island of Ely,' I said. 'You came here to find work, and you had an accident. You stuck an eel gleeve into your foot, and you have had a high fever.'

He absorbed that in silence for some moments. Then he said, 'My head hurts.'

Yes, it would. 'I'll try to relieve it.' I got up and squeezed out a fresh piece of linen in cold water, placing the cloth on his forehead.

'Nice,' he whispered. His eyes drooped closed.

I left the cloth in place until it grew warm, then removed it and plunged it back in the water. Then I put a drop of lavender on the fingers of each hand and, making small circles, very gently worked across his face from temples to the middle of his forehead and back again. He murmured and stirred but did not speak. Presently, I wrung out the cloth again and replaced it, leaving him to sleep.

I set about preparing the next batch of medicine. Now there were other ingredients to add besides the willow bark, and I frowned in concentration as I brought to mind Edild's instructions. I was absorbed in my task, and when Morcar's great cry rang out it made me jump so much that I scattered the contents of a sachet of dried hemp all over the floor.

I rushed to his side, reaching out to push him back for he was twisting and turning, trying to sit up, and I feared for the stitches in his foot if he went on moving so violently. 'There, now, there, lie back, Morcar,' I said, trying to make my voice steady, for I read pure horror in his wild eyes.

He collapsed back on to the bed, his face an agony of fear. 'Don't let it get me!' he moaned. 'Oh, they are there, and they are so *dark*! I am afraid – so afraid!'

I put my hand on his head, holding it down, my other hand resting against his shoulder. 'Be still,' I crooned, 'rest, Morcar.' I sensed Sibert behind me. 'We will look after you.'

'Don't let it get me!' Morcar whimpered again.

They? It? I wondered what ghastly enemies he saw in his feverish mind. Suddenly, he caught sight of Sibert, and his terrified scream hurt my ears.

'Hush, hush!' I said. 'Don't be alarmed, it's

only Sibert. He's my friend, and he has been helping me look after you.'

'I have, she's right!' Sibert piped up anxiously. 'You're safe,' he added.

Morcar stared from one to the other of us, his eyes still dark with fear and his lips moving soundlessly. Then he said, 'Is it nearly morning?'

I was close to tears, pity for him undermining me. 'Yes, Morcar.'

I saw him relax slightly. 'They will not come while it is light, will they?'

'No.' I hastened to reassure him, although I had no idea what he was talking about. He went on staring up at us, and then slowly his eyes closed. His breathing deepened. He was asleep.

Slowly, I stood up, turning round to Sibert.

'What on earth was that about?' Sibert whispered.

I shrugged. 'He's still feverish. He was probably just rambling with delirium.'

Sibert looked down at him. 'Poor man.' Then, after a moment, 'What shall I do now?'

I was so grateful for his support. So much so that, following on so closely after my moment of emotion over Morcar, for the second time I almost broke down. That, however, would have been self-indulgence, and, as Sibert had just reminded me, there was work to do.

'Find Morcar a pisspot,' I said firmly. 'I've been pouring liquid into him on and off all night, and soon there will be some coming out. If we can judge the moment right, we might save ourselves having to change his bedding all over again.'

Evidently seeing the very good sense of that, Sibert nodded and, pulling his tunic over his head even as he unfastened the door, set out to resume his foraging.

I went to stand in the alley and took some breaths of the damp, morning air. Then I went back inside and went to look through Sibert's pack to see what I might find for us to eat for breakfast.

The day seemed to crawl by on feet of lead. Sibert managed to find not only a pisspot but also fresh bread, a little jar of honey and a piece of cheese that was dry only round the edges. He sat with Morcar for a short time to allow me to go outside, relieve myself in the communal privy and stretch my legs, walking by the water. After my long night and morning, it felt like a feast day.

Morcar slept until twilight. Then, as if the onset of darkness had reawakened his fears, he opened his eyes, stared at me and said with total lucidity, 'Hello, Lassair. I think I should warn you that they are trying to kill me, and it is my belief that they will not rest until they have done so.'

SIX

'They pushed me into a filthy ditch,' my cousin said, in a voice that even the least experienced healer would have judged was quite rational, 'and they waited up on the bank until they thought I was drowned.' A shudder went through him. 'I could see them, looming up above me: huge, dark shapes like ghosts in their shrouds.'

I smoothed his brow with my hand, and he turned to look at me. 'I'm sorry,' he muttered.

What had he to be sorry about? 'It's all right,' I said gently.

'It was unspeakable down there,' he said, eyes unfocused as he confronted the horrors in his memory. 'There was a corpse, nothing but bones and slimy, rotten flesh.' He shuddered again, his whole body shaking. 'But I had to stay there, I *had* to!' he cried, as if Sibert and I had questioned his judgement, 'I had to hold my breath and make them think I was dead. I let out a few bubbles, then I made myself stop.' He put a hand over his eyes, and I guessed he was trying not to weep.

'They were up there watching you?' Sibert asked.

Morcar removed his hand. His eyes were indeed wet with tears. 'Yes. Still, quite still, like marble images. Dear God in heaven, I thought I would die down in that foul water! I could feel ... *things* floating around me, brushing against me, and I started to think there were maggots and leeches and foul things crawling on my skin, sucking my blood, and that ... that body, still in its rusty armour, bumping against my face.' The horror overcame him and he retched, bringing up a mouthful of yellowish bile. Quickly, I reached for a cloth and wiped it away. He gave me a look of thanks.

'When I could stand it no longer I broke surface and took in a mouthful of air,' he said, calmer now. 'I didn't know if they were still there or if they'd decided I was drowned and gone away. Either way, I didn't care. Death was preferable to another instant in that ditch.' He drew a steadying breath.

'They'd gone?' Sibert asked.

'Yes,' Morcar said with the ghost of a smile, 'or else I'd not be here now. I managed to get myself up out of the water and half way on to the bank, although how I did it I'll never know. Then I lay there calling out, and in the end a monk came by and went for help.'

'They brought you back here?' I said softly. I was still very perplexed as to why the monks had not instantly taken him in to care for him.

Morcar fixed his eyes on mine. 'I told them to!' he said in a hoarse whisper. Then, realizing that I did not understand, 'I thought the robed figures who tried to kill me were monks, you see. Now I'm not so sure, but then, in my panic, I did not dare let my rescuers take me

73

within the abbey.'

'I see.' Yes. It was all too clear. Morcar had faced a frightful choice between surrendering to the first-rate care of the monks, two of whom might have just tried to kill him, or being taken to his meagre, dirty lodgings where he would probably die.

He was looking at me anxiously. Hastily, I wiped the deep frown off my face, but it was too late. 'I'm so sorry, Lassair,' he said. 'I found someone to take a message to my mother to send help, and it never occurred to me that the task would fall to you. I have brought you here to danger and to the deeply unpleasant task of nursing me. Can you ever forgive me?'

'There's nothing to forgive!' I said, putting all the sincerity I could muster into my voice. 'Edild would have come herself but she is presently occupied with several very sick people back in Aelf Fen. I volunteered to come,' I added, stretching the truth a little, 'because this sort of experience is quite invaluable to an apprentice healer like me.'

'That's what she told me too,' Sibert put in, obviously keen to add verisimilitude to my tale.

Morcar managed a crooked grin. 'Really?'

'Really,' Sibert and I chorused together.

Morcar stretched experimentally, then very, very carefully moved his right foot. Surprise flooded his face. 'Oh!' he exclaimed.

I leapt up. 'Does it hurt?' I was already running through what stronger pain-relieving drug I could administer that would not risk sending him into a permanent sleep. He had already had

74

several drops of poppy...

But, 'No, it doesn't hurt,' Morcar was saying, still looking amazed. 'It throbs a bit, but otherwise it's just numb.'

I breathed a sigh of relief. 'You should drink,' I said, pouring some watered-down willow infusion into a cup. 'As much as you can, for it will help reduce the fever.'

Morcar looked embarrassed. 'Speaking of drinking,' he began.

It was Sibert who made the leap of understanding. I was ushered outside while he helped my cousin fill the new pisspot.

Morcar was still very sick. He managed to drink most of the infusion, but then, with a petulant, almost spiteful gesture that I blamed entirely on his feverish state, he pushed my hand away, spilling the dregs of the drink on the skirts of my gown.

I made him as comfortable as he could and sat beside him as he twisted and turned, muttering under his breath. I feared he was growing delirious again and, indeed, soon his moans grew in volume although he was deeply asleep, if not unconscious. I put my hand on his forehead. He was very hot.

Sibert crawled over to me, awakened by Morcar's mutterings and cries. 'Is he all right?'

It was a singularly dull question, but I realized Sibert was still half asleep and therefore had only a part of his wits about him. 'No,' I replied shortly. 'His fever's creeping up again.'

Sibert studied Morcar for a few moments.

'Can't you do anything?'

'No,' I repeated, cross that he was making me confront my inadequacies. Then, relenting, I said, 'Sibert, do you think you could go and fetch me some freshly drawn water?' We had our own supply – Sibert made sure to keep the bucket inside the door filled – but it had grown stale and warm from the fire. Sibert nodded, drew on his boots and slipped outside into the darkness.

I reached into my bag and found my little bottle of lavender oil. Pouring a few drops into the palm of my hand, I dipped in my fingers and, kneeling beside Morcar, very gently began to massage his head, from his temples across to his brow and then right up into his hairline and over his skull, extending the process I had begun earlier. Fevers were usually accompanied by severe headaches, and it could be that poor Morcar, deeply asleep though he might be, was suffering pain.

Presently, Sibert returned. The water in the bucket was icy-cold and smelled sweet. Quickly, I dipped in a cloth and, wringing it out, folded it across my cousin's forehead. As wet cloth encountered hot skin, I imagined I heard the hiss of steam.

I willed Sibert to go back to bed because I was not at all confident about what I was going to do next, and I didn't think I could even attempt it with an audience. Sleep, Sibert, I thought, staring hard at him. You are so sleepy. *Go to sleeeeep...*

Sibert yawned, his jaws stretching impossibly

wide. 'Do you mind if I go back to bed?' he whispered.

I hid a smile. 'Of course not.'

'If there's anything you need, wake me.'

'I will.'

He hovered beside me for a few moments – *just go!* I yelled inside my head – then he crept away. I heard rustling as he settled down, and then quite soon his breathing lengthened and he gave a few little snores.

I made myself forget him. Totally. Moving smoothly and quietly, I sat up cross-legged and deliberately forced my mind inwards. I was heading away from the familiar everyday world and venturing out among the spirits, as Edild and, lately, Hrype had taught me. I had done all I could for my cousin; now I needed help.

My aunt and Hrype, the healer and the sorcerer, have each in their own way taught me of the world beyond vision, the world where the true power lies and which is accessible to those with the skill and the strength to journey there. It took me months of summoning my courage before I even dared make my first attempt, for I knew I was not worthy and for someone like me to be audacious enough to try would surely make the spirits so furious that I would swiftly be annihilated.

I do not care to recall those first few occasions. The first time I threw up all over my aunt. The second time I scared myself so much that I wet myself. The third, fourth and fifth times nothing happened. The sixth time I had the tiniest glimmer of what lay beyond the smoky veil. Now I had ventured there twice without serious damage to myself (other than a splitting headache all the next day), and I was at last beginning to understand the vast power that lay concealed out there.

It was enormously helpful that I had found my spirit guardian – or rather, as Hrype would have it, my guardian had found me. Hrype had told me how to seek out my guardian, and for an alarming three days I'd been alone in the forest up around the Breckland, fasting, with only sips of water to drink, wandering lost along unfamiliar tracks and so bemused by fear, hunger and fatigue that I had not known if I'd remained in this world or had accidentally strayed into some other. When at last I'd collapsed I'd believed it was to sleep and dream – that's what it felt like at the time – but Hrype told me afterwards that this was a trance, dropped on me like a soft blanket by the spirits I had come to seek, under the influence of which I was permitted to see through new eyes.

See I did. *Watch for the first creature that comes to you*, Hrype had commanded. *He is your spirit guardian, and his essence is already within you. He will recognize you and seek you out.*

The creature that came up to me, watching me intently from bright golden eyes and gently pushing his snout into my hand, was a fox. He was a young adult, lithe and slim, his rich, reddish-brown fur thick and glossy. He had spots of white on his chin and chest and his slim feet were as black as the tip of his brush.

A fox! I knew the tales they told of foxes. I had heard tell of the supernatural power that informed them when death was near; their tricky ways; their cunning and their ability to move silently and secretively. Already, I was forming a bond with my guardian, although I did not know it, for alongside these flashing images came memories of Edild as she revealed to me my web of destiny. *You are air and fire*, she told me – air like the feather-light footstep of the fox, fire like his fiery red coat – *restless, uncompromising and direct, yet you possess the ability to conceal your true self with a plausible false skin*, she had concluded, which I thought described my ability to lie fluently and credibly in a very flattering light.

I stared at the fox and he stared back at me, so intently that I felt his intelligence boring into me, questing, searching. I tensed so tight that it hurt. Then suddenly he released me, and it was as if he smiled; I swear he gave a little nod of recognition. Then there was a moment's intense pain as something entered my mind – or perhaps something went out from it – and I understood that the fox and I were somehow united. I can't remember any more; I slept then, or perhaps passed out, and when I woke I felt calm and strong. I got to my feet – it was dusk – and walked the many miles back to Aelf Fen without stopping to eat, drink or rest; without fear, too, for I knew my fox padded silently and invisibly beside me. It took me all night, and when I was back in Edild's house I slept solidly for two days.

* * *

Now, as I sat on the floor beside my sick cousin, I sent my inner self striding off in search of Fox. Soon I felt him take up his place pacing at my side. He stretched his head up, and I felt his cool nose briefly touch my hand as he greeted me. He knew what we must do, for he was a part of me and had experienced all that I had experienced that day. Together we walked on, and my feet fell as softly as his. Presently, we came to the place we sought, and in my mind I cried out the words that would invite the spirits to come to us. Fox left my side, trotting round in a perfect circle, pausing briefly at east, south, west and north.

After some time, I knew the spirits were there. I opened my heart and begged them to help me.

When I returned to myself I could make out a very faint glimmer of light filtering through the gaps around the ill-fitting door. Very carefully I stretched, easing the cramp out of my legs; my feet had gone numb, and I gritted my teeth against the pain as the feeling returned. I must have been sitting there in my trance for many hours; the night was almost over.

For a moment I had forgotten why I'd set out on my journey to the spirits, but then it flashed back into my mind like a spring tide. Barely able to contain myself, I leaned over Morcar.

He was still alive. He was breathing steadily, and when I touched his forehead he was hot but not burning. He stirred briefly, smacked his lips, grunted and then, turning on his side, relaxed again. He was asleep. He was not unconscious or in the dread coma that leads down to death; he was just asleep.

Very quietly I got up and crept outside. I had a brand from the fire in my hand, and I hurried down the track to the water that rose and lapped at the far end. There I bent down and with my free hand scooped up a clump of mud. I walked right to the edge of the dark water, and then, closing my eyes, I turned my attention to the kindly spirits who had answered my appeal and thanked them from the bottom of my heart. Then I took a deep breath and let it out, softly and smoothly, giving my thanks to the spirit of air. I leaned down and plunged the glowing brand into the river for the spirits of fire and water. Finally, I dropped the ball of mud on to the shore for the spirit of earth. I stood for some time and gradually my racing, excited heartbeat slowed. When I felt ready, I turned my back on the darkly glistening water and returned to Morcar's lodging.

Morcar woke up shortly before mid morning. I was alone with him, Sibert having set off to find food. I was not sure Morcar could be persuaded to eat, but I was ravenous and I'm sure Sibert was too. I was also drooping with tiredness, longing to put my head down and sleep. I planned to do just that later, once Sibert was back.

I watched as my cousin's eyes slowly roamed round the sordid little room. Admittedly, the thorough clean-out had improved matters, but it was still a hovel, however you looked at it.

Morcar finished his inspection and turned to me. 'Thank you, Lassair,' he said gravely.

'Oh, it was nothing a bit of hard work couldn't manage,' I said lightly.

Morcar did not smile. 'I was not thanking you for improving the room.'

I looked down, embarrassed by his expression. 'I'm a healer,' I muttered. 'If I can't do my best to save my own cousin, there isn't much hope for anyone else.'

He did not reply. I remembered him as a silent sort of a man – and, indeed, I had put his sudden garrulousness the previous evening down to the ramblings of fever. I was just thinking that, as he hadn't yet mentioned people trying to murder him, perhaps that had been a delusion of sickness, when he cleared his throat hesitantly and spoke again.

'Lassair, we cannot stay here,' he said, lowering his voice to a whisper. 'It's not safe.'

'We can't possibly move you yet,' I whispered back. 'You are far too weak to walk even as far as the end of the track and—'

'Then you must get me a ride with a carter or find a mule,' he hissed fiercely. As if I could conjure an obliging carter or a mule up out of thin air! 'We have to get off the island, Lassair, for they tried to kill me once and will undoubtedly try again.'

I decided to go along with him. 'They won't if they don't know where you are,' I said very softly. He looked very slightly reassured, or that might have been my wishful thinking. Encouraged anyway, I added, 'Even the monk at the abbey gate hadn't heard of you and had no idea where you were.'

My words had the opposite effect from the one I'd hoped for; Morcar's pale face went ashen and sweat broke out on his forehead. *'You asked for me at the abbey?'* he said, the words a sort of strangled croak as he tried to shout and keep his voice down at the same time. 'Oh, Lassair, you fool, you've killed us all!'

I was offended at being called a fool and, besides, he was being overdramatic. Or I hoped he was. 'Shh! Be quiet! It's all right, I just told you, the monk said quite plainly he knew of no one called Morcar of the Breckland who was a flint knapper!'

Morcar rolled his eyes. 'Did you relate the long line of my ancestors while you were about it?' he demanded furiously. 'Dear God above, Lassair, you should have had more sense!'

I almost retorted that I hadn't been aware there was any need for secrecy and how else was I to have sought him out other than by asking for him? I managed to bite back the words; he was still very sick and dependent on me. At no point in a healer's long training is he or she taught that it's permissible to yell at a patient. 'I'm sorry,' I said when I had myself under control. 'I went to the abbey because I had no idea where you were, and I thought it possible the monks might be caring for you.'

'You know why I couldn't risk that. I told you,' he said. He didn't sound quite so angry.

'Yes, I know *now*,' I said patiently. 'I didn't *then*.'

83

My cousin didn't comment, except to go, 'Hrumph!'

I hurried on. 'I'm sure there's no need to worry, Morcar. As I just said, the monk I spoke to had never heard of you.'

'He might have mentioned your enquiry to his brethren,' Morcar said, face twisting in anguish, 'including the two that want to kill me!' He tried to force himself into a sitting position. Quickly, I pushed him back. I had to use more force than I'd expected. He glared up at me out of terrified eyes. 'Lassair, we have to go!' he wailed. 'It's not only that they want to kill me, there's something—' Suddenly, his jaws clamped shut, as if someone had hit him hard on the point of his chin. The fear in his eyes intensified, and he gave a low moan, such an awful sound that my heart quaked.

'What?' I whispered, barely able to get the word out.

But he shook his head. 'No. *No,*' he muttered. Then, eyes on mine again, he repeated urgently, *'We have to go!'*

'We can't,' I said. Smiling, trying to look reassuring, I added, 'You don't even know that these two men were monks, Morcar. And I'm quite sure they weren't trying to kill you – they probably just brushed against you and you slipped.'

He closed his eyes briefly, muttering under his breath. Then, opening them again, he fixed me with a furious stare and said coldly, 'You weren't there. They tried to kill me, girl. One of them took the gleeve I was using to hold myself up and the other barrelled into me like a charging bull. They thought they'd drowned me. When they find out I'm still alive, they'll come after me and have another try, and they'll kill you, too, if you stand in their way.'

He spoke with such certainty that I began to feel afraid. I allowed myself to imagine them, two dark, hooded shapes looming huge in the dim light of dusk, creeping along the alley, slowly opening the door to fall on Morcar, Sibert and me...

It was a mistake to have let the images into my mind.

Mentally, I gave myself a severe scolding. 'You cannot be moved and that is an end of it, Morcar,' I said firmly. He opened his mouth to protest, but I held up my hand. 'Tomorrow, if your condition continues to improve, I will send Sibert to find a way of transporting you off the island and away from here. I promise,' I added, risking my soul because just then I had no idea how I was going to manage it. And where, even if we got him away from Ely, would I take him? Home to his mother? To Aelf Fen and Edild's care? I thought it best not even to think that far ahead.

Morcar was watching me closely. 'I have your word?'

'Yes.' I'd just promised, hadn't I? 'When Sibert comes back you'll have to try to eat something, Morcar, because if we're going to move you you'll need to build up some strength. I will—'

We both heard the footsteps pounding along

85

the alleyway. They were approaching, fast.

Morcar's eyes widened in terror. I grabbed the blanket off the bed where Sibert had slept and threw it over him, covering him from head to injured, bandaged foot, then I lay down in front of him, so close that I could feel the thumping of his heartbeat pushing against my back. I drew his discarded hooded cloak over me like a cover and, propping myself up on one elbow, prayed to every spirit that might be listening that when they came bursting through the door they would see nothing more than an angry young woman woken violently from her slumber and none too pleased about it. *You're angry*, I told myself. *You aren't afraid because you don't know there is anything to fear. You're angry. Very, very angry...*

The hurrying footsteps stopped right outside. They must know Morcar was in here. I raised my chin, going over the words I would shout out as soon as they appeared.

The door opened.

'What do you think you're doing,' I cried, 'bursting in here without my permission? Waking me up with your noise, making me jump out of my—'

One person stood there, tall, slim, looking very upset.

It was Sibert.

I felt myself slump with relief. I leaned down to Morcar, quickly uncovering his head and saying, 'It's all right, it's just Sibert.'

I rolled away from my cousin and stood up, preparing to yell at Sibert for scaring us so badly. But his face was white – almost as pale as Morcar's. As we stood there face to face, the provisions he had brought back fell out of his hands. A small apple rolled across the floor. 'What is it?' I whispered urgently. 'What's happened?'

Sibert looked at Morcar and back to me. 'Someone's been murdered,' he said. He was trembling. 'They've found a body, down at the end of a narrow stream where some of the men have been catching eels.' He shuddered, putting up a hand to wipe his mouth. I smelled vomit.

'Did you go and look?' I demanded.

'Yes.' He moaned, briefly closing his eyes. 'It was ghastly. He'd been pinned face forward to the abbey wall with an eel gleeve. It can't have pierced his heart, for they're saying it took him most of the night to die. There's so much blood!' he exclaimed, and now both of his hands were over his mouth.

I tried not to imagine the victim's torment. To bleed to death, feeling the blood seep out of you and unable to do anything to save yourself ... *Stop it*, I ordered myself. *This is not helping.* 'Sit down,' I said to Sibert, 'and if you feel faint, or sick, put your head between your knees.' He obeyed. I fetched him a cup of water, standing over him while he sipped it. 'Better?'

He looked up and I saw that his colour was returning. 'Yes. Thank you.'

I began collecting up the dropped provisions. 'When you feel like eating, I'll prepare something,' I said, trying to make my voice calm and untroubled. 'Mmm, this bread smells good. I'm very hungry and—'

Sibert was staring at something on the floor, just in front of where Morcar lay. The shock from Sibert's announcement was still written all over Morcar's face. I would have to do something to help him very soon, I thought, for this talk of murder would surely work on his terrified fancies about hooded assassins.

I looked to see what had caught and held Sibert's attention. He was staring at Morcar's cloak, which I had thrown off as I stood up.

'What's the matter?' All my efforts to appear unflustered had flown away and I sounded exactly like what I was: a very frightened girl.

'Whose is that?' Sibert pointed a shaking finger at the cloak.

'It's mine.' Morcar's whisper was all but inaudible.

Sibert knelt down right in front of him. 'Where did you get it? *When* did you get it?' he demanded.

Morcar frowned with the effort of trying to penetrate the mist of fever and answer the urgent question. 'Er ... two, three days ago,' he said shakily. 'It had started to rain, and it went on raining. A peddler came out to where we were fishing, and he had a load of cloaks on a barrow. He said they'd keep the wet out, but it's a useless thing, and what's more it stinks.' He must have realized he was rambling and stopped.

Into the silence Sibert whispered, 'The murdered man wore one just like it.'

I was beginning to understand. As I did so, my fear rapidly escalated. 'You say the peddler had a load of cloaks?' Reluctantly, Morcar nodded. 'And he sold many?'

'Three or four,' Morcar managed.

I turned to Sibert and, meeting his eyes, I knew he had reached the same awful conclusion. The men who had attacked Morcar must have found out somehow that they had failed to kill him. They had seen a man in an identical cloak to Morcar's and, believing it to be their victim, they'd had another go. They can't have known that men other than Morcar wore similar cloaks; they hadn't even bothered to check they had the right man by looking at his face.

They had struck him from behind, spearing him to the abbey wall face forward.

My thoughts flew around like a flock of sparrows disturbed by a cat. I forced them still and tried to work out what we should do. It was surely only a matter of time before the murderers realized they had the wrong man – if, that was, Morcar was the intended victim and the dead man had been mistaken for him rather than the other way round. Assuming the worst, that it was Morcar they wanted dead, when they found out they had failed again they would come after him. Sick and injured as he was, with only a youth and a girl to protect him, they would succeed next time. As Morcar had predicted, they would probably kill Sibert and me too.

I was by no means ready to die. I was sure the same applied to Sibert and, as my patient, Morcar was my responsibility.

I turned to Sibert. 'We need to get Morcar off the island,' I said. 'As soon as it's getting dark you must slip out and find a boat. If we have to use a boatman, we'll pay him well because he'll have to keep his mouth shut. Once you're over the water, beg, borrow or steal a mule and get Morcar on it, then take him to Edild as fast as you can.' I stopped, breathing hard.

'What about you?' Sibert demanded. Morcar was looking at us in horror. 'Aren't you coming?'

'No.' I knew what I must do, and even as I hatched my plan I knew that someone had done it before me; I was repeating the actions in someone else's tale. It had worked for them, I reminded myself, or anyway this bit of it had. If the spirits were with me, it might work for me.

'Why not?' Morcar whispered, although from the expression in his eyes I think he already knew.

I looked down at him. 'Because the murderers must not know you've gone. If we all leave, there will be nobody to keep up the pretence that you're still here.' Sibert began to speak, but I knew what he was going to say and didn't let him finish. 'It has to be me,' I said firmly, 'because I'm the healer and I know what to do. I'll bustle about asking for various herbs and preparations as if I'm still treating my patient. I'll even go to your precious monks, Morcar, and ask their advice.'

Both men were staring at me, neither looking very confident. It was depressing, since I'd hoped they might have more faith in me.

'It's dangerous,' Sibert stated flatly, just as Morcar said, 'I cannot let you do this.'

I sighed. 'You don't *let* me do things, Morcar, you're my cousin not my father or my husband,' I said tetchily. 'As I keep reminding you, I'm a healer. I have a duty, and if I don't fulfil it I'm in trouble.' That was not strictly true, but I hoped neither of them would appreciate it. 'As to danger, Sibert, there's only danger around Morcar, so if you take him away and leave me here you'll actually be making it safer for me.'

There had to be a flaw in that argument, but I couldn't see it. Nor could Sibert; grudgingly, he muttered, 'Very well then.'

Quickly, I bent down to Morcar. 'Now, drink, eat if you can and rest. I will check your foot later, and we'll wrap you warmly. As soon as night falls, you must go.'

It said a lot about the state my poor cousin was in that he didn't argue any more but instead gave a feeble nod and fell back limply on his bed. I immediately busied myself with preparing food and hot drinks, going through my herbal supplies in my mind and deciding what remedy I should give to Morcar next. Anything, really, to take my mind off the prospect of that night, after they'd gone.

When I would be quite, quite alone.

SEVEN

There were several hours to wait until it was sufficiently dark to sneak Morcar away without anyone seeing us. I wished it were not so, for it was very hard to fill the time and keep the lid on my nervous anxiety. I gave Morcar a sleeping draught; the more he slept, the stronger he would be for the ordeal of the journey. Sibert and I soon ran out of harmless, non-worrying things to say and with relief – certainly on my part – eventually returned to what was uppermost in our minds.

'You really think someone tried to kill him?' he whispered, nodding down at the sleeping Morcar.

'Yes. Why, don't you?'

'Oh, yes. There seems no doubt now that the other poor man has been so brutally killed.' Sibert frowned. 'Although we still don't know which of them, Morcar or the dead man, is really the intended victim.'

I, too, had been worrying about that. 'Why would anyone want to kill Morcar?' I wondered aloud.

'I have no idea,' Sibert said. 'He's your cousin. Can't you come up with anything?'

Slowly, I shook my head. 'No. Until he came

here to Ely, he's always lived the quiet life of an industrious and not very sociable flint knapper. He's respected, well liked, as far as I know, and he's never been in any sort of trouble.'

'Then maybe it's the other man who's the real victim,' Sibert said eagerly, 'which would be good because, although of course I'm very sorry for him, at least if the killers know the right man is dead there's no danger for Morcar any more.'

'Ye–es,' I said slowly. I was thinking.

When I said no more Sibert, too, fell silent. I think he even managed to doze, although sleep was very far from me. Late in the afternoon he stirred, stretched, got up and announced that he needed some cool fresh air to clear his head.

'Be careful,' I warned.

He grinned. 'I will.' Then, his face serious again, 'I'll have a look around for a boat, preferably without a boatman in it. It would be good to earmark one for later.'

'It would,' I agreed. 'Good luck.'

Morcar woke up while Sibert was out. To my enormous relief he looked better. The bright-red flush of fever that had stained his cheeks had all but faded away. His eyes were bright, and he looked alert. When I asked him how he felt he grinned briefly and said, 'I'll do.'

My cousin is, as I think I've said, habitually a man of few words.

While we waited for Sibert to come back I encouraged Morcar to eat – I'd made a sort of savoury porridge which, even though I say it myself, smelled appetizing – and he drank a mug of my febrifuge infusion. Not wanting to put him off his meal I waited till he had finished, then I said, 'Morcar, if you were the intended victim of the killers, can you think of any reason they would want you dead?'

He smiled grimly. 'Lassair, since I've been able to think clearly again I've thought of little else.'

'And?' I prompted.

He shook his head. 'I can think of nothing.'

It was starting to look as if the dead man had been the true target. 'I—' I began.

The door was pushed open and Sibert slipped quickly inside, closing the door behind him and leaning against it. I could tell from his face that something was wrong. 'What?' I whispered.

He looked down at Morcar and me. 'There's been another murder. They found him just now, down in a ditch by the eel fisheries.'

'Drowned?' I asked, horrified.

'No.' Sibert's face was grim. 'Stab wound in the back that went straight through the heart.'

I tried to control the shaking that all but made my teeth clatter. 'Was he wearing a cloak like Morcar's?'

Slowly, Sibert nodded.

I crouched beside my cousin. 'Morcar, I think they really are after you!' I said urgently. 'They attacked the right man first time, but you managed to live. Now they have tried twice more, and two innocent men have—' I bit down on the rest of the sentence. Morcar undoubtedly knew already what I'd been about to say. 'There must be a reason why they want you dead!' I said instead. 'Can't you think of *anything*? Has any small incident happened recently that you've forgotten about? Something you saw or over-heard? Something somebody told you that seemed insignificant at the time but now—'

Sibert nudged me. 'Let him speak,' he said.

I realized Morcar was smiling – very faintly – as he waited for my flow of words to stop. 'Sorry,' I muttered.

His expression deepened fleetingly into a real smile. Then he said, 'There was something.'

Together Sibert and I said, 'What?'

'It was when Lassair asked if there was any-thing I saw,' Morcar said slowly, frowning as if thinking hard. 'There was something, when I was going home after a long day's eel fishing. I was tired and dispirited, it was raining like the Flood was coming back and my new cloak was letting in water. I was trudging along under the abbey wall and I could see a gate house up ahead. Not the main one; this was a small one that they don't use much. I heard a shrill cry but it was quickly muffled, and I peered into the shadows to see who was there. I could make out four figures, maybe five. They were monks, or I *thought* that was what they were – robed men, anyway, and at least one wore the dark, hooded habit of the Benedictines.' He paused. I noticed that his breathing had quickened and I hoped it was with the effort of telling his story and not from rising fever.

'I thought they were just horsing around,' he went on. 'One of them was a younger man. He wasn't much more than a lad, maybe fifteen or sixteen, and he was slim, slight, with bright, very pale hair. I reckoned the older men were teasing him, maybe even bullying him a bit. I guessed the hastily suppressed cry was him – the pale lad – and probably one of the others had quickly shushed him because they were close by the abbey gate and the older monks didn't want anyone to hear the horseplay and get them into trouble.' He stared into the distance, eyes unfocused. 'I don't reckon they hold with monks being boisterous,' he remarked.

I was trying to make sense of it. The monks had been roughing up the pale boy and they knew they'd get into trouble if their superiors found out. Was that it? But not that much trouble, surely – not enough to kill the man who had seen the incident...

Sibert said, 'Perhaps the pale boy doesn't want to be a monk and they were taking him inside the abbey by force.'

It was a better idea than mine. 'They knew someone had seen them, that someone being Morcar' – I picked up the thread – 'and, because what they were doing was wrong, the witness had to be silenced before he told anyone what he'd seen.'

Sibert and I both turned to Morcar. 'What do you think?' Sibert asked him. 'Does that make sense?'

Morcar thought about it. 'I suppose so,' he said. 'But why would it matter to anyone but the lad if he were made to be a monk when he didn't want to?' He glanced at me. 'Who did they fear I'd tell?'

96

I had no idea. 'Er—'

'It would matter,' Sibert said slowly, 'if the pale boy is someone important.'

Silence fell as we all thought about that. Eventually, I said tentatively, 'What, like some lord's son who was supposed to make an influential marriage?' We all knew how the wealthy and powerful in our land used their children as pawns in their complicated games, marrying them off where their presence would most benefit their fathers.

'It's possible surely?' Sibert said. 'And whoever is trying to shut him up with the monks doesn't want this marriage to happen.'

It was possible, certainly it was. 'Yes,' I replied. With an effort I turned away from the interesting avenues of speculation that were flooding my mind. 'We must work out the why later,' I said firmly. 'For now, we have something far more important to do.' I edged closer to Sibert, lowering my voice. 'Did you find a boat?'

He nodded. He was smiling, excitement thrumming through him. 'Yes. It lies tethered to a post right at the end of the track, and it looks as if nobody's been near it for years.'

'Is it watertight?' I demanded. It sounded too good to be true.

'It floats,' Sibert hedged. 'But listen, I've got some really good news – it's raining again, very, very hard!'

Morcar, hearing this, groaned aloud. Thinking of him, my poor, sick patient, I said sharply, 'Why in the Lord's name is that *good* news?'

97

Sibert looked happily at Morcar and me. 'Because the water's started to rise once more, very fast. Already, many of the lower-lying areas around the island are flooded.'

I still did not understand. Morcar did. He said kindly, 'When it floods, Lassair, you don't need to find a mule or a carter to take you from Ely to Aelf Fen. With a boat and a strong oarsman' – he shot a grateful look at Sibert – 'you can go by water all the way.'

I did my very best for my cousin. I checked the wounds in his foot, which were angry looking, the surrounding flesh red and swollen, but which showed no signs of putrefaction. I dabbed on more comfrey ointment and re-dressed the foot, wrapping a generous amount of linen around it to pad it. The wounds would hurt like fury if Morcar so much as touched his foot to a hard surface, and I knew I must do what I could to soften the impact. Then Sibert and I helped Morcar into his outer garments, wrapping him closely in his woollen cloak and putting the new short, hooded cloak over the top. I prepared a pack of food and medicines – not many of the latter, for with any luck he would be with Edild in a few hours – and Sibert slung it on his back. Then we gathered up Morcar's blanket and the sack containing his tools, and together Sibert and I got him to his feet.

Sibert checked the alley outside. It was dusk and there was nobody about, which was hardly surprising as it was raining so hard that we could barely see three yards in front of us. I dived back for my own blanket and put it over Morcar's head. He needed it more than I did.

We set off, keeping under the eaves of the hovels as much as we could, and Sibert led the way down to the isolated spot where the boat lay all but hidden in the rushes. Its bottom held several inches of water, which Sibert baled out as best he could with his cupped hands. Then we helped Morcar down into it, settling him on the thwart that ran across at the stern. The boat had a framework over the stern and the tattered remnants of a cover for it lay folded under the thwart. The cover was made of canvas, hard and brittle with age, full of dusty dried leaves, cobwebs, dust and general dirt; by the time Sibert and I had draped it over the frame we were both filthy as well as soaked. The cloth did a little to keep the worst of the rain off Morcar and as he looked up at me I could just make out his white face.

He must have seen my anxiety. 'I'll be all right,' he said. I could hear his teeth chattering and I leaned out to him, trying to tuck his blanket more tightly around him, rocking the boat dangerously.

'Stop it, Lassair!' Sibert said in a harsh whisper. 'We're wet enough without you spilling us into the water!'

I drew back on to the bank. I felt utterly miserable, worried out of my mind for my patient and not at all sure I was doing the right thing. It would do him no good if we got him away from the men who were trying to kill him only to have him die out on the fen in an open boat...

It was as if he read my thought. 'I won't die,' he said with a grin. 'Takes more than a drop of rain to see me off.'

His uncomplaining courage all but undid me. 'Go on, get on your way,' I called out softly to Sibert. 'Take him straight to my aunt.'

'I will.' Already, Sibert had coiled in the painter, and now he was nudging the little boat away from the shore with an oar. As I watched he slid the other oar into the water and, as soon as he was clear of the bank, he began to row, quickly getting into a rhythm so that the boat gathered speed. The craft and its passengers disappeared into the teeming rain.

'Goodbye. Good luck,' I whispered.

They wouldn't have heard me. Over the deafening sound of the rain on the water, they wouldn't have heard me even if I'd yelled.

The little hovel seemed lonely and empty without them. I tried not to think about them out there on the fen; there was nothing I could do now to help them and they must take their chance, relying on Sibert's oarsmanship and knowledge of the area to get them safely to Aelf Fen. It ought not to take long; going straight across the floodwater was much more direct than going the long way round on dry land. Edild would not mind being woken up in the predawn, and she would—

Stop it, I commanded myself.

I tidied the room, sweeping out the straw that Morcar had lain on and stacking it inside the door for disposal in the morning. I shook up the bed where Sibert had slept and spread out his blanket. I no longer had my blanket, having given it to Morcar, so I made up the fire, banked it carefully with ash to make sure it stayed in till morning, then wrapped myself in my shawl, pulled the end of Sibert's blanket up over my legs and closed my eyes.

I had not realized how exhausted I was. The next thing I knew, I was opening my eyes to daylight, sunshine was filtering through the cracks around the door and there were sounds of people stirring in the houses either side of me.

The new day was here.

I took advantage of being alone in the room. I heated water, stripped to my skin and washed, then quickly dressed again. I had spread my gown in front of the fire while I slept and now it was more or less dry. I combed out my hair and re-braided it, then I made myself sit down and eat some breakfast. The bread was dry, but I was so hungry that I barely noticed.

As soon as I had finished I set about my self-appointed task. I had remained in Ely to make the killers think Morcar was still there, being looked after by me; it was time to make a start. I tied a clean, white cap over my neatly braided hair and set off.

I knew where the apothecary's shop was situated; I had spotted it as Sibert and I had searched for Morcar. Now I pretended to be the dullest-witted healer ever to walk the earth, asking again and again for directions and finally, with a flirtatious little smile, forcing a young

101

merchant to walk me right up to the shop door. The more people that got to hear of the silly young healer who could not find her way, the better. From the apothecary I was careful to buy the ingredients I would have required to go on treating Morcar; I needed them in any case, having used up almost all of the supplies I had brought with me. Then I went up to the main gate of the abbey and, very meekly, asked if it were possible to speak to the infirmarer.

The monk at the gate said, 'We do not permit the entry of lay women into the abbey save with special permission.' He was a different type from the monk I had seen on my first day, a nicer, more charitable type, for he managed to put regret into the official words, and he looked at me quite kindly.

'I see,' I said, eyes cast modestly down. 'I am sorry to have troubled you, brother.' I gave a sad little sigh.

As I turned to leave he said, 'Wait.' I stopped. 'What did you want with the infirmarer?' he asked.

I risked a quick look up into his face. 'I am nursing my sick cousin,' I said. 'He fell in the ditch and has a fever, and he also has a deep wound in his foot.' That ought to be sufficient to describe Morcar, if anybody were interested. 'I'm doing my best to treat him' – quickly, I reeled off the standard remedies for fever and grave wounds – 'but I wanted to ask someone with much, much more experience than I have if I'm doing right.' I bit my lip, staring at my boots.

There was a pause. Then the monk said, 'Wait here. I will send word.'

I waited. I wanted to cheer with jubilation, but I restrained the urge. Presently, my monk returned. 'He's on his way,' he muttered. Then he went back to guarding the gate, glaring out across the street as if pretending to be the very last monk in the abbey to be caught in a simple act of kindness for an anxious young healer.

I waited for some time. Then a gruff voice behind me said, 'I'm Brother Luke. Are you the girl with the fever patient?'

I spun round to him, bowing my head as I admitted that I was. Curtly, he ran through his version of how I ought to care for my cousin, which was pretty much what I'd been doing anyway. When he'd finished, I thanked him profusely and, reaching into the little leather purse at my waist, took out a coin. 'Please put this in the poor box, Brother Luke,' I said.

He looked at it, surprise in his eyes. I had given him more than I could afford, but I wanted to make quite sure he remembered me and, hopefully, spoke of me to all his brethren.

It was almost midday before I returned to the little house. I knew someone was inside, for the leather strap that I had wound around the latch to hold it firmly closed was hanging loosely from a nail on the door post. Hoping it was Sibert, I went in.

Sibert lay fast asleep on the straw mattress, mouth open, snoring rhythmically. I found myself smiling broadly; it was such a relief to see him. I burned to ask him if Morcar was all right, but he needed to sleep. I left him to it and set about unpacking the clutch of small, linen bags containing the supplies I had purchased from the apothecary. You just never knew when you might need a fever remedy...

Sibert woke up late in the afternoon and said he was hungry and was there anything to eat? While he slept I had been out to find food, and I had prepared a generous meal. I'd visited the area where stalls had been set up to serve the huge workforce, buying dumplings made of flaked fish, flour and spices, a bread and mush-room poultice, a pot of honey-glazed carrots and slices of a sweet loaf flavoured with ginger, spices, berries and walnuts. I also had a jug of mead. I had spent far more than I ought to have done – we would have to exist on meagre sup-plies from now on, unless Sibert managed to go foraging – but there was something that I had to ask Sibert to do, and I badly needed him to agree.

We ate hungrily, having first raised our mead cups and drunk to Morcar's good health. Sibert had already told me he was all right and had survived the journey; the first thing he'd said when he woke up – well, actually the second, after *I'm hungry* – was, 'Don't look so worried, Lassair, Morcar's tucked up safely at Aelf Fen and both your aunt and my uncle are looking after him to the very best of their abilities.'

I made myself relax as Sibert and I worked our way through our feast. It was too good to waste by being so anxious that I didn't notice what I was eating. When we had finished and were relaxing on our straw piles, I gathered my courage and said, 'Sibert, we can't stay here for ever pretending to nurse a man who isn't here. Sooner or later someone will discover the deception, and besides I've got better things to do with my life.'

Sibert grinned. 'Me too.'

'We have to find out who tried to kill Morcar and why,' I hurried on, 'and so far the only thing we have to go on is that strange scene that he saw at the abbey gate.'

'Yes,' Sibert agreed. 'The pale boy who does not want to be a monk.'

It was a grand conclusion to draw from such a small incident but, as I had just said, all we had. If it had been this that Morcar had seen, and that the killers had to keep secret, then it was indeed the right place to begin. Before I could start to doubt myself I said, 'You've got to go into the abbey, Sibert. You have to find this pale-haired boy and speak to him. If he's there against his will, we'll try to help him. Even if we can't, we must tell someone' – the abbot, I supposed – 'and bring the whole thing into the open, because only then will the killers stop hunting Morcar.'

Sibert obviously followed the logic of this, nodding as I spoke. Then he fixed me with a glare and said, 'You said *you* must go into the abbey. Don't you mean *we*?'

I took a breath, slowly letting it out. Then I said, as calmly as I could, 'No, I'm afraid not. It's an abbey full of Benedictine monks and they only admit lay women when they really have to.'

'You're not a woman, you're a healer,' Sibert protested.

I knew what he meant. 'Yes, but I don't think they make the distinction.' I explained about my visit that morning and how, even having described myself as a healer, I had not been allowed in.

'Oh.' He sounded forlorn. Accepting, but definitely forlorn.

I reached over, the mead jug in my hand, and topped up his mug. 'Come on!' I said bracingly. 'A man who has just rowed across half the fens and back again is surely not afraid of a bunch of monks!'

He grinned. 'It's not the same,' he said vaguely.

No, I was sure it wasn't. I dug him playfully in the ribs. 'What's the matter, afraid they'll make you stay in?'

I had been joking, but from the sudden heat in his face I realized I'd hit the bull. He muttered something, his face still red, and I reached for his hand. 'They won't.' I stated it flatly. 'If they do, I'll come and get you.'

His smile widened. 'Promise?'

'Promise.'

He gave a deep sigh. 'Very well. I'll go in as soon as they open the gates in the morning.'

EIGHT

We made Sibert as unmemorable as we could next morning. I fashioned a cap for him out of the woven scarf he was wearing round his neck, pulling it forwards to conceal his forehead and brows. His tunic was muddy from his trip across the fens, and I resisted the urge to brush it clean; cleanliness stood out more than dirt among a hard-working population, and it would be better if nobody remembered any details about the man who had come looking for the pale-haired monk. Just in case.

I didn't let myself think too much about *just in case.*

As we ate our breakfast we concocted a story: Sibert would say his name was Faol and he worked with his father, who was a rat catcher, and did the monks have any areas of the abbey that were infested? If they said no, then Sibert was to pretend to have seen ominous signs, upon which we hoped the monks would be alarmed into inviting him to have a good look round. Once inside, it ought to be easy. This was, after all, an abbey that at present was in the throes of a major redevelopment, with a huge, new cathedral rising in place of the little Saxon church. Workmen were going in and out all day, no doubt swarming all over the building site. Indeed, our first idea had been to have Sibert pretend to be one of them. We had, however, realized that this disguise would not give him the excuse to venture into the abbey's private areas; hence the rat-catching plan.

I saw him off with a hug and an encouraging word. I watched him as he hurried off up the alley. Then I went back inside and started to pray.

The pale-haired boy lay on his hard bed. He knew he could not stay alone there for long. One of the worst things about this new life into which he had been so abruptly thrust was the almost total lack of privacy. Not that he'd ever had much of that in his humble village home, but what he had always sought – and quite frequently managed to achieve – was solitude. Now every instant of the day and the night was spent in the close company of other people. Those people were monks, moreover, and to the last man senior to him in the religious life, which meant they were entitled to tell him what to do and make sure he did it. He had never in his life felt so many pairs of eyes studying his every move, and it unnerved him so badly that he barely knew himself.

As if that were not bad enough, he was terrified.

There was something quite dreadful within the abbey. He knew that without a shadow of a doubt. He had seen it. *It* had seen *him*, or it would have done if it had— *No*. He forced himself to arrest the thought. Wasn't it enough that the fearful spectre haunted his brief snatches of uneasy sleep, without imagining it in his waking hours?

They called him Brother Ailred, but that was not his name. He was not sure that he ought to be called brother, for he was quite certain he had not taken any vows in the short time he'd been at Ely. But to whom could he protest? The other monks barely let him speak, and he was quite sure that if he tried nobody would listen.

As far as the pale-haired youth was concerned, his name was Gewis. He was fifteen years old, and he had been born and bred in a small village called Fulbourn, on the edge of the fens some five miles to the south-east of Cambridge. His home had been out to the south of the village, close to where the Gog Magog hills rose up. His father had died four years ago when Gewis was eleven. Gewis wished he had fonder memories of him, but the truth was that his father had been an embittered man, self-absorbed with little time and few kind words to spare for his young wife and son. His name was Edulf and he was a carpenter, or so he claimed, although Gewis had rarely seen a man less handy with the tools of his trade. As Gewis grew towards maturity and began to think about his childhood he realized that his mother Asfrior must have had an income of some sort, for otherwise the little family would surely not have survived. As soon as he was old enough, Gewis had picked up sufficient skill to take on carpentry jobs, at first only the simplest work that other men rejected as beneath them, then gradually progressing to more demanding tasks. The fact that the household depended on the young son and not the father for its income must, Gewis thought, have served only to increase Edulf's anger with the world and resentment at his place within it.

Life at home with his mother had been in some ways easier without his father's gloomy presence, although his mother had grieved long for her husband and, to Gewis's dismay, now appeared to be as resentful as Edulf had been at her lowly lot. Gewis did not understand; it was as if both of them, first his father and now his mother, were angry about something. What it was, Gewis had no idea. All the thoughts he had wasted on trying to puzzle out the mystery led nowhere, and in the end he'd concluded only that at some time someone had somehow cheated his father out of some possession that would have made the family's life easier, although what this possession might be he had no idea. He guessed that his father must have passed on this secret to his wife as he lay on his death bed, so that now she, too, was soured by constantly dwelling on what might have been.

It was a thin, unsatisfactory conclusion, and Gewis had never really been happy with it. There was something else, something he tried hard not to think about, especially now when he was away from his home and could not look after his mother. The unwelcome fact was that both of them, first Edulf and now Asfrior, had grown very, very afraid.

Given the underlying mystery that lay hidden

in his past and the very evident fear of both his parents, Gewis had hardly been surprised when *they* had come to Fulbourn to seek him out. His mother's reaction had been strange; it had almost been as if she'd expected the visitors. There were four of them, dressed in the robes of Benedictine monks, and all were broad, strongly built men. Even had Gewis thought to refuse the request that sounded like an order – that he accompany them there and then to the abbey at Ely – he would have stood no chance of evading or escaping them. They provided him with a garment that looked very much like a monk's habit, similar to the robes they wore. He was given a moment to bid his mother farewell – she seemed to be encouraging him to go with the monks, so presumably it was all right – then they'd set off.

For most of the journey north to Ely he had felt too stunned to speak, and the presence of the four men who stationed themselves around him as they walked had been powerful enough that he'd dared not pose any of the dozens of questions that had flown to and fro in his mind like gnats over a summer meadow. It was only after they'd crossed the water to the island and were on the point of entering, through a gate in a shadowy alley, into the abbey itself that he'd managed to protest. His moment of rebellion had been very brief: one short cry, then the hard hand of the biggest monk had crushed against his lips and they'd bundled him inside.

In the days since then they had kept him very busy as slowly he learned the daily round of the monks. They told him virtually nothing. His only comfort had come when an old monk, with what he fervently hoped he was right in thinking to be a kindly smile, had leaned across to him and whispered, 'Welcome. You're safe here.'

Safe? Safe here? That suggested to Gewis that he had not been safe out in the world in his village. Why not? Where, or what, was the threat? Gewis had no idea. But, if he had been asked, he would have bet it had something to do with the oddities of his past...

Gewis heard footsteps, many of them, pacing steadily along the passage outside the long dormitory. Hastily he got to his feet, straightened his robe, ran a hand over the unfamiliar shaved patch on the crown of his head and went to join the other monks. They were going to pray, as they did several times a day for what felt like hours. It would have been difficult to concentrate anyway for someone like Gewis, here through no wish of his own. As it was, somehow the necessary detachment had to be summoned to ignore the fact that the abbey was now a building site and to fix the heart, mind and soul on God.

Gewis stood in his appointed place. His eyes were not fully closed and carefully, moving as little as possible, he looked around from under his eyelids, trying to assess what progress had been made in the time since he had last been summoned to prayer. What he observed made his heart drop; weary, lonely, sad, he closed his eyes and gave himself to the prayers.

The image, however, stayed right there in his

mind. They had almost done it, those hard-working, tough and ruthlessly determined men who took the Norman coin in return for their job of violation. Only a fragile shell remained, and soon that, too, would be gone.

They were building a huge new cathedral on the very spot where the little Saxon church had stood. There was no way that the two structures could coexist and so almost the entire Saxon church must be demolished. Some of its core elements would survive: the south side chapel, it was rumoured, would form the north wall of the new monks' quire. Within a precious and much-loved building, the south side chapel had been particularly special for it was here that the bones of Ely's early abbesses and benefactors had been interred, together with the remains of other beloved figures who had been involved in the abbey's life. Even this little chapel was not immune from the wreckers' destructive mallets, and the signs of the attack were evident. This onslaught was, according to the whispers, both a disrespectful and a dangerous thing to do; rumours abounded, the most frightening of which was that something had been disturbed that would have been far better left in peace.

Nobody seemed willing to describe what that something was. Gewis's eyes fluttered open as he recalled what one of the other young monks had said yesterday about a misty shape that had loomed up out of the shadows beneath the abbey wall. Hastily, he tried to crush the memory of those furtive whispered words, but it proved too strong. *It was shrouded all in white ... It held out*

113

a hand like a claw ... There was something terribly wrong with its face...

Gewis felt fear churn in his bowels. *Dear God,* he prayed silently, *help me! Save me!*

But help did not come.

For the morning's work he was sent to sweep the many passages that wound through the abbey. Building sites made a lot of dust and dirt, and the monks spent many hours every day trying to keep their living quarters as clean as they could. Gewis was sent with two other monks to the maze of apartments to the south side of the new cathedral. Presently, he found himself alone, sweeping the length of a narrow corridor between high walls. There was a little door at the other end, and he was aiming to deposit his growing pile of sweepings on the far side of it.

He heard footsteps. Turning, expecting to see one of his brethren, he found himself face to face with a young man perhaps a couple of years older than himself. The newcomer was tall and slim, with fair hair styled quite long and blue-green eyes that held a wary expression. He wore a shabby, shapeless cap pulled forward over his forehead.

He wasn't a monk and this alone was sufficient to make Gewis approach him eagerly. 'Can I help you?' he asked.

The stranger was staring at him intently. Then, taking Gewis totally by surprise, he grinned and said, 'Yes, I think you can.'

Gewis had no idea what the young man meant and, before he could ask, there was the sound of

114

running feet and three older monks came hurrying along the corridor. The one in the lead drew to a halt, composed his face into a smile and said, 'Thank you, Brother – er, Brother Ailred, we will deal with this.' His two companions had hastened to take up positions either side of the stranger and, so subtly that Gewis wondered how they had achieved it, they had swiftly turned him round and were ushering him back along the passage.

'You say you saw a rat scuttling away down here?' the first monk said to the stranger as he followed the group back up the corridor. The young man muttered something in reply and the monk said, 'That is most helpful and we shall take steps immediately to deal with the problem. Now, if you would be so kind, let us explore this way...'

Gewis stared after them, his broom hanging from his limp hand. He tried to fight the thought, but he was fairly sure he had just seen a helping hand from the outside world smoothly and efficiently snatched away.

The morning seemed endless and as the hours crept by I had to fight the increasingly horrible scenes that my imagination threw up. *Sibert can look after himself*, I kept saying to myself. *He is in no danger. He has gone into an abbey full of monks – God's men, for heaven's sake! – and he will come to no harm.*

That was all very well, but the logic and the good common sense were having a hard job holding their own against images of eel fishers

115

in hooded cloaks lying dead on the sodden ground, murdered in ways too brutal to contemplate...

Frustrated, anxious and sick of the sight of the four walls that enclosed me in that small room, I drew my shawl around me and went outside, quickly walking the short distance down to the waterside at the end of the alley. It was not exactly raining this morning, but moisture made the air heavy and already hundreds of tiny droplets had settled on my shawl. I clutched my fingers into the fine wool, remembering my beloved sister Elfritha, who had made it for me. The thought was reassuring, and just for an instant it was as if she stood beside me, hugging me close. I wondered if she was thinking of me just then, even as I thought of her. Love is God's miracle, the men of the church tell us, and I have often thought that if it is indeed miraculous then it probably can unite people across distance.

I went on standing there, barely aware of the brownish water slipping by just below my feet. It was only gradually that I realized I was no longer worrying about Sibert. I was, in fact, quite calm.

It was perhaps the absence of that anxiety that made me appreciate something I should have thought of ages ago, something which, as soon as it had occurred to me, drove out the calm. Oh, I thought, *oh*. How could I have missed that?

Morcar had witnessed the pale-haired monk being bundled into the abbey, and for that the men with the young monk had tried to kill my cousin, making two more attempts when somehow they found out that he had survived. They had killed two men whom they had mistaken for Morcar. Did they know that their true victim still lived? I had feared they would find out, which was why it had been imperative to get Morcar off the island and divert his would-be killers by pretending he was still here, being nursed by Sibert and me. So far, so good, but what would they do when they started to wonder if Morcar had told anyone – Sibert and me, for example – what he had seen?

Morcar's life was in danger because he had seen something he shouldn't have seen. This perilous secret was now also known to Sibert and to me. Try as I might, I could see no way that the two of us did not also now share the danger.

I wished I could fly away down the waterside path, opening my mind and letting my dowser's gift seek what I so desperately needed. I wished I could let my feet find the safe paths across the fenland so that, safe in a place that meant death to everyone else, I could evade those who must surely be hunting for me. Had it been just me, I would have done just that. My ancestress had known how to cross the treacherous water; in my heart I knew I could do so too.

It was not just me. There was Sibert, to whom I was bound in some way that I did not really understand. As well as him there was the pale-haired young monk, possibly trapped inside the abbey against his will and without doubt in-volved in something so serious that men were driven to kill.

I yearned to flee, but I had to stay.

I turned away from the water and walked slowly back to the little room.

I found Sibert waiting for me. It was a relief to see him, and for a moment that drove the greater fear aside. He was tense with excitement and I made him sit down on the straw while I made him a hot drink and tore off a hunk of bread.

'I found him!' he said through a mouthful of bread.

'He's alive? He's not hurt?' I don't know why I thought they might have harmed him.

'No, no, he was busy sweeping a passage, and he looked fine.'

'You're sure it was the right one, the pale monk who Morcar saw?'

'I can't be absolutely certain, naturally,' Sibert said reasonably, 'but the boy I saw was pale all right.'

'Describe him.' It sounded very curt, and I shot Sibert an apologetic smile.

He grinned in return. 'He's quite slight, slimly built and not very tall,' he began, 'and he looks sort of insubstantial, as if he might float away. He was sweeping quite slowly and rhythmically, as if he were moving in a trance.'

Interesting. 'What did he look like? His face, I mean?'

'His skin is very fine and very white – more like a girl than a boy, really. His eyes are ... I'm not sure. Grey, I think, and very light, without much colour at all. His hair is white.'

'*White?* What, like an old person's?'

Sibert thought. 'No, not exactly. Old people's hair goes dry and straw-like. The boy's hair is glossy, and it swings when he moves his head.'

'But it's white?' I insisted. I had never heard of a young person with white hair.

Again, Sibert paused to think, this time screwing up his face as he tried to describe what he had seen. 'White's wrong,' he said eventually. 'The young monk's hair is cream.'

Cream hair, white skin, eyes with barely any colour at all; what on earth *was* this boy?

I turned to Sibert to find his eyes – his lovely, familiar, blue-green eyes – on mine. The moment felt heavy with menace. Trying to break the mood, I said flippantly, 'He sounds more like a ghost than a living person.'

And Sibert gave a shudder so powerful that I saw him tremble.

I felt his fear like a living thing, and it seemed to leap from him to me so that suddenly I, too, was shaking. 'What is it?' I managed, my voice barely audible.

'A ghost,' Sibert whispered, eyes wide with dread. 'Oh, dear God, supposing he *was* a ghost? And I was right beside him. I could have reached out and touched him!'

For a moment we were both frozen with horror. Then I said, forcing a grin, 'Sibert, whatever else ghosts may or may not do, I don't think they sweep corridors.'

After several heartbeats, Sibert laughed. An uneasy, nervous laugh, yes, but still a laugh.

I wondered why the very mention of the word *ghost* should have provoked such a reaction, for

I knew from personal experience that Sibert could be brave when danger faced him. There was obviously something he hadn't told me, and I reckoned there was only one way to find out. 'Sibert, is the abbey haunted?'

He paled again and, hand like iron on my wrist, said urgently, '*Shhhhhh!*' Then, recovering, with an attempt at nonchalance that touched me to my core, 'Yes. They do say so.'

He was obviously so very reluctant to say more, but we both knew he must. I twisted my wrist out from his grasp – I'm sure he didn't realize it but his fingers were hurting me – and held his hand. 'Tell me,' I said simply.

He drew a deep breath, then another. Then: 'The monks are scared and their superiors try to pretend that it is not so. They say the men are merely unsettled because the building work is so disruptive to their normally tranquil life. They cannot easily hear God's voice amid the uproar, and this is disturbing them.'

I was quite surprised at the idea of God not being able to make himself heard to one who tried to listen, even above the tumult of a construction site. What were the senior monks trying to cover up? 'You spoke to some of them?' I asked.

Sibert nodded. 'Yes. They are quite approachable, really, or anyway the younger ones are. They're just like anyone else and they seemed eager to come and chat to me, although I noticed that they kept looking over their shoulders in case the men in charge noticed.'

'What did they say about the ... the ghost?'

Sibert swallowed nervously. 'The rumours say that something's been seen in the area where the old Saxon church stood.'

'Something—?' I began, but Sibert shook his head and I stopped. My curiosity burned me, but I would have to let him tell his story in his own way.

'The new cathedral is much bigger than the old church,' he went on, 'but it's being built on the same spot, so they're having to demolish most of the church. The shingle roof and the outer walls went ages ago, and the tower was the first thing to be knocked down. The most sacred part was the little chapel in the south aisle, because its walls are full of bones.'

'Bones?'

'It's a place of honour, Lassair, reserved for the remains of people like old abbesses and Saxon lords. They told me that St Etheldreda's bones are in there.'

I was beginning to suspect what the nature of this rumour might be. 'And one of these worthies is resenting the disturbance?' I suggested.

Sibert clearly disliked my light tone. 'It's nothing to joke about,' he said sharply. 'You didn't talk to them. You didn't sense the terror they're feeling in there.' He jerked his head towards the abbey.

'No, that's true,' I acknowledged meekly. 'What have they seen?'

Again, Sibert drew a steadying breath. 'It's a shape, clad in white,' he said, 'like a corpse in its shroud. Its face is deadly, ashen, and its hair is

121

pale as snow.' He, too, was pale, and I heard him suppress a couple of wrenching, retching sounds.

Fear, I suddenly understood, was making him physically ill...

'And it's got pale eyes too?' I asked, trying to bring his attention back to me.

He turned to stare at me, horror all over his face. His mouth worked, but no words emerged. He tried again, this time successfully, and instantly I wished he hadn't.

Because he said, 'It hasn't got any eyes.'

NINE

We sat there on the straw, clutching each other's hands, as the fear flowed around us like a dense, dark cloud. A ghost with no eyes ... Dear Lord, what sort of a creature could it be? What had been done to it, and how terrible would be its wrath now that its uneasy peace had been so violently disrupted? Was it even now plotting its unspeakable vengeance?

I squeezed Sibert's hand. It was warm, human, living, and it squeezed back. I sensed the fear retreat a little. 'Sibert, we must leave the island,' I said. 'It's not safe, we—'

'The ghost has only been seen within the abbey or, at the worse, just outside the walls,' he said quickly. 'We're not in danger out here, or at least I don't think so.' He looked uneasily around the little room.

'It's not the ghost I'm afraid of.' It was – of course it was – but I wasn't going to admit it. 'There's something else.' Briefly, I explained to Sibert what I had realized while he was in the abbey. 'The killers must surely suspect that Morcar told us what he saw, and they'll come for us. Morcar's safe now, but you and I will be as helpless as chicks when the fox breaks into the henhouse.'

'I can fight!' Sibert protested, stung.

'Four, maybe five of them?' That was what Morcar had said.

Sibert frowned. 'Hmm.'

Sensing a breach in his defences, I pushed on. 'We needed to pretend I was still here looking after Morcar only for as long as it took you to get him to safety,' I pointed out. 'You managed that, and now he's tucked up snugly in Aelf Fen, and you must admit it's very unlikely the killers will find him.'

'I went over the water,' Sibert said musingly. 'I left no trail for even the most expert tracker to pick up.'

'There you are then!' I exclaimed. 'Morcar's perfectly safe. It's you and I who are in danger now.'

'Yes,' he said, still in that thoughtful way. Then he spun round, looked straight into my eyes and said, 'You can go if you want. I'm staying here.'

I sighed in exasperation. 'Sibert, *why*? It's dangerous, you've just admitted that, and you said yourself that the pale monk hasn't been harmed, so maybe Morcar was wrong and the boy isn't—'

'It's nothing to do with the pale boy.'

Surprised, I said, 'What then?'

A half-smile twitched at his mouth. 'Don't you know? You touched on it when we were on our way here.'

Then I understood.

I tried to recall exactly what he had said. *I've always wanted to go to the island. There's some-*

thing strange about the story of what happened to my father.

His father, poor Edmer, fatally wounded in the Ely rebellion. Yes, of course. There had always been another, deeper motive behind Sibert's eagerness to accompany me on my mercy mission. I let my shoulders slump. Against the huge attraction of delving into a mystery from the past, what chance did my fears for our safety have?

I straightened up and turned to him. 'Come on then.'

He was already smiling. 'Where are we going?'

'*You* won't leave till you've done all you can to unearth what you need to know, and *I* won't leave without you, so the sooner we start, the sooner we can go home.'

It was past noon, however, and I was very hungry; Sibert was too, and he needed more than the heel of bread I'd thrust at him when I'd returned to find him waiting. I set about preparing a meal, and while I worked I recalled all that I knew of Sibert's recent family history.

His father Edmer, Hrype's brother, had fought with Sibert's grandfather under King Harold at Hastings. After the defeat, in which the grandfather had died, the family had lost their estate of Drakelow, on the coast near Dunwich. Hrype had taken his and Edmer's mother, Fritha, and fled to the Black Fen, where eventually Edmer found them. Old men spoke with pride of the network of spies and informers that had operated all over the fens after Harold's defeat as men

125

loyal to him tried to regroup after the disaster; it was thrilling to think of how such secretive men had strived so hard to protect each other. Edmer, Hrype and Fritha had then made their way to the Isle of Ely, where Edmer wished to join the Saxon resistance under Hereward – although Hrype warned him repeatedly that this act would cost him dear.

Edmer, however, would not – and did not – listen. Not only was he suffering from the profound mental wound of having fought and lost, and from being forced to watch his father die in the battle, but in addition he had a new wife: Froya. She had been Hrype's pupil, and Edmer had fallen in love with her the moment he set eyes on her. Edmer fought for revenge, for the pride of the Saxons and for the future, for now that he had a wife he knew that he might also have a son. The rebellion was the first step to the recovery of Drakelow, the family estate, and Edmer did not hesitate.

He took a Norman arrow in the thigh, and the wound became infected. Hrype did his best, with Froya right beside him fighting for her man, but they had to watch helplessly as Edmer's life force began to fade. It was too much for his poor mother; Fritha had been gravely traumatized by the defeat and the loss of her home, and in the course of the flight across the fens she had suffered a seizure that left her partly paralysed. Her son's wound was too much. She turned her face to the wall and quietly died.

Hrype amputated his brother's leg. As soon as he was well enough to travel, they found a mount and got him away, leaving Hrype behind pretending that he was still nursing his sick brother. Froya fled to Aelf Fen, but the safety of its sanctuary came too late for Edmer; he succumbed to his hurts and died in his wife's arms. Her son, my friend Sibert, was born a few months later. The only kin he had ever known were his mother and his father's brother.

It was no surprise, really, that he was so very keen to find out more.

We set out in the early afternoon. Once again Sibert arranged his scarf so that it hid his head and brow. I fastened my white cap over my braided hair and, for good measure, pulled up the hood of my dark cloak to cover it. Without actually saying so, both Sibert and I realized that if we were going to go about asking possibly awkward questions about the recent past, when Saxons had rebelled against the Norman invaders, then it would be best to do so as anonymously as we could. If it were to be discovered that two young people had been too curious, we did not want the trail to lead back to us.

'Where do you plan to go first?' I said softly to Sibert as we hurried up the alleyway.

He grinned briefly. 'Where do the gossips gather?'

'In the alehouse,' I answered promptly.

'Quite so. There's an alehouse on the market-place, and it's usually busy. We'll start there.'

I was content to follow his lead. It appeared that he had given some thought to his investigation, and I agreed with him that this was a good initial step. As we emerged from the alley into the market square we were all at once in a crowd, and I kept close behind Sibert as he shouldered a way through the throng. The alehouse was over in a far corner, the bundle of branches that marked it out now ragged and almost bare of leaves. It was a long, low building that occupied the entire corner of the square. A wide entrance opened on to a short corridor with rooms opening off on either side. It was clear from the noise which was the tap room.

Sibert got mugs of weak beer for us and then stood looking around, a slight frown making a crease between his eyebrows. Then he nodded over to the left and, following the line of his gaze, I noticed a group of half a dozen old men sitting on crude benches on either side of an upturned barrel. Old they might be but several pairs of keen eyes looked out with lively interest on the comings and goings all around them.

I edged my way over to the group. One of the benches had a little space and, with a smile, I asked its two occupants if they would move up so that I could sit down.

'Aye, right gladly, my pretty maid,' said the nearest old man, baring his gums and two remaining teeth in a smile. He shuffled his skinny bottom along the bench and patted the shiny wood in invitation. 'You perch here beside me and ... oh.' He had just caught sight of Sibert, a few paces behind me and now preparing to squeeze in beside me.

Sibert's presence did not deter his flirtatious advances for long. Soon he had his scrawny hand on my knee, only removing it to pinch my cheek as he commented on my 'rosy little face'. I bore it with a smile. For one thing, if I did not discourage him it might make him and his friends more receptive to Sibert's questions. For another, I didn't really mind.

Sibert exchanged a few general comments with the old men by way of an introduction. I joined in, offering an opinion on the weather and the likelihood of more rain. Then there was a short, reflective pause, and I sensed Sibert go tense.

'It's a bit of a disruption, that there,' he offered, jerking his head in the direction of the abbey. 'Going to be a monster, that new cathedral!' His eyes popped with wonder, and I was impressed with his yokel-overawed-with-the-sights act.

There was an exchange of rumbling, grumbling remarks among the old men. Then one of them, sitting on the other side of the one clasping my knee, leaned forward and said in a low voice, 'They've knocked down St Etheldreda's chapel, you know. Her that's been our beloved saint since time out of mind.'

'Have they?' Sibert whispered, wide-eyed.

'Aye, lad, they have, with no respect for her that we all love nor no more for us that love her. What's more, they—' Whatever further sedition he was going to add was abruptly cut off by the old boy next to me, who dug him smartly in the ribs with a muttered, 'Dangerous talk, Teb. Dangerous talk.'

Silence fell. Then Sibert leaned forward – all six old men mirrored the gesture – and said, so

129

softly that even I barely heard, 'My father fought with the Wake.'

The old men did not exactly leap up and welcome him like a long-lost grandson – they were too careful for that – but nevertheless you could see they were delighted. One or two of them nodded, and one muttered, 'So did we, lad.'

We all sat smiling at each other and then, when the initial euphoria had subsided, the old man next to me – Teb – leaned across me and said to Sibert, 'Is your father with you?'

'No,' Sibert replied shortly. 'He died of his wound.'

There were mutters of *God save him* and *God bless his brave soul*. Then Teb said, 'You've come to pay your respects, then, at his grave?'

'He does not lie here,' Sibert replied. I prayed he would not reveal the fact that Edmer was buried at Aelf Fen, and he didn't; he must have known as well as I did that it would not be wise to give away the fact of where we lived, even to our new friends. 'He received a Norman arrow in the thigh, and those who treated him could not save his leg. After the amputation my ... his friends managed to get him away from the island and away across the fens, but it was no good.'

The old men bowed their heads, and for some time nobody spoke. It was a mark of respect for a fallen warrior, I knew that, but not quite what Sibert must have hoped for. If he had been expecting the tale of amputation and flight to prompt one of the old men to leap up and exclaim, 'Yes, I remember him!' then he'd be

130

disappointed.

I thought of something. 'Where were the houses of healing?' I asked shyly, as if, being a mere girl, I was hesitant to speak in front of a group of men. 'Where would my friend's father have been taken?'

Teb gave my knee a kindly pat. 'Many were tended by the monks,' he said. 'Not that our holy brethren were all in favour of the rebels, oh, no. Still, the healers among them are decent men in the main, and they did not refuse their aid.'

Edmer had not been treated by the monks; his brother and his wife had cared for him. 'Was there any other place where healers gathered?' I persisted, giving Teb what I hoped was a sweet and innocent smile.

'Interested in healing, are you, pretty maid?' he asked, patting my face.

'Oh, yes!' I said with total honesty. 'I hope that I may make it my life's work.'

Teb nodded his approval. 'Well, if you'd been here during the rebellion you'd have learned enough to last a lifetime,' he said grimly. He glanced around him, then leaned closer to me and whispered right in my ear, 'There was this man, magic they said he was, and it's told that he could put a man into a deep, dreamless sleep and whip off a limb without his victim even noticing!' He leaned back, triumph in his eyes, as if to say, what do you think of *that*?

I knew exactly what I thought of that. I was aware, because Sibert had told me, that his uncle Hrype had somehow sedated Edmer before the amputation. The magic man whom my friend

131

Teb had just described must surely be Hrype. Teb was waiting for my reply. It was not hard to sound thrilled as I said, in an excited whisper, *'Oh!* I wish I knew how he could have done that!'

Teb gripped my knee and shook it warningly. 'You mustn't go blabbing about what I've just told you!' he said urgently. His eyes flicked briefly in the direction of the abbey – it was as if he and his friends were aware of it all the time like a watching, listening presence – and he said, all but inaudibly, 'Them monks are funny about things like that.'

I understood what he meant. In the course of my long and ongoing training with my aunt Edild, she had told me repeatedly that many of the skills she was teaching me were frowned upon by the men of the church. They tended towards the view that if a man or a woman suffered sickness or grave injury it was God's punishment, and it therefore followed that any alleviation of their agony was contrary to God's will. The prime example was, of course, childbirth; Edild knew of several palliatives that could ease a long labour, so that there was less risk of mother or child – or both – dying because the mother was too exhausted by pain to go on. The church, however, was adamant: women must bear their children in pain because of Eve's sin of disobedience.

Edild and I did not see it that way.

'I won't breathe a word!' I whispered now to Teb. I licked my finger, drew it across my throat and then sketched a cross over my heart.

He nodded, apparently satisfied. 'That's a good girl.' I squeezed his hand, still on my knee but now quite a lot further up my thigh. It worked. Once again speaking right in my ear, he hissed, 'The magic man lived in a little reed-thatched house at the end of the alley that runs east under the abbey walls. They'll remember him there.'

Then, laying his forefinger alongside his nose in the time-honoured gesture implying secrecy, he sat up straight again.

I wanted to leap up there and then and hare off in search of the reed-thatched house, but it seemed wiser to wait. My old Teb seemed anxious that his information should go no further, so he was hardly likely to tell anyone what he'd just told me. But it was better to be safe than sorry, and if Sibert and I went on chatting to the old men about other topics then nobody would be able to say that we'd shot off like a couple of scalded cats the moment we'd been told about the magic man's house.

The magic man ... While the superficial part of my mind gossiped with the old men and giggled with my elderly admirer, my deeper self was walking with Hrype.

Finally, Sibert and I got away. There was no need for words as quickly we crossed the market-place, which was still busy with townspeople, monks and the ever-flowing stream of workmen passing in and out of the abbey, and made our way down the alley that led off under the abbey walls to the east. At first houses and little hovels bunched tightly together in a mass of packed humanity, but quite soon the dwellings thinned. Right at the end there was a row of reed-thatched cottages.

One had its door ajar. I went up to it and peered inside. A woman of around my mother's age sat on a stool by the hearth. She was spinning wool. Without turning she called out, 'Close the door, Mattie, it's cold enough in here already.'

I slipped inside, Sibert right behind me, and he closed the door. 'Not Mattie, I'm afraid,' I said softly.

The woman turned. 'So I see,' she said. 'Who are you and what do you want?'

'My friend here is looking for people who might remember his father, fatally wounded during the ... er, in 1071,' I said, keeping my voice low. We had no idea where this woman's sympathies lay; she neither looked nor sounded like a Norman, but that did not necessarily mean she had supported the rebellion.

She nodded slowly as she looked us up and down. 'Who sent you here?' she asked. Her tone was not unfriendly, merely wary. I did not blame her for her caution.

'An old man in the alehouse said there was a healer who used to live here,' I said.

Again she nodded. 'Aye, there was.' She stared down at her hands, fallen idle in her lap. 'He was a good man,' she muttered.

'You remember him?' Sibert said eagerly.

The woman gazed up at him. 'No, for I was not here.' I sensed the sag of disappointment that flooded through him. Then, as if she noticed too, her face spread in a tight smile, and she said, 'You want to talk to my mother.'

The woman's name was Yorath. Although she did not admit as much, we gathered that her menfolk had fought with Hereward. From what she said, it sounded as if her mother was a wise woman, and it appeared she had been both willing and eager to work with the magic man.

As I listened to Yorath's quiet voice speaking of the events of twenty years ago, I felt as if her words were casting a spell on me. Such was my enchantment that it was almost a surprise when I heard my own voice ask, 'Who was he? Who was the magic man?'

And Yorath said, 'My mother never knew his name. He was here when they needed him, and he did not spare himself in his care of the sick and the wounded.' She sighed, her eyes soft as she remembered the old tales. 'Then he was gone, and none of them ever saw him again.'

Her mother, who was called Aetha, lived somewhere out on the fens; Yorath did not specify exactly where. She undertook to send word to her to ask if she was willing to see us. If we were to return the following afternoon, she would give us her mother's answer.

We promised to be there. I sensed that Sibert wanted to stay; we were standing in the very place where his gravely wounded father had been brought, where Edmer's brother had tried so hard to save his life, where Edmer's wife, desperately anxious for her new husband, had done all she could to help. The central drama in his family's recent history had happened right here. Had I been in his boots, I should have wanted to stay too.

I took his hand and gently led him away. I muttered a farewell to Yorath, catching her looking with deep sympathy at Sibert. 'We will see you tomorrow,' I said, and she nodded. Then Sibert and I were outside in the alley, and I hurried him away.

TEN

Sibert's tension did not dissipate as we made our way back up the alley and across the market-place. I was not surprised, for I understood how hard it must be for him to sense the mystery of his past so close but still outside his reach. When he cast a longing look at the alehouse and asked if I minded if he went back to talk some more with those within, I said no, of course I didn't.

I watched him go, my heart flooding with sympathy. If he thought it would help to drink a lot of ale, so that eventually he would fall asleep on the floor of our little dwelling in a beery stupor, then I could not blame him.

I walked on to our room, planning how I would fill in the remainder of the afternoon and the long evening that stretched ahead. I would take the unexpected free time to have another tidy up, I resolved, and when I had done that I would go through my satchel of remedies and medicaments. It was not often that I had access to an apothecary's shop, and it made sense to check my supplies and think about whether there was anything Edild and I needed back at home.

I swept out the room, shook up the straw and prepared Sibert's and my own sleeping places, then I fed the fire to make a good blaze and

137

banked it down with ash so that it would burn long and slow. Next I sat in the light from the partly opened door, unfastened my leather bag and started going through the contents. I was already aware, in the back of my mind, that this task would not take much time and that the remainder of the evening loomed ahead with nothing to fill it. It was probably this that prompted me, for when I picked up the bottle of Edild's special remedy for pain in the joints – it is full of comforting, warming herbs such as ginger and cinnamon, with a good portion of willow and a little devil's claw – I suddenly knew how I was going to spend the rest of the day.

I had a good supply of oil, and it did not take long to prepare several bottles of the warming rub, diluting Edild's remedy in the proportion she had instructed. Then I set to preparing myself.

I always carry lengths of clean, white cloth folded at the bottom of my satchel, for use as dressings and bandages. Hoping I had some large pieces, I spread them out and soon found what I wanted. Then I took my knife and, with its sharp point, cut out the shapes I needed. I fetched needle and thread and sewed the seams, testing the fit and, when I was satisfied, neatly hemming the raw edges. Then I unbraided my hair, brushed it back off my face and wound it in a tight, severe bun at the back of my head. I put on the wimple I had just fashioned, relieved to find how closely it framed my face. I put my cloak on over my gown and pulled up the wide folds of my hood; the fabric was dark, the material inexpensive and, like all my clothes, well worn. I stood up, wishing I could see what I looked like and fervently hoping that I looked sufficiently like my sister Elfritha: like a nun. I did not suppose I would have fooled one of Elfritha's superiors, but I trusted that the average Ely monk would only have a sketchy idea of what a Benedictine sister wore.

I knew, because they had told me, that the monks did not let women inside the abbey without a good reason. Did the same rule apply to nuns?

I was just about to find out.

The monk on duty at the abbey gate greeted me with a smile and said, 'Good day, sister, what can we do for you?' which was promising.

'Good day to you, brother,' I replied, careful to keep my eyes cast down. 'I have been sent with supplies of a new remedy for the joint and muscle pains that torment so many of the elder members of our community.' So far, I had spoken the truth, except that nobody had actually *sent* me. 'Many of the sisterhood are badly afflicted in this persistent wet weather' – that too was true; Elfritha had mentioned it last time I had visited her – 'and if I may help any of the brethren, then I would dearly like to do so.' I was a healer; I wanted to alleviate suffering wherever I found it.

The monk was looking at me with interest. 'A new remedy, you say?' I nodded. I had noticed that nuns didn't speak unnecessarily. 'Your own creation?'

'No.' I smiled modestly, as if to imply that I was far too lowly to be allowed free rein to experiment in the herb store.

'Many of the older brethren suffer greatly,' the monk said. He paused, then said, 'You may enter.'

He ushered me inside a tiny room just inside the gate and, calling out to a monk emerging from one of the buildings, asked him to fetch someone called Brother Philius. I waited, trying to make my face calm. Elfritha's fellow nuns always manage to look serene, as if they're confidently waiting for something lovely that's just about to happen.

Brother Philius appeared. He was young, dark-eyed and quite short, with a restless air as if he was eager to get on with God's work. He bustled into the little room, his energy instantly making it feel cramped. 'Sister—?'

I bowed my head. 'Sister Hilde.'

'You have brought a new remedy for damp-induced pains, I'm told?' Already, he was hurry-ing me out of the room and marching off in the direction of a passageway that ran between two low buildings.

Thankful that his professionalism had made him ask straight away about the remedy, where I was on safe ground, rather than my credentials as a nun, where I most certainly was not, I agreed that I had.

Brother Philius fired questions at me as we marched, and I described the different elements that Edild and I had prepared for the remedy.

140

When he got down to the exact proportions of these elements and the details of how they were blended, I had to confess ignorance. Edild had not permitted me to watch, although this was, I was pretty sure, because she had uttered a power spell as she worked and it was dangerous for someone as inexperienced as I to listen.

I certainly wasn't going to tell Brother Philius about *that*.

We had reached a small building tucked away behind the clamour of where the men were working on the new cathedral. With a wry smile, Brother Philius opened the door and said, 'Come in. It's remarkably peaceful in here, given the present circumstances.'

I preceded him into the room. It was long and narrow, with three simple cots down each side. A fire burned in a hearth at the far end of the room, making the temperature pleasantly warm. Two of cots were occupied by very old monks.

'I know what you're thinking,' Brother Philius muttered. I thought he sounded furtive, almost guilty. Wondering why, and also wondering what he thought I was thinking, I did not speak but sent him an enquiring look, eyebrows raised. 'It's a great luxury to have the fire,' he said, 'and in truth there is no need of it for someone like me, blessed as I am with good health and vigour.' He leaned closer and I caught his smell – of herbs, oils, incense and all things clean, which was so typical of healers. I bent my head to hide a smile; I liked Brother Philius. 'The warmth is for the old ones,' he whispered. 'They are both very poorly. They protest sometimes, for they have spent all the years of their adult lives vowed to poverty, but we tell them that the heat aids them and so releases those who nurse them for other duties.'

Yes, it made sense. It was clever to have manipulated the old men's instinctive selflessness in such a way. 'Wet and cold are the true causes of their pain, are they not?' Brother Philius added, sighing. 'And here we are on an island in the midst of water.'

I opened my satchel and took out a bottle of the new remedy. I held it up and Brother Philius, his face eager, took it from me. He drew the stopper and, tentatively at first, sniffed at the contents. A slow smile spread over his face. 'I can almost smell the potency!' he said softly.

Again, I had to hide a smile. Edild had explained how the energy that the healing spirits bring can be captured in a remedy and that it bursts out, eager to get to work, when the jar or bottle is opened.

Brother Philius was striding over to the patient in the cot to his left. 'Brother Anselm, we have a treat for you!' he exclaimed as the old man struggled to sit up. 'The sister here has kindly brought a new remedy, and I'm going to try it out on your hip!'

Either Brother Philius had forgotten that, although garbed as a nun, I was still a woman, or else he was treating me as a fellow healer used to bare male flesh. Whichever it was, he swiftly unfastened the old man's robe and pushed it down so that it sagged below his hips. Brother Anselm rolled over on to his side and I had a glimpse of his aged genitals beneath the fringe of white hair. Then the scent of Edild's new remedy filled the air, and I watched, fascinated, as the hands of a true healer got to work.

You could tell from Brother Anselm's groans of pain that quickly turned to moans of pleasure that the remedy and the strong hands were doing good. Brother Philius was clearly impressed. After only a short while he turned to me with a huge grin and said, 'Whoever made this is all but a miracle worker!' I saved that up to tell Edild. He returned to his work but then, as if the thought had suddenly struck him, he spun round again and said, 'Have a go at Brother Matthias over there.' He indicated the monk in the opposite cot. 'His pain is in his left shoulder,' he panted – massage is hard work – 'extending up into his neck and down under the shoulder blade.'

I nodded. I knew that pain; I suffer from it myself when I spend too long hunched over my work. It sometimes feels as if someone is sticking a knife into me.

I reached for another bottle of the remedy and crossed the room. The second old monk was perched on the edge of his cot and had already bared his shoulder. With a smile, I put down my satchel, took off my cloak, rolled back my sleeves and poured oil into the palm of my hand. I rubbed it between my hands to warm it a little and then advanced on my patient.

I worked on my old monk for some time, gently at first and then, as I felt his flesh warm and soften beneath my hands, more vigorously. I

143

was embarrassed by his thanks; I did not really deserve such profound gratitude when I was here on a mission of my own and the healing was only to cover up my true intentions.

Word of my presence must have spread. Several more old monks appeared and, before Brother Philius and I were done, we treated nine men. When we had finally finished, we stood together wiping our hands, both of us red-faced and sweaty.

'Thank you, Sister Hilde,' he said. 'I understand that you cannot reveal the recipe of this wonder remedy, but...?' He left the question unspoken, hovering in the air.

I reached for my satchel, extracting a bottle. 'This is the concentrate,' I said, giving it to him. 'Mix it with oil in the following proportions' – I described various concentrations for different ailments – 'and remember it is strong, so don't be tempted to use more.'

He held up the bottle as if it were the Holy Grail. 'Thank you,' he said. 'On behalf of my old monks, thank you so much.'

I rolled down my sleeves and reached for my cloak. 'May I make a request?' I asked. I felt mean, as if I were taking advantage of his gratitude and choosing the exact moment when he couldn't refuse me.

'Of course!' he exclaimed. 'Name it.'

I squashed down my guilt, reminding myself firmly why I had needed to get into the abbey in the first place. 'I have heard tell that St Etheldreda's church is being demolished to make room for the new cathedral,' I said. 'Would it be permitted for me to look?'

'Yes, indeed,' Brother Philius replied. We were at the door now, and I saw that afternoon had merged into evening. 'There won't be many workmen there at this hour, for it's getting dark.' He glanced back inside the room. 'I need to get back to my patients – it's time I saw to their supper. If I show you the way, may I leave you to look round on your own?'

It was what I'd been praying for. 'Very well,' I said meekly.

He led me along a dark passage that abruptly opened into a huge open space. Skeletal walls rose up in the distance and high above our heads a frame of wooden falsework stretched up into the evening sky. The detritus of demolition and the tools of construction were all around but, other than a group of workmen huddled around a brazier and a carpenter planing a length of pale oak, the site was deserted.

'The little Saxon church stood just there.' Brother Philius pointed. 'Now, if you don't mind, I must leave you.' I bowed my head in acknowledgement. 'Farewell, sister – it was a good day for my old monks when you came along!' He grinned, gave me a wave and hurried away.

I stood in the soft light, staring round me. Where should I look first? Where might the pale monk be at this moment? The immediate thing was to get out of sight so that, with any luck, everyone would forget I was there in the abbey. Then I could pursue my quarry until either I found him or they found me and threw me out.

I slipped into the deep shadow cast by one of the new walls, already high above my head. Then I set about my exploration.

I had failed. I had tiptoed up what seemed like dozens of passages, and I had forced myself into countless hiding places when footsteps echoed and discovery loomed. Each time I had prayed that the footfalls would be those of the pale monk, and each time I had been disappointed. It was hopeless and I knew it.

I seemed to have gone round in a big circle, for now I was once again approaching the building site. Now only a couple of watchmen remained, seated either side of the brazier and muttering in low voices. I slipped behind a pillar, working out a route to the gate that would keep me out of their sight. Go *there*, I thought, to that ancient stretch of wall out in the middle of the site, then dodge over to the far side, keeping behind the screen made of the wooden falsework. It looked easy.

I gathered up my skirts and ran light-footed to the old wall. I was about to hurry on but just at that moment I sensed something snag at my attention. A stab of horrified fear sheared through me, instantly followed by pain so severe that it was all I could do not to cry out. Then I was assailed by a fury so great that it drove me to my knees.

I crouched on the ground, huddled down in the shadows. I covered my head with my arms in a futile attempt to defend myself, although I knew enough about the deep, dark mysteries of the

146

spirit world to recognize that it was no living hand that threatened me. Slowly, the dread faded, and in time I was able to straighten up.

I stared at the ground around me. I could see the outline of the Saxon church; it had been quite small, with narrow aisles on the north and south side forming side chapels. It was the wall of the south side chapel that I stood beside. Immediately to my left, at the west end of the church, I could make out the scar where the foundations of the tower had been ripped out.

The wall of the south side chapel was where the old bones had been stored. Every bit of common sense and self-preservation told me to get out of there, but I watched, almost as if I were outside myself and a mere observer of my own actions, as my hand stretched out to investigate.

The shock went through me so fast that at first I thought it had come from whatever it was within the wall that I had just touched. An instant later, I realized that somebody stood beside me, someone warm-blooded, mortal, someone who had just grabbed my arm.

I spun round. He was white-faced, white-haired and his eyes – his strange, pale eyes – were wide with horror. He whispered, 'Did you see it? Oh, is it true then? It really exists?' Then his grip on my arm weakened, and I watched in horror as he slumped to the ground at my feet.

Gewis knew he must open his eyes. He had set out for what was left of the little Saxon church without permission, and if they found him there he would be punished. He did not understand why, any more than he understood any of what was happening to him. He'd been brought here, and he had to pretend he was a monk. His mother had approved, and they had told him he would be safe here. Safe from what? And how long would the threat last? Would he have to stay here for ever?

He groaned and, without his volition, his eyelids fluttered. *No*, he thought, *no! It is better to remain unconscious, for reality is too much to bear.*

Then he remembered where he was and what he had seen. The terror grabbed him in its fierce claws. Instinctively, he rolled himself into a ball, seeing again that looming, white shape with its face of horror and the blood, oh, the blood...

Hands were on him, strong hands, and a scent of sweet oil was in his nostrils. 'Do not screw up your limbs so violently,' said a soft voice, 'for you will do yourself damage.'

He froze. Had the spirit spoken? If he found the courage to open his eyes, would he see it bending over him, stretching out its hand to drag him into whatever hell it inhabited?

Ghosts do not speak soft words, the voice of reason said in his head. Nor do they smell of ginger and rosemary.

With what felt like a huge effort, he opened his eyes.

A young woman was leaning over him, her expression anxious. She wore a white wimple, and over it what looked like a black veil. A nun then. He stared back at her.

She was slender, her figure quite boyish. She was around his age, perhaps a little older. Her skin was very smooth, pale in the dim light. Her features were fine, the nose small and straight, the mouth wide and well formed. There was a haunting beauty in her face, and her watchful eyes held intelligence. Her eyes ... He stared into them, for they fascinated him. They must surely be blue, or perhaps green, but in the twilight they appeared silvery, the irises surrounded by a rim of indigo...

It was the face of someone who watched carefully, observing others while holding back their own essence. It was a face that could easily make others uneasy.

Gewis, alarmed all over again, shrank back. But then she smiled, and suddenly everything changed. She reached down and stroked his shoulder, and under her touch he felt his limbs unclench. She went on stroking him for some time, rather like an intuitive groom with a frightened horse, and a sense of calm spread through him. Finally, he felt able to speak. 'Who are you, sister?' His voice was barely above a whisper and, to his shame, it shook.

Her smile deepened. 'I'm actually not a nun. My name's Lassair and I've come to look for you.'

'*Me?*'

'Yes.'

'But why?' He fought down the sudden surge of optimism. What good could one skinny girl do against an abbey full of monks?

She leaned closer, speaking quietly into his

ear. 'My cousin saw you being bundled into the abbey, and they tried to murder him,' she whispered. 'He's safe now, but others have died. Whatever secret they are trying to keep clearly centres around you and is worth killing for.'

He shook his head in frustration. 'I don't understand!' he moaned. 'I wish I did, I wish I could explain to you what's happening, but I can't!'

She was staring at him intently. 'Who are you?' she breathed. 'What is this mystery that surrounds you?'

'I don't know!' he hissed. 'Don't you think I haven't been wondering the same thing myself? There's nothing special about me – I'm a carpenter's son from Fulbourn!' His voice had risen with his anxiety.

'Shhhh,' she soothed him. 'Hush, or the night watchmen will hear. Can't you think of anything that—'

She heard the footsteps before he did and, tensing, drew back right against the ancient wall. He met her eyes; hers were wide with alarm. 'They're coming!' she hissed.

He got up and cautiously peered around the wall. His worst fears were realized: the quartet of burly monks who now strode out across the cathedral site were the four who had brought him to the abbey.

'Go!' he said to her. 'Quickly, now – get away from here!'

She did not move. 'What about you?'

He smiled grimly. 'I'm allowed to be here in the abbey, for they seem to have turned me into a monk. You, on the other hand...' He did not think he needed to finish the sentence.

She understood. 'I will not abandon you,' she said urgently. 'I promise. I'll help you if I can.' She was already on her feet, crouched to spring away.

He heard the monks' footsteps echo on the ground. They sounded like the herald of some dread fate. *'Go!'* he repeated.

She shot him a last anguished glance, and then she fled. The ancient stretch of wall was between her and the four monks, and he was almost certain they could not see her. Nevertheless, his heart beat hard with alarm, making him feel sick. He watched her closely, and as she flew across the one place where she might be visible to them – between the base of some of the falsework and the foundations of a vast, new pillar – he stood up and faced them.

They would not kill him. They wanted him safe within the abbey, but they wanted him alive.

Or so he fervently hoped.

He stepped out of the shelter of the old wall and went to meet them.

ELEVEN

Hrype was almost at the stage where he could no longer hide his anxiety from Froya. Almost. He was accustomed to spending the majority of the hours of daylight away from the house, either at work on the land or else busy with the mysterious intricacies of his calling. Froya did not appear to have noticed that, at present, she barely saw him, except briefly in the morning, as they ate breakfast together, and last thing at night, when he would slip inside, exchange a few words with her, and then throw himself on his bed as if he were worn out and desperate to sleep.

He rarely slept nowadays. As Froya, too, went to her bed and the lamp was extinguished, he would lie there in the dark, keeping his body perfectly still while his mind roamed free, always making straight for the same place in the past.

Behind closed eyes he watched the drama re-enact itself over and over again. The flight from Drakelow and the illusion of hope and safety that beckoned him and his poor blighted mother to the Isle of Ely. The voice of Hereward as he stood up on a block and addressed his loyal followers, inspiring them with his ferocity and making them truly believe they could oust the Normans and send them back to where they came from. The mocking laughter as the rebels watched the Conqueror try again and again to find a way across the fenland; the howls of derision and the screams of triumph when the hastily constructed causeway collapsed and King William's army choked and drowned in the dense, black mud.

Their fierce joy had been short-lived. Hrype remembered too well that sick dread in the pit of his stomach when he'd learned that the monks had betrayed the rebels and given away the secret of the safe ways across the water. He had foreseen in that instant what would happen; he had seen all of it, unfolding in his mind as if the images had been put there by a master story teller. He had taken Froya aside – his pupil, his bright-eyed pupil, now his brother's wife – and instructed her to help him prepare for what was to come. Together they had gathered all the supplies of bandages, medicaments, splints, slings and gut for stitching wounds that they could lay hands on. Others had had the same idea, and Hrype had not been surprised when a woman had tapped on the door and said she had come to help.

The fighting had been savage and intense. The Conqueror gave no quarter, and his soldiers advanced like a spring tide. So many were injured; so many died. The woman – Aetha, her name was – had turned her attention to laying out the dead.

Then they brought in Edmer. At first Hrype

looked down at his patient through the eyes of a brother; here was Edmer, dear Edmer, little companion of childhood, beloved friend of adulthood. The wound in Edmer's leg made Hrype shake with dread. Edmer had been struck just above the knee by a Norman arrow and somebody, perhaps even Edmer himself, had tried to wrench it from the flesh. At the base of the deep, bloody pit could be seen the head of the arrow ... Then the healer took the place of the brother. Hrype emerged from his shock and, cool headed, got on with what he must do.

Froya was beside him, and with a part of his mind he noticed, admiring, that she, too, had managed to put her fear for her husband aside while she focused on nursing him. They washed out the wound, Froya keeping a pad of linen ready and mopping at the blood that went on welling up like a spring so that Hrype could see what he was doing.

The first touch on the arrowhead caused Edmer to shriek in pain. Hrype stopped then and, selecting his most potent herbs, made a draught for his brother so strong that the muscles tensed against the agony seemed to relax before their eyes. Edmer, barely conscious, managed a smile and said, 'Get on with it.'

Hrype dug and delved. Froya mopped and wiped, repeatedly throwing blood-saturated cloths on to the fire as she reached for more. Hrype tried to work faster – his brother's life force was ebbing away, and he seemed powerless to call it back – and, steeling himself, he made one more great effort, pushing back the strong sinews of Edmer's thigh and driving the pincers deeper, deeper, until his grip on the arrowhead at last felt secure. He closed his eyes, very aware of the great brown bear that was his spirit guide hovering somewhere close, and then he pulled.

The arrowhead emerged with a nauseating squelch, bringing with it pieces of Edmer's flesh. Instantly, Froya set to work, washing out the terrible hole with water that had been infused with lavender and rosemary oils, and when she was done, and Hrype was satisfied, he re-assembled the pulp of the thigh and stitched it together.

The shock claimed its first casualty: Hrype and Edmer's mother, already devastated by the seizure that had grabbed her on the flight to Ely, gave her maimed son one last smile, nodded with love in her eyes to his sound brother and, giving up her spirit, quietly died.

They had done all they could for Edmer. Hrype knew that, although it did not assuage his guilt. The damage had probably been done the moment the arrow struck, carrying with it whatever foul matter that soon began to spread through Edmer's body. He was a strong man and he'd fought back but it had been no good...

When after a week the lower leg was turning black, streaks of dark red running like tracks up from the wound towards Edmer's groin and the smell of dying flesh filling the little room, Hrype knew what he had to do.

Edmer's fever ran high and he slipped in and out of consciousness. Hrype dosed him with the strongest potion he had ever administered, and then he sharpened his knives and his saw and took off his brother's leg.

He made a fine job of it; he knew that there was no element in all his medical treatment of his brother for which he could berate himself. He had performed many amputations, and he knew how to leave a flap of healthy skin to stitch over the stump of limb. He and Froya kept Edmer clean, they fed him skilfully blended remedies and whenever he would, to please them, try to eat, they were ready with mouthfuls of nourishing food. Edmer held on.

He might have lived had they not had to move him. But the Conqueror was savage in his vengeance, and Edmer was a wanted man with a price on his head.

Hrype spent all his remaining money on a sway-backed old mare that was worth at most a quarter of what he paid, and by night he carried his brother out of the little house and set him on its back. The he watched as Froya led the animal away.

Not for long; he dried the tears that seemed to have escaped from his eyes and got on with what he had to do. The Normans believed they had all the time they needed to come for Edmer; they knew where he was, and they knew he now had only one leg. Hrype kept up the pretence of nursing his brother, even making a man-shape out of straw and tucking it beneath the covers where Edmer had lain and suffered. If anyone peered into the room, they would think Edmer was still there.

He stayed there for four days. Then one dark night he slipped away.

He did not know where Froya and Edmer had gone, and for some time he did not try to find them. He had done all he could for his brother, and Froya would nurse him as well as Hrype could have done; perhaps it was better to leave them be.

But he could not fight his own deep self. By night he dreamed of them; by day his inner eye saw them. Edmer was dying and Froya...

Even now he could not bear to think of it.

He had given in to what his heart commanded. He had crept from the ruined barn where he'd been camping and, by the light of a bright young moon, he'd lit the special fire, entered the trance state and humbly asked the spirits to show him the way. Two days later he'd arrived at Aelf Fen.

It was exactly as the vision had shown him. Edmer died a week later, his head in his wife's lap and his hand in Hrype's. He whispered a hoarse blessing, and then his spirit flew away.

Froya's child was born in the depths of the harsh winter that followed. The birth was hard and the labour long; Sibert came into the world yelling his protest.

Sibert.

Wearily, Hrype opened his eyes. It was deep night, dark and profoundly still. Sometimes, when he had suffered the parade of scenes from the past as it scoured across his mind and finally relinquished him, he managed to sleep afterwards. It would not be so tonight. Sibert had not returned from Ely, and Hrype was very afraid he

157

knew why. Morcar was safely ensconced in Edild's little house, and thanks to both Lassair, who had administered the original treatment, and now Edild herself, he was quickly recovering. Sibert had brought him home, rowing him across the flooded fenland in a leaking old boat, but he had set off back to Ely as soon as he had handed Morcar over. Hrype had not even seen him; Edild had reported calmly that Sibert was anxious to return to Lassair, busy keeping up the pretence that her patient was still on the island, just as Hrype had done before her, so that those who wanted to kill him would not realize he had gone.

Hrype could not protest. Sibert and Lassair were acting courageously and sensibly, and on the face of it there could be no argument with their chosen course of action.

Only Hrype knew there was more to it. His own instincts had told him why Sibert wanted to stay on the Isle of Ely. To confirm it, he had looked into the scrying ball and seen into Sibert's mind. There was confusion there, as well as anger. Above all there was determination. Hrype had at last cast the runes, and then he'd seen everything.

He will not come home, Hrype thought. *Not until he knows*. He sighed, for he knew what he must do and he did not want to do it. Froya's mood was already low and troubled, and if he, too, went away he knew she would descend into the melancholia that so often afflicted her. But there was no choice; Sibert's course was set and the runes said he would not divert from it.

The only thing that Hrype could do was make sure he was there when the inevitable happened. He might not survive – he recalled Sibert's anger, to which he had been a reluctant witness – but he would have to take that chance.

He lay in the dark and formulated his plans. When dawn began to send a paler light into the eastern sky, he was already up. His pack stood ready by the door, and he sat by the hearth waiting for Froya to wake up. She opened her eyes and looked right at him. She knew. He watched as her face crumpled and tears overflowed down her pale cheeks. But she did not try to stop him.

I tried to think. I was still shaking with fear, for now that I thought about it I realized that I had surely just seen an apparition. Had it truly been there, with its face of horror and the long streaks of blood down its white shroud? Or had I picked up the pale youth's terror and seen what he believed he had seen? Either way, the thing in the old church had been an abomination, and I felt as if I were disturbed in some frightful way right to my very roots.

As if that were not bad enough, the four broad, thickset monks who had come looking for the pale monk had seen me. They could not but have noticed that the boy and I had our heads together and were whispering; would they jump to the conclusion that he had imparted to me the essence of the dread secret that lay at the heart of this mystery, and would he then be able to persuade them that he hadn't? Our encounter had been brief, but even in that short time I had

159

sensed that he was honest and decent. I was sure he would do his best to protect me, even...

No. It was no good. I was suddenly convinced that it was the pale boy himself who was the secret. Even if he had not uttered a word, I knew he was in there and the four monks now knew that. They had tried to kill Morcar, and they had killed two men they mistook for Morcar, merely because he had witnessed the pale youth being smuggled inside the abbey. What were my chances now that *I* had seen him in there?

My fear escalated, and without any conscious effort I found I was running, my satchel bouncing on my hip, the skirts of my robe and my cloak threatening to trip me. I gathered them up and ran for my life.

I fled across the marketplace and into the maze of narrow, ill-lit streets opening off it. It was late now, fully dark, and there were few people about. I ran on, panting, a stitch in my side. The houses thinned and petered out; I found myself on the edge of a rain-soaked stretch of open space that sloped gently down to the water. There was a shelter of some sort at the water's edge, and I hurried down to it; it was a wash house. There was nobody within – people don't do their laundry late in the evening – and I went inside and slumped on to the stone bench that ran along its rear wall.

My heartbeat gradually slowed. I took deep breaths and, as the sweat cooled on my body, clutched my cloak tightly around me, pulling the hood over my head.

The hood ... With a stab of profound relief, I

thought of something. It wasn't much but it gave me a glimmer of hope. I had gone inside the abbey as a nun, wimpled and veiled like a Benedictine. I had been wearing my disguise when the four monks approached. With any luck, they would not have realized that the nun whispering to their pale boy was the healer who had tended the man they attacked.

With any luck.

I closed my eyes, concentrated so hard that it made my head throb and summoned my guardian. He came quickly – I'm sure he had been with me all evening – and I sensed the tip of his cool nose push into my hot hand. In my mind I saw him, his luxuriant red coat glowing in the starlight, his deep, dark eyes quietly watching me. It was strange because just for an instant I thought I saw the shadowy shape of another animal standing behind him. It was a silver wolf; Edild's spirit animal.

Already comforted by the reassuring presence of Fox, now I smiled in the still night, for I knew my aunt was thinking about me and her thought was so powerful that her guardian had materialized in the dark place where I was.

Slowly, I reached up and took off the wimple, folding it neatly and stowing it in my satchel. I unwound the tight bun – I had drawn my hair back so severely that the skin of my forehead felt unnaturally stretched – and shook my head, feeling my long hair swing around my neck and shoulders. I sat quite still, composing myself and putting my essence back into my true self. Then, recalling all that Edild had taught me about invisibility – which actually is no such thing, just a way of blending into the background so that nobody notices you – I got to my feet and set off up the alley and back into the town.

I kept to the shadows until I reached the market square. I had to cross it to reach the alley where our little house was and I knew that, if unfriendly eyes were looking out for me, then what I must not do was appear furtive. I slid along right in front of the houses that bordered the square, keeping under the overhanging roofs, walking steadily but not hurrying. I am a healer who has been called out to tend a patient, I repeated to myself. I have laboured long and I am tired, so that my feet drag a little. I stumbled, quickly righting myself. I am heading for my home and a well-deserved rest. I let out a little sigh, which turned into a yawn.

I was in the alley now. I risked a glance over my shoulder at the abbey gates; I would be out of the line of sight of anyone looking out in an instant, so I felt it was safe.

The great gate was not quite shut. I could not see anyone but nevertheless I knew he was there. I felt eyes like bright lights searching the darkness; searching for me.

Either he did not see me or he'd realized that I was no nun and so he had no interest in me. I did not wait to find out; I gathered up my skirts again and ran for home.

I did not appreciate how very much I was looking forward to Sibert's presence in the little house until I got back and found he wasn't there.

I let myself in and closed the door, trying not to let the panic take over.

Where could he be?

He was not still at the ale house, I was sure, because I had just passed it and no lights showed, nor were there any sounds of human activity within. The drinkers had left, and those who resided there had turned in for the night. Had Sibert fallen into conversation with someone and, desperate to know more, gone home with him or her to continue the exchange? Oh, he might have told me!

But you weren't here to be told, my reason protested. *You were out on an errand of your own that Sibert did not know about. It's entirely possible that he came home hoping to find you and was as disappointed, puzzled and, yes, alarmed as you are now.*

I collapsed on to my straw mattress. I thought about going to look for him, but I had no idea where to start. Besides, someone had been on watch at the abbey gate and to go out again was surely pushing my luck too far. I was so tired that I knew I would not get far, and the fact that my mind was exhausted too meant I was highly likely to make stupid decisions.

Go to sleep, said a voice in my head. I smiled; someone with more sense than I appeared to be guiding me. I slipped off my boots, loosened my belt, pushed my knife under the mattress within easy reach of my hand and lay down, drawing my cloak around me. There was a moment when I held on to wakefulness – *Sibert, where are you?* – and then I let myself go.

* * *

It must have been very late when I drifted off, or perhaps I was more in need of sleep than I had realized, for when I woke the light streaming in through the small window told me that it was getting on for noon. I stretched and yawned. I was thirsty, and my stomach was growling with hunger. I pushed the cloak off me – I was too hot – and was turning my thoughts to food when I remembered.

I shot up, twisting round to look at Sibert's straw mattress so fast that my head spun. He was not there, but someone else was.

My mouth opened and closed again as I tried to form the words. He beat me to it; with a cool smile Hrype said, 'Good morning, Lassair. I was starting to think you were enchanted and would never wake up.' The smile widened. 'You are all right. You have not been harmed.'

It was a statement; Hrype did not need to ask, being able somehow to sense hurt or malaise in the auras that he claims he sees around all sentient beings, humans included.

'No, I'm fine,' I agreed. I knew what he would ask next, and I steeled myself to tell him the truth.

He already knew that too; apparently, he knew much more than I did, which admittedly would not be difficult. 'Sibert has left the island,' he said softly, as if he were chanting the words; it was the voice he used when he was describing what his inner vision showed him. 'He seeks someone, one who he hoped was to send for him, for he grows impatient and will not wait.'

164

Then, relief flooding his stern face, he said in his normal tone, 'But it's all right; she is not ready to be found.'

'I'm not sure he—' I began, but he raised a hand and I fell silent.

Then, as if the short and strange exchange had not happened, he said, 'I don't know about you, but I'm hungry. Let's go and find some dinner.'

I hurried to get up, brushing straw off my gown and surreptitiously trying to tidy my hair. He waited patiently until I was ready, and then we left the little house and, side by side, set off up the alley.

TWELVE

The food stalls were crowded, catering to the needs of a workforce of hungry men who had been busy since first light. Hrype led the way to one where the queue was long enough to suggest that the food was good but not so long that it would be ages before we were served. We stood in silence while we waited, and when it was our turn Hrype ordered steaming bowls of cabbage soup and rye bread sprinkled with poppy seeds. We found a place to sit down – a partly demolished wall over on the abbey side of the market square – and tucked in. The cabbage soup had been thickened with barley and flavoured with pork stock; it even contained some quite generous pieces of the meat. I dipped in my bread and sucked in my first mouthful. The soup was delicious, and very quickly I had eaten the whole bowlful.

With a smile, Hrype tipped some of his into my bowl. 'You, evidently, are more in need than I,' he remarked.

I hesitated fractionally, purely for the sake of politeness, and then resumed eating.

When I had finished, Hrype asked me to tell him all that had happened since Sibert and I had arrived in Ely. I did so, concentrating hard to make sure I told him the important facts without too much elaboration or speculation. I forced myself to think only about the pale youth and the murders to which his presence on the island had led. I knew that if I so much as let the thought of Sibert's private mission cross my mind then Hrype would somehow spot it and pounce.

'So you see, it really looks as if this pale monk is at the heart of some dangerous secret, although he claims to have no idea at all what it could be,' I concluded.

Hrype was silent for quite a long time. Then he said thoughtfully, 'Pale.'

It was a pretty typical Hrype remark: enigmatic and, as a conversational contribution, not in the least informative.

'What do you mean?' I asked after a pause during which I cast around frantically – and fruitlessly – to see if I could divine what he meant.

'Describe *pale*,' he ordered.

Ah, yes. 'His face is white, but not the greyish pallor you get when you're very sick or in great pain.' Edild suffers from the dreaded hemicrania, often with disturbed vision and nausea, and I know from one look at her when the pain is bad because her face goes corpse-white and her eyes seem to sink in her head. 'He just looks as if he's naturally white-skinned. His eyes have very little colour. The light was poor so I could not determine exactly, but I'd say they were very light grey. His hair is cream.'

'Cream,' Hrype echoed.

'Yes, cream. Not white, like a grandmother's,

167

not blonde like a child's. *Cream,*' I insisted.

Hrype smiled. 'Yes, all right, Lassair, I do not doubt your word.'

That was a relief. I sat waiting for him to comment, but he said nothing. Eventually, I could not contain my impatience. 'Hrype, I'm sorry if I'm interrupting your thoughts, but what should we do? This pale boy was forced inside the abbey by four big, strong men who may or may not be monks, and it appears that they watch him closely even now he's tucked away inside the walls. They saw me talking to him last night' – I said that quickly, hoping to minimize the shiver of fear that shot through me when I thought of those four bulky forms advancing through the dusk – 'and, although as I explained I was dressed as a nun, it's still very likely they know who I am. They might have followed me, or—'

'You are not in danger at the moment,' Hrype interrupted, 'but it might nevertheless be wise to leave Ely.'

'But the pale boy's all alone in there, and he doesn't understand what is happening!' I protested. 'Those men have killed already, and they might be planning to kill him too!'

A smile twitched at the corner of Hrype's long mouth. 'I think not,' he murmured. 'Although there is indeed much danger...' His eyes went unfocused, as if he were contemplating distant things, then he snapped back to me and said, 'You care about this boy?'

'I—' Did I? I had become entangled with the mystery at which he was the heart, that was for sure, and my curiosity was thoroughly aroused.

168

I pictured his face. I saw him trembling with fear. I imagined them holding him down, coldly planning how to dispatch him. It hurt. 'Yes, I care,' I admitted crossly.

Now Hrype's smile spread. 'It is nothing to be ashamed of,' he murmured.

'I'm not.'

He waited while my anger subsided. It did not take long. 'What will you do?' he asked softly.

I like to think the idea was mine alone, although my experience of Hrype leads me to believe that he could easily have put the thought into my head. He had, after all, just said it would be wise to leave Ely. 'I'm going to see if I can find out something about him,' I said decisively. 'I'm going to Fulbourn.' In case he thought I was running away, I added, 'But I'll be back!'

It was about sixteen miles to Fulbourn, and I knew the way, having enquired of the ferryman who rowed me across from the island. It lay a few miles east of Cambridge, and for much of the way the path to take was the Ely to Cambridge road. The only slight problem was the rain-drenched land, which meant that some of the lower-lying tracks were under water. I hoped there would be opportunist boatmen ready to make a few coins wherever this had happened.

It was only when I was well on my way that it occurred to me to wonder what Hrype would do while I was absent. I didn't have to wonder for long, and indeed I was cross with myself for having walked right into his little trap. Something had brought him to Ely, and I did not have to think very hard to work out what it was. Sibert was trying to discover what had happened at Ely when his father took the wound that had ultimately killed him; even without Hrype's extraordinary ability to see into the minds of others, it would have been clear to him that Sibert had other business on the island apart from escorting me as I went to tend my cousin Morcar.

I had been so proud of not letting Hrype catch a glimpse of what Sibert was up to via the medium of my thoughts. My care and my caution had been quite unnecessary, I now realized, because he'd known all along. Now, by either suggesting or agreeing to go to Fulbourn – I was not sure which – I had given Hrype all the time and the space he needed to go after his nephew and stop his enquiries when they had barely begun.

I was so sorry. I spoke to Sibert silently, inside my head, warning him that Hrype had arrived in Ely and was no doubt trying to find him. I also sent him my humble apologies. I don't know if he heard but it made me feel very slightly better.

Then, with some effort, I put Sibert, Hrype and the puzzle of their past to the back of my mind and strode out for Fulbourn.

The road to Cambridge was busy, and I got a ride on the back of a farm cart in exchange for giving the farmer a pot of chickweed, camomile and foxglove ointment for his piles. It still surprises me the way complete strangers reveal intimate facts about themselves as soon as they know I'm a healer; I hadn't been in this man's company for more than half a mile before he began telling me much more than I wanted to know about his back passage. Still, we both got what we wanted. He would soon have relief from his pain, and I had saved myself ten miles of walking on muddy, soggy ground.

I said goodbye to my farmer just outside the town, setting off on a path that skirted around it to the east and then branching off down a track to the village of Fulbourn. Everyone else, it seemed, was making for Cambridge – my farmer had said there was a market there today – and the winding track was deserted. At least it was dry, although black water lapped, at what seemed to me to be a worryingly high level, in the ditches on either side. It was not raining right now, but the skies were dark and lowering.

If it rained I would get soaked, for the sparse and leafless alders and willows that grew in places along the track offered no protection. But there was nothing I could do about the weather.

I trudged on, my boots already caked with dark mud and weighing twice as much as when I had put them on. Presently, I saw a huddle of buildings in the distance. If my bearings were right, this ought to be Fulbourn.

The narrow path crossed the remains of an ancient track, and for a moment I stood to contemplate it. In the winter-bare landscape I could follow its line as it stretched, straight as a die, into the distance on either side. For some reason I felt a shiver of awe. Or was it fear?

I think some instinctive part of my mind had

picked up the danger before I was aware of it because, without my volition, suddenly I found myself hurtling towards a thicket of hazel and bramble that had grown up some twenty paces down the straight track to my right. It was not much of a cover but better than nothing. I got down on hands and knees and wriggled under the dying vegetation. I felt the prickle of a bramble cut a deep scratch into my scalp and crouched lower, my face pressing against the cold earth. I covered myself with my cloak, drawing up my hood, and left just a small space to peer out.

A man was coming along the path from Fulbourn. He was broad and powerful, walking purposefully as if he marched to a beat I couldn't hear. Even before I saw his face, I knew who he was. I tried to curl up even more tightly, making myself as small as I could.

He was almost at the place where the path crossed the ancient track when he called out. I shut my eyes, in that instant of pure terror reverting to childhood and the belief that if I couldn't see him then he could not see me. I held my breath, my heart pounding and sweat breaking out all over my body. How would he kill me? With a knife? With his hands around my throat choking the life out of me? I put my hand down to my waist and, trying to stop the tremor in my fingers, drew my knife from its sheath.

I waited.

Nothing happened.

I heard the man talking. What was he saying? Was he asking his gods for strength to do what he must and kill me? I raised the edge of my hood a tiny amount and looked out.

Now there were two men. Another of the quartet from Ely had come to meet him.

I pushed the heavy hood back so that my ears were clear and listened.

The man who had come from the village was nodding his head in answer to something his companion had asked. The companion asked again, and this time the first man said, loud enough for me to hear, 'It is safe now.'

This seemed to satisfy the other man. He said something – I think he was complaining about a wasted journey – and the first man gave a harsh laugh and said, 'I told you I could do it alone. It was your choice to follow me.'

They were already moving off. I risked another look and saw that they were not going in the direction of Cambridge, behind us to the west, but up the straight track – which, I had reckoned, went almost due north. Well, if they were striking out back to Ely then it would be a more direct route.

I watched them stride away. They moved fast, and quite soon they were no more than two dark shapes in the distance. I waited a little longer. When at last they were out of sight, I crept out of my hiding place, brushed myself down and hurried on to Fulbourn.

The faint shiver of dread was now escalating very rapidly into all-encompassing fear.

The village had grown up around the church and the green. Rows of small, dark houses huddled close to each other as if for security from the wide, flat land all around. I smelt bread and my nose led me to a baker, busy extracting fresh loaves from his oven. I wished him good day and asked where I might find the carpenter's house.

He wiped his sweaty face with the back of his wrist and gave me a grin. 'Which one?' he asked.

Oh. 'Er – the carpenter I'm looking for has a son of about fifteen,' I said, embarrassed. I hadn't prepared for the possibility that there would be more than one carpenter in the village, which was pretty stupid of me.

To my relief the baker was nodding. 'I know who you mean now,' he said. 'Young Gewis is about that age and he's Edulf's son and Edulf was a carpenter, only Edulf died ... ooh, let me see, now.' He paused, a thoughtful frown creasing his cheerful face. 'Three, four years back? Four, I'd say.' He nodded, as if agreeing with his own estimate.

Gewis's father was dead. I hadn't prepared for that, either. Perhaps it was the wrong family; there was an easy way to find out. 'Gewis lives in the village?'

'Aye, that he does.'

I cursed silently. 'And he's here now?' I would have to look elsewhere for my pale youth's family.

The baker scratched his head. 'Come to think of it, I don't reckon I've seen him for a few days.' His frown deepened. 'A couple of weeks, maybe...' My hopes shot up again. 'His

174

mother'll be at home,' the baker went on, and my optimism rose even more. 'I saw her yesterday evening. She bought a flax-seed loaf and we spoke about whether there'd be more rain before nightfall, and she said—'

'Where would I find her?' I tried to cushion my interruption with a smile.

'Now that I *can* tell you,' the baker said helpfully, taking my arm and drawing me so that together we were looking along the street. 'Go up to the end of the row, past the church and round Norman's Corner, then head on down that row and you'll come to four cottages all together. Asfrior's is the third one.'

Asfrior. Edulf. Gewis. I memorized the names. 'Thank you,' I said to the baker, 'you've been very helpful.'

He beamed at me. 'I like to be of assistance to a pretty maid.' He reached out a swift hand and pinched my bottom.

I spun around and hurried away.

As I made my way to the quartet of cottages I planned what I would say. I would tell the pale youth's mother that I had come from Ely and was concerned about her son, worried in case he was in the monastery against his will. I'd say we had talked, her son and I, and that I'd sensed he was uneasy. If she, too, were worried about him, this would surely give her the chance to reveal her anxiety to me in the hope that I might be able to help.

I approached the four cottages. They were well kept, the walls and roofs in good repair, and smoke spiralled up out of the reed thatch of three of them. I went up to the third one and tapped on the door. There was no answer so I tried again, harder this time. I was just about to call out when the door of the cottage on the far side opened, and a short, plump woman of almost my granny's age emerged on to her immaculately swept step. She wore a gown of some dark-brown shade, over which she had tied a voluminous apron. She wore a neat, white headdress; her face was round and red; and her small, dark eyes bright with interest.

'If you're after Asfrior, she's not at home,' she said.

'Oh.' The disappointment was crushing; somehow I had not thought for a moment that I would find nobody at home. 'Do you know where she is?'

'Gone to market, I expect,' the old woman replied promptly. 'I heard her very early, getting ready. Heard voices, see, and then a bit of a bustling about; then the door closed and all went quiet.'

'When do you think she'll be back?' If she had set out so early, perhaps she would have finished whatever business had taken her to market and even now be on her way home.

The old woman was staring out up the road. 'I'd have thought she'd be here by now,' she said, a slight frown creasing her already lined brow.

I was struck with the alarming thought that maybe Asfrior had not gone to market at all but to Ely. How ironic – how *annoying* – it would be if I'd come all this way to find her and she'd gone to the very place I'd just left. 'I'm sure she won't be long,' the old woman was saying. Then she added, 'Want to come inside and have a warm and a bite to eat? You look as if you could do with it.' She was eyeing me, taking in my thin body.

'I'd love to,' I said. Never mind her prurient interest in my skinny body; she had just offered me comforts that I hadn't expected until I got back to Ely.

She led the way inside. Her cottage was tiny, much of the space taken up by a bed against the far wall. A fire burned brightly in the hearth, and I caught the savoury smell of whatever was bubbling in the pot suspended over it. The old woman pushed forward a stool, told me to sit down, take my boots off and warm my feet, and while I did so she fetched two wooden bowls and ladled out generous portions of barley broth. She fetched a loaf and tore off two chunks of bread.

I fell on the food, and my old woman did not speak until I had finished. Watching as I wiped my bowl with the last of the bread, she said, 'Coleman bakes a good loaf. If he could only keep his hands to his craft, and not let them wander all over pretty girls' bottoms, he would be perfect.'

I smiled. 'It was he who directed me here.'

'Did he pinch *your* bottom?'

'He did.'

The old woman cackled. Then, while I, too, was still chuckling, she said in a very different tone, 'What do you want with Asfrior?'

I sensed she cared about her neighbour and was protective of her. I said quickly, 'I mean her no harm. I heard that she had lost her husband and—' I was floundering, for I did not want to touch on the highly sensitive matter of the pale youth – Gewis – and his mystifying secret unless I had no choice.

Fortunately, the old woman appeared to be convinced that I had no malicious intent towards her neighbour. 'She's not done well since her man died,' she said.

'How did he die?' I asked. It might be relevant.

'He was quite a bit older than Asfrior,' the old woman said with a shake of her head. 'Twenty years or so, I'd say, and when the lad was born some took Edulf for his grandfather. Asfrior weren't much more than a girl, see.'

'They were happy?'

'That they were, or as happy as Edulf would ever be. He loved his young wife and his babe, no doubt of that, but he were ever a melancholy man, sad, brooding, as if something was eating at him.'

I thought about that. Could this something be related to the deadly secret? 'Did he ever hint at what it might be?' I asked tentatively.

The old woman slowly shook her head. 'No, I can't say that he did. There were hints that something had happened to his father – that'd be Gewis's grandfather – and I once heard a whisper that he – the grandfather – had suffered some terrible fate. As for Edulf himself, though, I never knew what ailed him.' Then the sharp eyes met mine. 'Didn't stop me speculating though.'

'And what did you conclude?'

'Didn't like the life he led,' she answered promptly. 'Resented the hardships. Seemed to think he deserved better.' Edulf, clearly, had got up her nose with his attitude. 'Instead of appreciating what he had – good, hard-working wife, pretty little child, plenty of jobs to get on with and a fair reputation as an honest craftsman, for all that he didn't have much flair – he sat around moping and complaining.'

'Did he—'

But she hadn't finished. 'Course, he always looked too fragile for this world,' she said critically. 'That deadly white skin and the strange, pale hair made him look more like something from the spirit realm than a flesh and blood man, and he were so straw-straight and thin that you'd think a good easterly wind would blow him away.'

So my pale youth had inherited his colouring and his shape from his father ... Realizing that the old woman still had not said how he had died, I asked again.

'He went off to work on some grand new building where they wanted nothing but the best craftsmen,' she said with a disapproving sniff, 'and *that* were a surprise in itself because, like I said, you'd get a satisfactory job out of Edulf but no more than that and he weren't what I'd have called the best, nowhere near.' Her eyes narrowed as she thought back. 'Went off all in a lather and in such a hurry that he forgot his tools and Asfrior went after him with them. Next thing we know, he's had an accident and he's broken his neck.'

'An accident?' I felt a thrill of apprehension.

'Story went he was perched up high on the scaffolding working on a carving and reached too far.'

It was utterly plausible and such accidents were common. Building sites were perilous places, and I had heard muttered dark tales out of the past to the effect that each great new construction had to have its human sacrifice. With an effort I brought my thoughts back to the present. I exchanged a glance with the old woman, and I had the clear impression that, despite the dangers inherent in a carpenter's work, she didn't believe the story of Edulf's accident any more than I did. Whatever violent drama was being played out around Gewis appeared to have had its origin in the earlier generation: with his father Edulf. Or perhaps even further back, with his grandfather who had met a terrible fate...

The old woman was chattering on, describing how Edulf's body was brought back for burial and how his widow had been desperate in her grief. But I was barely listening. Asfrior still hadn't returned – we would surely have heard her if she had, for the walls of the cottages were thin – and I was struck with the thought that I had sixteen miles to walk before nightfall. I stood up, thanked my old woman and, with a haste that was far from courteous after she had been so hospitable, made my excuses and left.

The cottage next door was, as I had expected,

still empty. I wrapped my cloak round me and headed out of the village.

I had cleared the village and was walking fast towards the place where the ancient straight track branched off to the north when suddenly something caught at the edge of my mind. I pinned it down: it was a remark that my old woman had made, and I concentrated hard, trying to remember exactly what she had said. She had said she'd heard Asfrior early in the morning, getting ready to go to market. She'd heard sounds of movement then it was quiet. Yes, all that was unexceptional, but it wasn't what had aroused my interest – and, I had to admit, my alarm. The sounds of movement were not all, and in my head I listened to the old woman's words: *Heard voices, see.*

But Asfrior had been alone. Her husband was dead and her son, as I well knew, was in Ely. I saw those four burly men in my mind's eye, and I heard again what one of them had said only an hour or so ago: *It is safe now.*

Dread filled my mind.

What should I do? Where should I look? I had seen him approaching the crossroads, and his remark suggested he had already done what he had come to do. I went over to stare down in the ditch on the right side of the path, still looking intently as slowly I walked back towards Fulbourn. When I was close enough to the village that anyone happening to look up could have seen me, I turned round, crossed to the opposite side and, still staring into the ditch, headed back to where I had begun the search.

I found nothing in the ditch. But, just before I reached my starting point, I became aware of the sound of carrion birds, cawing loudly and repeatedly. I looked up. In a small copse in the corner of the field before me I saw perhaps fifty crows, settling on the ground, pecking, fighting among themselves and fluttering up in the air, only to settle back down again almost immediately. They were so intent that many did not move away until I was all but on top of them.

They had already taken the eyes, and the pale face that gazed sightless up into the sky was bloody with peck marks. The blow to the head that must have killed her stood out big as an apple and dark against the smooth brow.

I turned and ran as fast as I can back to the village. I went to the baker and as soon as he saw me all thoughts of chancing his luck for another pinch fled. With nothing but concern on his friendly face, he said, 'What is it, lass? You look terrible! Sit down, let me—'

'There's a body,' I gasped. 'A woman. She's in the copse at the end of that field.' I pointed.

'Are you sure she's dead?'

'Yes! *Yes!*' The living do not allow crows to peck out their eyes. I fought off the nausea as with my mind's eye I saw her again.

The baker was already busy. He called out three or four names and other men materialized on the road. He muttered something and the group hurried away towards the copse. One slipped inside a house and returned carrying a hurdle. I followed behind.

When I caught up with them they were standing, heads bowed and caps in their hands, around the body. I already knew who she was and when one murmured, 'Poor woman. Poor, sad Asfrior,' I was not in the least surprised.

There was a long silence as the men absorbed the shock. Then one said, 'Reckon she must have tripped and hit her head.'

The others nodded their agreement.

Two of the men leaned down to the body and gently put it on the hurdle. It didn't look as if Asfrior weighed very much. Then they took up the ends and slowly bore her back to the village.

I stood beside the baker. His happy face was drawn with sorrow. He put a companionable arm around me. 'Want to come back to the village?' he asked. 'I'll do you something to eat and a hot drink. I could put some honey in it – give you some heart.'

It was kind of him. However, he seemed for the moment to have forgotten I'd come to the village asking about the dead woman's family, and it seemed wise to leave before he remembered. His companions had decided this death was a horrible accident – apparently, none of them had thought to ask himself why Asfrior had left the path and why, if she had tripped and hit her forehead, she was found lying on her back – but I did not want to disabuse them.

'Thank you but I must be on my way,' I replied.

'You have far to go?' He was still eyeing me anxiously.

'No, no, not far,' I lied. 'My father will have

183

set out to meet me by now,' I added, compounding the lie.

The baker nodded. 'Well, if you're sure.'

'Quite sure. Thank you for looking after me,' I said meekly.

'That's all right.'

'Goodbye then.'

'Goodbye, lass.'

As I hurried away I was sure he was watching me. I increased my pace, hoping he would not notice, and soon I was nearing the crossroads. I turned round. The baker had gone.

I set off along the ancient track. It was rough and overgrown, but it went in the direction I had to go. After what seemed like a very short time, I emerged on to the Cambridge to Ely road. I did not meet up with my farmer of the morning, but a merchant heading home with a load of market goods picked me up. This time the treatment I bartered in exchange for my ride was for his wife; I supplied a costly cream made of rose petals and honey that smoothes a woman's wrinkles, although the effect is only temporary. I was so relieved to be on my way back to the four walls of the little room on the island that I would have given him whatever he asked.

I was rowed back to Ely Island on one of the last boats to cross that evening. When I finally got back, it was so good to close the door behind me that I was only a little distressed to find that I was alone.

THIRTEEN

Hrype set off as soon as he had watched Lassair cross the water and march off on the road down to Cambridge. He hoped she would get a lift; he admired her gallant spirit, but it was a long walk. Within the privacy of his own head he briefly stepped into the other world that ran parallel to his own and put in a polite request. When you asked for something for someone else, and there was no advantage to yourself, he had found that the spirits usually helped.

He looked around him. He remembered it all so well. Coming back to Ely was a torment, for at every turn the sights, smells and sensations of now were mingled and blurred with those of before. The marketplace was busy this noon time with a bustle of cheerful, hard-working people, and with his inner eye he saw as it had been during the rebellion. He saw desperate men, their eyes hard with resolve, encouraging one another with the justice of their cause. He saw hungry children who clung in terror to their mothers' skirts. He saw weeping widows, grieving mothers and daughters. He saw the sick and the gravely wounded; he saw himself shoulder to shoulder with other healers as, with arms that were red to the elbow with the blood of the

185

dying, he tried with all his skill and all his might to save a life.

He saw his brother.

Then the memories became too much. With a great effort he drew down a veil in his mind and covered them up.

Without his conscious guidance his feet trod the way to the house where he had laboured so long and so desperately. He wrapped his dark cloak closely around him, bent his long body to make himself shorter and cast his eyes down, so that he looked quite unlike himself. He imagined himself melting into the shadows of the abbey wall; in all likelihood, nobody noticed him at all.

He left the populous areas behind him, and soon he came to the row of little reed-thatched cottages at the end of the track. He stopped by the one outside which stood a lavender bush in a tub. He hesitated and then, barely pausing to knock, eased the door open and stepped inside.

The child he remembered had grown into a thin, tired-looking woman. She sat at her spinning, head bent, back bowed. She looked up at him as if she had been expecting him.

He said softly, 'Yorath. It has been a long time since we saw each other.'

'Yes,' she replied. He sensed wariness.

'I mean you no harm,' he assured her. 'I seek news of my nephew who, brought to the island on other business, has taken the opportunity to investigate what happened here during the rebellion.'

She was watching him closely, but she sat in the shadows and he could not read the expression in her eyes. He sensed her confusion and her fear. He waited.

'He was here,' she said eventually, her voice barely above a whisper. 'He was with a young woman. He asked about you, and I told him my mother worked with you trying to help the wounded and the dying.'

The rush of words sounded like a confession and he saw her fear had increased to terror. She was afraid of *him*.

'That is no more than the truth,' he said gently, 'and it was not unreasonable for you to tell him.'

'He wanted very badly to see Mother,' she went on; it was almost as if the words were being drawn out of her against her will.

'But your mother is not willing to meet him,' he murmured, half to himself.

'That's right, yes, that's right,' she exclaimed in a rush. 'I went out to see her and to ask, just like I promised the young man I would, but she's shut her mind to the past and wants no reminders.'

It is as I thought, Hrype reflected. *The vision was true.*

While she spoke he had been creeping steadily towards her, and now he crouched down at her side. He looked up into her face – he could make out her features now and saw that her eyes were wide and her face drained of colour – and very gently he reached for her hand.

'I laboured for many, many days with your mother, and I have the utmost respect for her,' he said, putting into his voice all the sincerity he could muster. 'I fully understand her wish not to

187

revisit those terrible times, and I uphold her decision not to speak to my nephew.'

He sensed Yorath slump with relief. With a small, wry smile he wondered if she had feared he would cast a spell on her and force her to do what Sibert wanted and take the youth to her mother, whether Aetha wanted to see him or not. And, he thought, how far *that* was from the truth of what he really wanted.

He was silent for some moments, sensing Yorath's mood. When she had at last mastered her emotion he said, 'Your mother no longer lives here on the island?' He knew she did not, but he turned it into a question. As a rule he found it wise not to disclose how much he managed to divine through methods that were not available to most people.

'No,' Yorath replied easily. There was, he noted with satisfaction, no apprehension in her tone. 'She never felt the same after the ... That is to say, she found she could not settle here under the new masters. She tried, and for some time after the rebellion I thought she was all right. Then they announced they were going to tear down our church and start on *that*.' She jerked her head violently in the direction of the new cathedral. 'Mother left. Said she wasn't going to stay here to see it rise up.'

Hrype saw Aetha in his mind, adding a couple of decades. He smiled. She had always been a courageous, determined and outspoken woman. He could well understand her decision to move away from the island before her sharp tongue that refused to shy away from the truth got her into trouble with the new masters. 'Where did she go?' he asked quietly.

He had been stroking the back of Yorath's hand all the while, the small repetitive movements designed to put her into a very light trance. It worked.

'She's gone over the fen to March,' Yorath said disinterestedly. 'Not the big island itself – she's settled on a smaller islet between March and Chatteris. Some call it Bearton. She keeps herself to herself, and nobody finds her unless she's a mind to receive them.'

'How does she live?'

Yorath smiled. 'She looks after herself, like she's always done. She grows vegetables, and she keeps bees and a few hens. Her wants are small, and she manages. She likes her own company.'

Hrype sent a tentative probing thought into Yorath's mind and saw the picture he sought. There was Aetha, looking much as he had pictured her and dressed in a patched old gown over which she had tied a coarse sacking apron. She carried a wooden bowl on one hip from which she was flinging out handfuls of grain for her hens. The tiny dwelling behind her was mud-walled and roofed with reed thatch, but it looked sound. The scene would have been tranquil except that Aetha's deeply lined old face wore a frown.

The frown sounded an alarm; Hrype stood up. 'It has been good to see you, Yorath,' he said. 'You look well.'

She smiled, suddenly looking much more like

the pretty girl he remembered. 'I look old, Hrype,' she replied. 'Life hasn't been easy, not for the likes of us.'

He knew what she meant. Memories were long, and the Normans were meticulous about recording who was with them and who was, or had ever been, against. Yorath and her mother had lost kin during the rebellion; Aetha had given far too much of herself trying to save the wounded and, when she failed, preparing their bodies for the grave. Ely had proved intolerable for her and so she had fled. Yorath had stayed right here with her memories...

Hrype held out his right hand, extending the fingers wide. He held it over Yorath's head. 'I wish you peace,' he murmured.

She met his eyes. 'Thank you.'

Then he turned and strode away.

Some call it Bearton, he repeated to himself. The place of the bears? He wondered absently what ancient fragment of folk memory was embodied in the name. He made his way to where the boats ferried passengers to and fro across the water to the north-west of Ely, the direction in which March and Chatteris lay. He did not even try to find a ferryman who would take him direct to Bearton, instead jumping aboard a substantial craft that was about to cross to March.

He deliberately stilled his mind during the crossing, not allowing the growing anxiety that threatened to gnaw away at him to gain the upper hand. Instead, he looked out calmly over the dark water, studying the places where islands broke the surface and noticing how the whole area appeared waterlogged.

When he reached March he asked among the people busy on the quayside if they knew where Bearton was. Nobody did. Not discouraged, he went on up the slight slope that led away from the water. He kept his eyes on the line where the land gave way to the sodden mud of the foreshore, and presently he spotted a place where a narrow causeway ran out across the water. It began as roughly a straight line but soon began to twist and turn this way and that, like a snake in a river. He looked right along the causeway – in places it was submerged by the high water – to its far end, which melted into the softly swirling mist. He stood watching and after some time the mist parted and he caught a brief glimpse of a low, dark hump of land rising out of the marsh. He glanced around him to orient himself. Yes; the islet fitted Yorath's description, for the causeway led out from March in the direction of Chatteris.

He had found Bearton.

He adopted his head-down, crouched pose and, careful to merge with the crowd and not draw attention to himself, soon reached the landward end of the causeway. Then he waited until the road was quiet, slipped over the low wall and set off.

The going was fairly easy to begin with, although the ground beneath his feet was very wet and worryingly yielding; it felt as if he were treading on clumps of saturated moss. After perhaps a mile he came to a place where the path was covered by the water. He bent down, removed his boots and rolled up his hose, then, not allowing himself any time to dwell on what he was doing, splashed into the water. It was icy, and soon his feet were numb. But, fortunately, it was not too deep, never rising much higher than his knees.

He waded on for another half a mile or so and then emerged on to land. He stopped, dried his feet, rolled down his hose and put on his boots. Then he made himself break into a trot, for he was by now cold all over and shivering to his bones.

The islet of Bearton was tiny. There were the ruins of several abandoned dwellings and, beyond them on the far side of the hump of land, a tiny cottage with a line of low outbuildings. Hrype could make out the regular shapes of several vegetable plots, now all but bare of anything but a few cabbages. Smoke rose from the reed thatched roof; Aetha, it seemed, was inside.

He hesitated, then, making up his mind, walked on. He was deeply apprehensive of what she would say to him, but it was surely better to know.

As he approached the cottage he smelt freshly baked bread. The door opened just as he raised his hand to knock, and he found himself face to face with Aetha.

'I thought it would not be long before you turned up,' she said with a grim smile. 'You'd better come in, Hrype.'

She turned and led the way back inside the tiny room that was her home, and he followed.

He looked around. He had always thought of Aetha as an efficient, tidy woman and the cottage supported that impression. The central hearth lay in a shallow pit, rimmed by carefully selected slabs of stone that were fairly uniform in size. The floor of beaten earth was swept clean. A stool was on the far side of the hearth, and roughly made wooden planks formed a set of shelves behind it. Along the far wall, supported by a simple wooden frame, was a narrow bed, on which sat a black cat with a white mark shaped like a star on its brow. The cat stared at him out of suspicious green eyes, and Hrype stared back.

'That's Callirius,' Aetha said with a smile. 'Take no notice of him.'

Callirius, Hrype thought. She named her cat after the King of the Hazel Grove...

He turned his mind to the purpose of his visit. She had just implied that she had been expecting him; because her daughter had told her that his nephew Sibert wished to see her? Or because ... No. He would not think about that unless and until he must.

'I have seen Yorath,' he said as he sat down on the stool that Aetha had pushed in his direction. 'She told me where you were.'

Aetha snorted. 'Only because you made her, Magic Man,' she said.

'I did not—' he began.

'Oh, I'm not saying you used force,' Aetha snapped. 'But I know you, Hrype. I know how your mind works on people.'

He bowed his head. He was quite surprised at

her challenge; usually nobody dared refer to his strange powers. As if she read the thought, she laughed again, a harsh, barking sound. 'I have not long in this world, and I shall not be sorry to leave it and go to the ancestors,' she said cheerfully. 'If speaking my mind to you means I get there a little sooner that I had expected it'll be worth it.'

He froze. It seemed to him that two opposing desires fought within him: one that wanted to lash out at this straight-talking, challenging old woman and one that wanted to laugh.

Laughter won. Soon she was chuckling with him. 'I would not hurt you, Aetha,' he said after a moment. 'My memories of working alongside you are strong in me still.'

'No, I never really believed I was in danger,' she replied. She was looking at him intently. 'Your power's grown,' she said shortly. 'I would fear you if I did not know you.'

He bowed his head as he considered her words. She was right in her assessment of his increased powers. In the years since they had laboured side by side he had studied hard and pushed himself to the very limit and beyond as he strove to open himself to the knowledge that the spirits offered. He had been wounded, he had fallen sick, he had suffered the extremes of terror and once or twice he had ventured far too close to death. Given all that he had experienced, it was no surprise that his power had grown. But it had come at a price.

She had just said she would fear him if she did not know him. Did she know him? He risked a quick glance and looked into her watchful eyes, then returned his gaze to his hands, folded in his lap. She had known him well enough when they were at Ely. She had seen him at his very best and at his very worst. As to what she read in him now, he was not so sure. He was always careful to veil his inner self from others and, although he recognized that Aetha had been bestowed with certain talents, they were surely nothing like those that the spirits had entrusted to him...

He raised his head and stared into her eyes. She flinched but then gathered her courage and stared right back. For an instant it seemed to Hrype that two glittering swords met and clashed together. Then the lesser one dropped. There was a moment when he saw right into her mind, but then she managed to get her defences up and the image was lost.

He knew he must not try again for he would risk hurting her.

Slowly, deliberately, he let the fierce tension drain from him. He was aware of her panting, as if she had been running very fast, and he listened as her breathing gradually returned to normal. Then she said, 'It's cold outside and you're shivering, Magic Man. I'll brew you a hot drink to put some heat in your bones.'

He was aware of her moving quietly around the room. He shut off the distraction, for he was trying to clarify the quick glimpse he had had into her mind. He had seen a tall, slender figure staring out along the very causeway he had just crossed. The figure was leaning forward, gazing into the mist; he was facing towards the islet, and the image had been from the far end of the causeway. Hrype was all but sure it was Sibert.

He cannot have reached this islet, Hrype told himself. *Aetha knows he wants to see her, for her daughter told her so, yet she refused, but if he had come here I would know.*

There would be signs for one such as Hrype to read had Sibert achieved his goal. The two were blood kin, and Hrype would have picked up his nephew's scent, no matter how hard Aetha had tried to disguise it. In addition, he would have read in her mind that she had recently spoken to the young man; the image Hrype had seen of the slender figure suggested strongly that she had only seen him, at the other end of the causeway.

Suggestion, however, was not enough.

'Have you seen him?' he asked softly.

She paused in her work. 'Yes.'

'He was trying to find you?'

'Yes.'

'But you did not wish to speak to him?'

'I ... No.'

Hrype smiled grimly. 'How did you prevent him crossing the causeway?'

'He was afraid to,' she replied. 'I saw him there, nerving himself to come to me.' Hrype guessed she did not mean she'd actually *seen* him, for it was a substantial distance from March to Bearton, and even the most long-sighted old woman would surely struggle to make out any more than the line of the far shore. No; Aetha would have seen him in her mind.

'Did you place the fear in his head?'

'He was already anxious, for the water was

196

high and in places the path across the causeway was submerged. There are fell creatures in that black water, Magic Man, as all fen dwellers well know.' She smiled, revealing strong, yellowing teeth. 'It was not much of a challenge to work on those fears a little.'

'You knew who he was?'

'I did, for hadn't Yorath just been to tell me he was looking for me?'

Hrype stared at her. 'You would have recognized him even without her warning, I think,' he murmured.

She met his eyes for a moment and then her gaze slid away. She sighed. 'Perhaps.'

He longed to ask her why she would not permit a meeting between herself and Sibert. He had been given a reason – hadn't Yorath said plainly that her mother had shut her mind to the past and wanted no reminders? Why, Aetha had taken the extreme step of abandoning the place that had always been her home and moving to this desolate islet in the middle of nowhere, cut off from humankind and with no company except her cat, her hens and her bees. Sibert, too, would not be just anybody, linked as he was with the terrible days of Hereward's rebellion and its aftermath.

It was enough, wasn't it?

Hrype's mind was working swiftly. Should he confront her directly, or would that merely serve to arouse her curiosity and send her thoughts flying straight back to the one time and place Hrype did not want her to dwell on? Or should he thankfully accept that she had not spoken to

Sibert, had no wish to, and undoubtedly would do whatever was necessary to make sure she didn't?

He was interrupted by Aetha's quiet voice as softly she chanted the words of an ancient spell for protection. Then she said, 'Do not worry. I remember it all, just as well as you do, but some things are best left in the past.'

She set a coarse pottery mug down on the floor beside him, its contents sending up spirals of steam. He smelt the sweet aroma of honey, accompanied by something spicy. He glanced up at her, intending to thank her, and he surprised her in an expression that was the last thing he would have expected.

She was sorry for him.

FOURTEEN

I was exhausted after my long day, and I slept soundly, despite worrying over the absence of both Sibert and Hrype. In a way, the fact that neither of them had returned eased my anxiety, for I told myself that they must surely be together and therefore much safer than if either had been alone. Well, Hrype was all right whether by himself or in company; he has a sort of infallibility about him, which I assume comes from being a cunning man. Not many men are willing to tangle with someone like Hrype. As for Sibert, he had certainly matured recently but he was still subject to fits of self-doubt when the least little obstacle could rear up like a tall cliff and stop him in his tracks, quaking with fear of what might happen. To think of him under the protective cloak of his uncle Hrype was very comforting.

I stirred once, for I had heard a small sound. I thought it was the door opening and was reassured, imagining that one or both of my companions had just crept in. Then I went straight back to sleep.

In the morning I discovered two things: I was still all alone in the little room, and someone had been inside during the night. I knew that without a doubt, for every night before I sleep I always make sure that everything is packed neatly away in my leather satchel and that the buckles are fastened. This morning, one strap was buckled but one lay loose.

I got up straight away, arranging my clothing and brushing the straw out of my hair, for instinctively I felt that whatever I had to face I would be better prepared for it if I were fully dressed and tidy. Then I made myself eat breakfast and drink a hot infusion, for we all do battle better with food inside us. Then I sat on my neatly made bed and thought about what could have happened.

There were no signs that anyone else had spent the night in the house, for the other mattress was undisturbed. I told myself the most likely event was that Hrype and Sibert – perhaps both of them – had returned briefly to our dwelling to fetch something from my satchel, and perhaps to check that I was safe, and then left again on whatever business he, or they, were pursuing. They would have seen me sleeping deeply and taken care not to wake me. Wouldn't they? No doubt they would return soon and tell me all about what they'd been up to.

Yes. That must be right.

The alternative – that some stranger with malicious intent had opened the door, stared down at me and gone through my belongings as I slept – was just too frightening to contemplate.

I reached for my satchel and, forcing my shaking hands to work, checked the contents. As far as I could tell, everything that ought to be there was there. Whoever had rooted through my potions, ointments, herbs and dressings had not disturbed them much, and nobody but me would even have noticed that they had even been touched. He – I knew instinctively that the intruder had been a man – had investigated the pieces of folded white cloth at the bottom of the satchel but only to the extent of pulling out a corner to identify the fabric.

It still could have been Hrype or Sibert, I told myself firmly. Both of them knew what I carried in my bag. Both of them would also know that I wouldn't object if they needed some herb or remedy and came to fetch it, and I tried to convince myself that, finding me so deeply asleep, they would have helped themselves rather than wake me up to ask me for assistance.

The problem with that comforting picture was that, as far as I could tell, nothing was missing from my satchel.

I sat there drowning in my fear for several moments. Then, with a greater effort than I'm prepared to admit, I fought back. *I'm still alive*, I told myself firmly. *Nobody has hurt me. Nothing has been stolen.* Although I did not know who had entered the little room, and what they had wanted of me, I was determined to find out. I wished with all my heart that Sibert or Hrype were there to find out with me – but they weren't, and there was nothing I could do about it. I tidied away my breakfast utensils, picked up my cloak, tied it firmly and set out into the morning.

* * *

How would you go about trying to find out who had crept into your house during the night and what they had been after? I'll tell you what I did: I tried to think why anyone might be interested in me, and straight away the answer flashed back that it must surely be to do with the pale youth. With Gewis, as I now knew him to be called. Yesterday I had gone to his village to find out anything I could about him. The four monks who guarded him must somehow have known where I was going. Perhaps they had made Gewis admit that he'd told me he was a carpenter's son from Fulbourn. I did not allow myself to dwell on how they might have forced him to tell them. So, knowing I was curious about him, they had forestalled me, and one of them had gone there before me. He had found Gewis's mother Asfrior in her little house and somehow persuaded her to set out with him; perhaps he'd concocted some tale about her son needing her so she'd gone willingly. Then he had struck her with something very hard, such as a lump of stone, and hidden her body under the trees. Again I heard those chilling words: *It is safe now.*

Safe? What did he mean? I was all too afraid that I knew, for surely he could only have been saying that, with Asfrior dead, it was safe for me to go to Fulbourn for my only source of information concerning Gewis lay dead with her head staved in.

Oh, *oh*, if I was right, what sort of men were they? What was it that had to be kept secret, so very secret that they had killed, and were going on killing, to prevent anybody finding out?

202

That thought was so awful that my mind shied away. Instead, I went over what I had learned from Asfrior's neighbour. I pictured Edulf, twenty years older than his young wife, a man who bore a heavy weight on his shoulders and whose own father had been involved in some tragic mystery. I thought of how he had died, falling to his death while working on some grand new building. Whoever had been in charge had demanded the finest craftsmen; I pictured Edulf, no doubt pleased and flattered to have been chosen, setting off with a spring in his step, his tool bag light on his shoulder. But then I realized that wasn't right, for he forgot his tools and his wife had to go after him with them.

I thought about that. The old woman hadn't actually said it sounded an unlikely tale, but she hadn't needed to. I agreed with her. A good workman with a reputation to uphold just doesn't set off on a new job without the tools of his trade. Edulf would no more have forgotten his bag than I would have gone to see a sick patient without my satchel.

I wondered what had really happened. Gewis, I realized slowly, was even now in a place where he was being kept apart from the rest of the population. Had this urgent summons that had come for his father been to achieve a similar result? Was that why he had not taken his tools, because the story of working on a magnificent new building was just that, a story, and in reality he knew quite well where he was going and why?

Something must have gone wrong. Whatever

203

they had hoped to do with Edulf, they had not succeeded, for there had been a frightful accident and he had broken his neck. He probably had not fallen from scaffolding while working on a carving; that, like the fictitious job itself, was nothing more than a cover story to satisfy the curious.

They – whoever they were – had wanted Edulf for some matter of great importance. They thought they had got him away to safety, but then something went wrong and he died. Now, four years on, they had come for his son Gewis instead.

Why? What did they want with the men of this family?

I had absolutely no idea.

My musings had achieved the desired effect: I had forgotten my fear. Well, most of it. I was hurrying along in the midst of the crowds of good Ely folk and, for the moment anyway, I felt quite safe. However, enemies were near, and I decided that, since they were taking an interest in my comings and goings, I ought to find out all I could about theirs. I knew that at least two of the quartet of burly monks had left Ely yesterday, for I had seen them just outside Fulbourn. I could not very well go inside the abbey to see if they were there, but I could check to see if they had set out across the water. Turning abruptly, I hurried down to the quayside from which I had embarked the previous noon.

I found the boatman who had given me directions and rowed me across – or, more accurately, he found me. He called out a cheery good morning and asked if I wanted to cross the water again today.

'No, thanks,' I replied. 'Actually, I wanted to ask you something.'

'Ask away,' he said with a grin. He was young, he was quite handsome and I think he was flirting with me.

I leaned closer, taking advantage of his interest. 'It's a little delicate,' I whispered.

His eyes widened, and he put a finger alongside his nose. 'I won't tell,' he hissed dramatically.

I smiled. 'I thought I saw a couple of the brethren from the abbey yesterday, when I was on my way to Fulbourn,' I said, keeping my voice low. 'Both of them are broad-set, tough-looking men and they have a sort of secretive, watchful look about them. I just wondered if you remember taking them across, or even if you told them, too, how to get to Fulbourn?'

Slowly, he shook his head. 'No, can't say as I recall anything like that.'

'Oh.' I'm not sure how I thought the information would have helped, but nevertheless I felt very disappointed.

But my ferryman was leaning close again. 'I remember rowing them back though,' he whispered.

'You do?'

He nodded.

'When?'

'Ooh, mid afternoon.'

'Did they—' No. I had almost said, *Did they*

look as if one of them had just done a murder?
But it would have been an absurd question.

Then the boatman really surprised me. I suppose, thinking about it now, men like him study their passengers, observing small things that most of us would miss. When you're pulling hard on the oars, endlessly rowing people to and fro, there can't be much else to do except indulge in a bit of speculation.

He said, again speaking so quietly that I had to strain to listen, 'I don't know what else they may or may not be but they're not monks.'

It took a moment for me to recover. Then I hissed, 'How can you be so sure?'

He smiled grimly. 'They were bearing arms.'

I realized that I did not want to believe him. 'Most men carry a knife,' I protested, 'even monks, if they have to go on a journey that takes them out of the safety and sanctity of the abbey.'

'That's as maybe,' he conceded. 'I'm not talking about some tiddly knife.'

'What then?'

He spoke right in my ear. 'One of them caught his hem as he got out of the boat. He had a sword in a scabbard hidden under his robe.'

A sword. Still I would not be convinced. 'But—' I began, my mind whirling.

'Anyway, they didn't talk like monks,' the boatman said with an air of finality.

'What do you mean?'

He smiled again. 'I know monks. I meet a great many of them, and I'm familiar with the way they address each other and how they speak. Believe me, your two burly men may have been dressed as holy men but they're not.'

I believed him. My mind racing, I understood then that the quartet must be inside the abbey of Ely with the knowledge and, presumably, the consent of the abbot and the brethren. Whatever they were doing there, whatever mystery Gewis was caught up in, it went right up to the highest authority in the abbey of Ely.

And that was the most alarming thought of all.

I left my boatman and walked on along the quayside. I walked aimlessly, for I had much to think about. I kept close to the water – perhaps its proximity was a comfort, giving the illusion that at any moment I could summon a boat and get away, back to my home – and soon I found that I had reached an area of hectic activity, where a boatload of passengers had just disembarked and another group were waiting to go across.

The waiting group included about half a dozen nuns, several of whom were white-faced and frightened-looking and one of whom was sobbing, her hand held against the front of her head. Drawing closer, I observed that she had a black eye.

The oldest of the sisters was only a few years older than I was and so I thought I would chance it. 'Can I help?' I offered, addressing the senior nun. 'I'm a healer, and I observe that one of your number is hurt.'

The nun spun round to look at me, her pale blue eyes chilly. 'We are perfectly capable of taking care of our own,' she snapped.

The injured nun let out a low moan. 'Please!' she whispered. 'My head hurts so, and it will be ages before we are safe back at Chatteris and in the care of the infirmarer.'

Chatteris! Hastily, I scanned the faces again but none belonged to Elfritha. Some at least of these women would know her though. The thought gave me courage.

'I have willow for head pain,' I said eagerly.

The wounded nun looked at her senior, and her eyes spoke eloquently. 'Please, Sister Maria?'

Sister Maria's frosty frown melted a few degrees. 'Well...'

I decided to take that as permission. I hastened over to stand by the injured nun and put my hands up to feel around her head. I felt the lump – it would have been impossible not to – and winced in sympathy.

'How did it happen?' I asked as I put down my satchel, opened it and drew out the willow-bark remedy. Then, touching her black eye, I added, 'Did you fall?'

She looked at Sister Maria, who nodded curtly and spoke for her. 'No, she did not,' she said tersely. 'She was attacked.'

A warning sounded in my head, clamouring for my attention. A nun had been attacked...

'Attacked?' I echoed, my hands busy preparing the correct dosage.

'On behalf of all of our sisters, we have come from Chatteris to pray one last time in the place that used to be St Etheldreda's church,' Sister Maria said, 'and to view the great new cathedral that rises in its place. We were asleep at our lodgings last night when an intruder slipped in. We have no idea what he wanted with us for, as is well known, we are vowed to poverty and have nothing upon us or with us that could be of interest to any thief, even the most desperate.'

No, I thought. But I already knew that theft had not been the intruder's motive.

'Sister Anne here woke up' – Sister Maria indicated a short, stout, whey-faced nun whose upper teeth protruded over her lip – 'and saw him. She was too terrified to cry out and alert the rest of us' – her tone gave away what she thought about *that* – 'and she watched in horror as he went from cot to cot, staring down at the sisters as they slept. Then he came to Sister Magda, who awoke as he crouched over her. Before she could open her mouth to scream he hit her, giving her that black eye, then he raised his hand, in which he carried some hard, blunt object, and hit her on the forehead. The sound woke us, and we all jumped up. He must have decided he could not fight all of us, and he shot out of the room and fled.'

I had been looking very closely at Sister Magda while I listened. The close-fitting wimple concealed her hair and her skin was light, her eyes blue-green. She was about my height and build. Of all the group, she was the only one who looked anything like me.

I watched as she drank the medicine, then I offered a little pot of catmint and caraway cream. 'Rub it around your eye,' I said. 'It will help bring out the bruise and lessen the pain.'

She smiled her thanks.

209

Sister Maria was clearly becoming impatient. 'The boatman awaits us,' she announced. 'Come along, sisters. Let us hasten away from this place.'

She let her cold eyes sweep along the quay, taking in everything from the rats under the piles to the sweaty ferryman who had just arrived and was resting, slightly breathless, on his oars. Then she ushered her nuns on to the waiting boat, stepped down after them and, keeping her back turned, lowered herself on to the thwart. I watched as she and her sisters were born away. Only Sister Magda risked a farewell glance; our eyes met and she mouthed, 'Thank you.'

I stood where I was for some time. I felt safe there among the hurrying people. Nobody would risk an attack in broad daylight with so many witnesses. Would they?

For I was in danger of an attack, and I had to admit it. The four burly monks – no, they weren't monks, were they? – the four tough men who guarded Gewis so closely knew that a young nun had been inside the abbey and spoken to him. They knew he had told her he came from Fulbourn and was a carpenter's son. One of their number had gone to Fulbourn to cut off the source of information there by killing Gewis's mother; a second had gone out to meet him to make sure the job had been done. They had not waited to see if the young nun reached Fulbourn; with Asfrior dead, it hardly mattered if she did or not. That night one or more of the quartet had gone out under cover of darkness to the place where a visiting group of nuns was lodging. He had looked at each face and, believing that he had found the one he searched for, he had attacked her. Perhaps his aim had been to scare her off the hunt. Or perhaps he had tried to kill her. Either way, the other nuns had woken up and he had fled.

They think I am a nun, I kept repeating to myself. *They do not know me in my true identity. I am safe. I must be, for they attacked not a healer but a nun.*

Perhaps I was safe, for the time being, unless – or until – they discovered their mistake. I would...

But then, with a stab of fear that felt like ice in my veins, I remembered that I, too, had had a visitor during the night. One who had searched through my satchel as if in need of something he knew that I carried. He...

Again, the progress of my thoughts was interrupted by something more urgent. This time the interruption brought sweet relief, for I was picturing the corner of white cloth that had stood out in the bottom of my bag. My intruder had seen it, investigated it but, thank all the good spirits, had not recognized it for what it was, or, rather, for the use to which it had recently been put.

I had used the cloth to fashion a wimple like my sister Elfritha's. My intruder had actually touched, unaware, my nun's disguise.

My guardians must surely be watching over me. The thought gave me so much comfort that, at long last, I felt able to leave the quayside and think about what I should do next.

FIFTEEN

As I was walking away from the quayside I heard someone call my name. I stopped, not turning round, for I knew who it was. I waited for him to catch me up then looked up at him and said, 'Hrype. You are back then.'

'Good day to you, Lassair.'

I thought he appeared dejected. 'You did not find Sibert?'

It was quite gratifying to see the surprise in his eyes, for when I left him to set out for Fulbourn he had given no hint at what he was going to do. He managed not to ask me how I knew; instead, he said, 'I went to the house where I dwelt during the rebellion, and I met a woman I knew. She was only a child when I was last here, but I remembered her. I worked with her mother. The woman – her name is Yorath – told me where to find her mother.'

'She does not live here at Ely,' I said absently. I remembered Yorath telling Sibert and me that the old woman lived somewhere out on the fens.

'No.'

Hrype had, I guessed, just got off a boat from some other fenland settlement. 'So you went to see this old woman to see if Sibert was there?'

'Yes.'

Nobody can extract information from Hrype when he doesn't want to give it. Nevertheless, I did not give up quite yet. 'Why did you think Sibert would seek her out? Because she was here on the island with all of you when your brother was fatally wounded and now he wants to—'

He did not let me finish. 'Lassair, enough.'

'But—'

'Enough.'

Just sometimes Hrype loses the tiniest edge of control and allows those close to him to see a pinhole glimpse of his awesome power. This was one of those times. I felt as if the sharp end of a whip had cut across my face, and I suppressed a cry at the sudden fiery pain.

He knew, of course he did. 'I am sorry,' he said. He put up his hand and very gently touched his fingertips to my throbbing flesh. It felt as if a block of ice was melting there, and the pain vanished.

So, I thought ruefully, *I'm not allowed to ask about Sibert.* It was hugely frustrating because it was the very thing I was desperate to know. My friend had gone off on a quest to find out about his past and, knowing him as I did, I was well aware he would be neither sensible nor cautious as he went about it. He was very likely to run into trouble and virtually certain to need someone to help him out. That someone ought to be me, but if I didn't know where he had gone and what he was doing how could it be?

My one consolation was that Hrype knew Sibert as well if not better than I did. Would he, who of course knew all about the family's past,

213

have a shrewd idea of what it was Sibert was trying to find out? Yes, he would, and if Sibert looked like running into danger then Hrype would go to his aid.

Wouldn't he?

It dawned on me as Hrype and I made our way back to our lodging that, if both he and Sibert had been off the island last night, neither of them could have crept into the room and stealthily gone through the contents of my satchel. I opened my mouth to tell Hrype about the intruder but something stopped me. Pride, probably. If he wasn't going to share his anxieties with me, then why should I involve him in mine? He was evidently far more concerned with Sibert than with my pale monk. Well, I could deal with that; I would just have to help Gewis on my own.

When we reached our little room it became clear that Hrype had only returned to see if there was any sign of Sibert, for after a quick look round his face fell into a deep frown and his shoulders slumped in disappointment.

'What will you do?' I asked.

Hrype did not appear to have heard. He was staring down at the place where Sibert slept, eyes wide and fixed as if trying to read news of his nephew from the straw. Then, with the most cursory nod at me, he drew his cloak around him and swept out.

Slowly, I lowered myself down on to my mattress. I could still sense the echo of Hrype in the little room – it felt like a whirling wind – and I waited until it had settled and all was still. Then I thought about what I was going to

214

do next.

I had already realized that it was up to me to help Gewis. The sensible thing would have been to decide, quite reasonably, that one sixteen year old girl on her own could do little or nothing against the sort of power that for some unknown reason was guarding him. If I was right, then whatever mystery surrounded him went back at least one and probably two generations. His grandfather had met an undisclosed but terrible fate; his father had died in a suspicious accident; his mother had just been murdered. In addition, two eel catchers had been killed because the men who held Gewis believed they were my cousin Morcar, who had witnessed them taking Gewis into the abbey. A young nun had been attacked because they thought she was the woman who had gone inside the abbey and actually spoken to Gewis.

I knew full well that I ought to pack up my belongings, admit that this was all far too big for me and set off for home there and then.

I didn't. I would like to say that it was because I kept picturing the fear in Gewis's eyes and because I wanted to be the one to break the news about his poor mother; I had a feeling none of his quartet of guardians would tell him. This might have been part of my reason, but it was not the driving force.

I had stumbled across a mystery and I knew I wouldn't rest until I found out what was going on.

I sat there for a long time. Then, realizing that the afternoon was swiftly passing, I made myself eat, although I was too tense with excitement and apprehension to have much appetite. Then I cleared away the remains, took my platter and mug to rinse them, and put them back on the shelf. I unwound my hair, brushed it out and then plaited it very tightly and wound the braids closely around my head.

Sibert could only have taken a small pack with him, for the majority of his possessions were in their bag beside his mattress. I took out his spare hose and a jerkin – they smelt of Sibert, and for a moment I just stood there full of anxiety for him – and, stripping off my own garments, put them on. The hose were too long, for Sibert is quite a bit taller than I am, but I folded them over at the top and they did not look too bad. I fastened my own belt around the tunic. Sibert is slim, so it was quite a good fit. My knife in its sheath was on my belt; I touched it for luck. I drew on my boots and pulled a woolly cap over my tightly wound hair. Then I ran my hands down over my body from the crown of my head to my knees, trying to see myself as I would appear to others. Thankful in that moment for my boyish figure, I reckoned I would pass muster to all but the most intent stare.

I was ready. Now it was just a question of waiting for the right moment.

I judged it right. As the light began to fail I made my way to the marketplace and stood for a while observing the comings and goings in and out of the abbey. The working day was ending and most of the traffic was coming out. A few men and boys were still going in; a man took a load of timber ready for the morning; a lad hurried through the gates carrying a loaf of bread and a mug of beer, presumably supper for some man still busy finishing a tricky task. I took a breath, sent a silent appeal to my guardians and, imagining Fox pacing on soft pads beside me, his ears pricked and his luxuriant tail slowly swishing to and fro, I slipped in behind two older men arguing about a delivery of stone and found myself inside the abbey.

I had already decided where I would hide. There was a cemetery to the north side of the site of the new cathedral, and its margins were being used as a store for materials. There were piles of stone, some dressed, some raw, and quantities of timber lay in tidy stacks. I slipped behind a delivery of timber that reared up as high as my shoulder and crouched down to wait for darkness.

Quite soon I regretted my choice of hiding place. As the light failed and the lamps were lit around the new build, the old stones in the burial site behind me threw deep shadows that seemed to move, as if the dead were creeping out of the ground. I told myself firmly not to be so silly.

To take my mind off my fear I thought about Gewis. He had appeared in the old chapel before, I reasoned; perhaps he made a habit of going there in the evening. Perhaps something drew him to those ancient walls ... I hoped very much that this was the case, for it was my only chance of seeing him again. I concentrated on silently calling out to him, letting him know I was waiting for him and summoning him to me.

I concentrated so hard that I made my head ache. Then, when I felt I had done all that I could, cautiously I stood up and looked at the scene before me.

The walls of the new cathedral rose up higher than when I had last visited. The site still looked like a confused jumble, but now I thought I could detect order in the chaos. The finished building was going to be *huge* ... But I was not there to inspect the work; I swallowed my awe and headed for the place where the old chapel had stood.

The ancient wall was still there, and I made sure to keep it in sight as I slipped behind a massive column that was growing up from the floor of the new cathedral. I stared out into the wide open space, trying to make sense of the oddly shaped shadows cast by the builders' materials and tools that were scattered all across it.

Perhaps Gewis's four guards believed that, having scared away the nun who had managed to get inside the abbey and speak to their charge, it was safe to let him wander out to the old church in the late evenings. Perhaps they had lessened their vigilance and he had evaded them. I did not know; the important thing was that he came. I made myself remain behind my pillar as his dark shape materialized out of the shadows, the light of the torches catching his white hair and his pale face. I peered out now and again, keeping watch on his progress across the vast space towards the place where the Saxon church had once stood.

The third time I looked, he had gone.

I stifled a gasp. Where was he? Had he sensed a presence – my presence – and hidden? Oh, but I meant him no harm – on the contrary, I wanted to help him, and by now I was quite desperate to reveal to him what had happened to his mother. The thought of her being dead and him not knowing, believing her to be safe and well back at their home in Fulbourn, was unbearable. I *had* to tell him.

I stepped out from behind the pillar and, very slowly, placing each foot silently, I crept towards the partly demolished wall that was all that remained of the ancient little church. Still I could not see him. Where was he?

Suddenly, he was right in front of me.

In that first, shocked instant I thought, *But he has changed his apparel! How did he do that? Why?*

Then I understood what I was looking at. The horrified cry rose up in my throat and it was only by a huge effort of will that I managed to keep silent. Inside I was screaming in terror as my panicking mind tried to make sense of the *thing* that stood before me.

It was clad in white. It wore a shroud, ravaged by the years into yellowing tatters; the cloth was deeply stained with rusty brown streaks that seemed to originate in the groin. The face was deathly white, the pallor tinged with green. The hair was long, reaching to the shoulders, fine-textured and cream in colour.

It was a face of nightmares. There were black bruises on the jaw and the forehead, as if it had

219

suffered a severe beating. Beneath the pale, well-marked brows there were deep, dark, bloody pits.

Someone had torn out the eyes.

The figure stood quite still in front of the ruined stones that had once formed the south-side chapel of the Saxon church. Then, very slowly, it raised its arm. The ragged sleeve fell back, revealing a hand like a claw. It was pointing ... I could not move, not even to look at the place that the claw-like hand indicated. It was as if death had taken me, stopping my heart and freezing me to the spot.

I could not go on staring at it. I closed my eyes.

When I opened them again, it had gone.

I forgot about my mission, forgot about poor murdered Asfrior, forgot about Gewis. Released from my petrifaction, I turned and fled.

I believe that my guardian spirit was helping me, for my feet were agile as a fox's running for his life before hounds as I leapt over obstacles, dodging and weaving between half-built pillars and the solid bases of falsework towers. I reached the outer wall of the new build and raced on along the shadowy cloister beyond.

Something was in my path. My foot caught against it – Fox seemed to have abandoned me – and I fell headlong, cracking my head hard against the stone floor. I think I stunned myself, for the next few moments were a blur. There was somebody there, someone who swore under his breath as he grabbed my shoulders and dragged me into the shadow of the cloister wall. I felt sick and my head throbbed with pain. I tried to moan in distress and instantly a firm hand was over my mouth.

'Hush,' a deep voice said right in my ear. 'Do not attract their attention.'

He spoke with an accent and I guessed he was a Norman. Who was he? What was he doing there in the abbey? My mind refused to work; all I felt was overwhelming fear.

He must have realized I was hurt. He sat propped against the wall and lay me down so that my head was in his lap. His fingers probed across my brow and I winced as he found the huge lump above my right eye. I started to push his hand away, but then I noticed that he was gently massaging the bump and that his light touch was actually bringing relief from the pain.

After a while he bent over me and, again speaking so softly that I strained to hear, said, 'Can you walk?'

I muttered something. He must have taken it for assent for, slowly and carefully, he raised me to my feet. Instantly, my head swam and the nausea returned. Again, he understood, not hurrying me but allowing me a few moments to recover. Then, moving gently and quietly, he helped me walk along the cloister to the far end.

I wondered where we were going. I wasn't afraid of him now – if he meant me harm he would have hit me while I was down, instead of trying to lessen my pain and helping me get up – but I was very curious. I tried to ask where we were going, but again he hushed me. 'I know a secret way,' he whispered.

We stood at the far end of the cloister for what

seemed ages. Sick, dizzy, I longed to lie down, but I did not dare. I stared around, trying to get my bearings. As far as I could tell we were on the far side of the cathedral site from where I had gone in. I had entered the abbey through the main gate that led off the marketplace; now, I believed, we stood on the south side of the church, and before us was a maze of buildings.

My silent companion must have satisfied himself at last that we were unobserved. Taking my hand – his was warm, square and strong – he led me at a swift pace over to our left. We passed passages, steps and low doorways leading inside the buildings – I had no idea what was within – and, after a lot of twisting and turning, we emerged into the open. We seemed to be standing in a garden. There was an orchard over to our left – I could see the skeletal shapes of apple trees, bare of leaves and holding up their branches like arms begging for help – and, beyond, a vineyard.

Still holding my hand, my companion led the way along a narrow path that passed between neatly clipped box hedges. I smelt rosemary and lavender, my nose attuned to the scents because of my profession so that even now, on a cold November night, I was able to detect them. We were in the herb garden.

We were hurrying now, all but running, and the pain in my head throbbed with each footfall. I folded my lips; I would not cry out. Then I saw the wall rear up before us. It was about ten feet high, and I had no idea how we would get over it. Perhaps there was a gate ... but a gate would be locked and barred, or even manned by some irate and sleepy monk who would far rather be in his bed.

There was a gatehouse – I spotted it over to our left. Clearly, we were not heading for it. Then the wall was right in front of us, and I watched in amazement as my companion, dropping my hand, appeared to fly into the air until the top of the wall was level with his chin. He put both hands on the stonework, raised himself up in an easy, fluid movement that suggested strength and sat astride the wall. Looking down at me, silently he beckoned me.

I looked down. His flight up the wall was revealed as no miracle; there was a compost heap at its foot, and he had simply run up it. I followed, trying not to think about what was squelching and slipping under the soles of my boots, and, as soon as I was standing on its summit, he reached down, caught me under the arms and lifted me easily to sit facing him on the top of the wall.

Despite everything – my anxiety about Gewis, my terror in the old church, my flight, the pain of falling and the alarming, furtive escape through the abbey – I found myself grinning at him. He grinned right back and, in the soft moonlight, I studied him.

He was perhaps twenty-two or three. He was broad-shouldered and slim-hipped, his hair was blond, neatly cut to the level of his chin, and he was fair skinned and clean shaven. The blond hair and light skin suggested his eyes should have been blue or grey, but they were not: they were dark brown. A thin scar cut through his right eyebrow, extending down so that it just touched the eyelid. He was suitably dressed for his night-time mission, whatever it was, for his hose were of some dark fabric and over them he wore a close-fitting black tunic. A long knife hung from his belt.

He slipped off the wall, landing soft as a cat on the far side. He held up his arms, and I jumped after him. I did not even think about it; I had known him for well under an hour, and already I trusted him not to let me fall. He was that sort of man. I felt his arms go round me as my feet hit the ground, and he grasped me close, lessening the impact.

It was only when I saw the surprise in his dark eyes that I remembered my boy disguise. My breasts may not be large, but they are there nonetheless – and, holding me to his broad chest, he must have felt them pressing against him.

He said very quietly, 'Not a boy then, after all. Good evening to you, pretty maid.'

Then he bent his head and kissed me full on the mouth.

Perhaps it was inevitable, given the various shocks, thrills and terrors of the night, for my heart was pounding and the blood ran like fire in my veins. I kissed him back, my mouth opening to his as I wrapped my arms around him. I had kissed men before – well, to be honest, most of them had been boys – and I thought I knew all about it. That night, as I stood in the shadows of Ely abbey's walls with my dark-eyed stranger, I realized I was wrong.

The kiss did not last long. Soon he reached up and gently unwound my arms from around his neck, pushing them down by my sides and squeezing my hands before he let me go. He smiled at me. Then he turned and walked away, his pace quickly escalating so that in no time at all he had vanished into the darkness.

I stood there still feeling the imprint of his lips, so fierce that I could feel my own swelling from the pressure. Had it not been for that very tangible proof of his presence, I might well have been left thinking that the whole thing had been a vivid dream caused by having fallen and struck my head.

Soon, realizing that I was very cold, I left the shadows of the wall and set out for the little house.

He had probably saved my life for, had Gewis's guardians found me lying stunned in the cloister, they might well have thought I had been talking to their charge and killed me as they had killed his mother.

My saviour then. And I didn't even know his name.

SIXTEEN

His name was Rollo Guiscard. He had been born twenty-three years ago on the island of Sicily to a Norman father and a Sicilian mother. His father belonged to the family of the great Robert Guiscard, a Norman adventurer who, with a band of like-minded men, had set out to carve himself a kingdom in the south and achieved his ambition in less than twenty years. It had been a day for celebration when, in 1059, the Pope himself had recognized the Guiscards' right to their hard-won lands. Not that there had even been any question of quitting them had the Pope withheld his approval, for the Guiscards were a law unto themselves.

Rollo's dark-eyed, fiery mother had not actually been wed to his father, but the Guiscards did not worry overmuch about such details. Rollo had been born in a castle – Troina, on its high hilltop in the Nebrodi Mountains – and in 1070, while Robert was engaged on the campaign to capture Palermo, the two-year-old Rollo moved with his mother to the new castle at Adrano, where his father ensured that Robert Guiscard's orders regarding its design were implemented. Robert was in the process of increasing the size of his Sicilian possessions by a considerable amount and he fully intended to hold on to what he had gained. Adrano, like all the new castles, was built tall, strong and with neither time nor money wasted on decoration. It might not have been a comfortable home but it was a safe one. As soon as he could hold a toy sword, Rollo wanted to fight. He quickly demonstrated that he had inherited in full the rebellious, fighting spirit of his forefathers, and Robert Guiscard, spotting the boy's potential, knew that one day he would accept the boy as a welcome and increasingly valued member of his private army. It was not long before he was put into training, and by the time he was thirteen he was already recognized as a very promising soldier. As he grew towards manhood he fought alongside his kinsmen and their supporters to consolidate the Norman hold on Sicily. The Kingdom of the South flourished; Rollo grew strong and skilled, and he feared no man.

In 1085 Roger Guiscard died and he named his son Borsa as his successor. Not many of the family were happy with the arrangement, for the love and loyalty of the fighting men was with Borsa's brother. Christened Mark, he was a mighty man in all ways, and his great size had been evident even as he kicked and squirmed in his mother's womb. He had been nicknamed Bohemond, after the legendary giant, even before he was born, and the name stayed with him all his life.

Bohemond did not meekly sit down and accept his fate. Typical of his bellicose line, he rose up against his brother, seizing key positions in both

Sicily and Calabria from Borsa's feeble grip. His onslaught was only stopped when he reached Bari, where his late father's brother, the Great Count Roger, at last checked him.

Rollo had fought with Bohemond, and he knew in his heart that, had events turned out otherwise, he would have stayed with him, making his life in the hot south where he had been born. But Bohemond had suffered a temporary setback and, for now at least, was no longer the victorious, infallible, irrepressible force he had once been; another man had halted his ambitions in southern Lombardy, and now he was turning his eyes to the east.

Something changed in Rollo. His life had suddenly soured, and he wanted more than anything to get away. *Besides*, he thought, as he found a comfortable place on the deck of the ship that was talking him north, *who wants to spend all their days on one small island when the rest of the world beckons?* The Kingdom of the South had been magnificent and would continue to be so, no matter who held the reins, but instinctively Rollo was aware that it could never be the true centre of power.

Slowly, steadily, by sea and on land, earning his bread by any means that offered, Rollo made his way across the Mediterranean and southern Europe, always travelling north and west, and eventually he arrived in Normandy. He threw in his lot with Duke Robert, the Conqueror's son, but Robert proved all too fallible a leader of men. When his attempt on his brother's kingdom of England failed – many said because Robert did not lead the onslaught himself but let other men do the work for him – Rollo lost faith in him. Now it was that brother of Duke Robert, King William of England, who called silently to him. One day in the early spring of 1089, he took ship from Le Havre in the guise of a merchant and landed in England.

He made his way to William's court, where he presented himself in his true identity as a son of the house of Guiscard, of the Kingdom of the South. He appeared to arouse King William's interest, and for some weeks the king kept Rollo close to him, asking him endless questions about everything from the new castles in Sicily to what he thought Duke Robert would do next. Rollo answered everything he was asked easily and fluently. Observation came as naturally to him as breathing, and his judgement was critical and sound.

King William had quickly realized that he had beside him, in Rollo, a man to value. He began to look out for a suitably testing opportunity, and it was not long before one arose.

The business at Ely was a worry. Not yet a grave worry, for King William knew where his quarry was and who guarded him. However, the anxiety never quite faded away. Attempts had been made in the past, as the king well knew. In these uncertain times, when he had occupied his throne for less than three turbulent years and already put down one major rebellion, might not others come up with the same idea? Was this not why the young man had been spirited away and walled up with the monks of Ely? *Ely*, thought the king. The location in itself was a matter for concern, for the monks on their island in the desolate fens had always had a reputation for independent thought...

The king deliberated for some time. Then in the late autumn of 1090 he summoned Rollo Guiscard, provided him with all the details of the situation and told him what he wanted him to do.

Rollo set out for Ely the next day.

Now, back in his lodging in a row of houses – well-built, but with a quality too subtle to make them stand out and therefore attract unwelcome attention – Rollo sat in a wooden chair before the fire and thought about what had happened that evening. He reached out for the goblet of fine wine – the king was generous to those whose services he valued, even when they were of a clandestine nature – and took a sip, letting the smooth liquid slip down his throat.

The lad was in the abbey; Rollo had seen him. It had appeared that the boy had been making for the site where the ancient Saxon church had stood. Rollo knew where this was because, typical of his thoroughness, he had gone to great pains to find out all that there was to know about the abbey of Ely, as it had once been and as it was now in the transition from Saxon to Norman. He smiled slightly. So the boy knew, too, what had lain buried in the ancient wall. It was a surprise, considering he had been brought up as a poor carpenter's son in some obscure fenland village, but perhaps someone had taken the trouble to tell him. Either that or the past had stretched out a silent hand and beckoned the lad...

Rollo knew he should not entertain such fancies. His Norman kinsmen would laugh him to scorn if they knew. But then, he thought, he was not pure Norman, for his mother was a woman of the south and she came from a long line of *stregha*. His smile deepened for it had been many years since he had heard the old dialect name for a witch. Then a thoughtful expression crossed his face as he recalled something he had heard regarding King William: that he had little time for the church and its ministers and his sympathies lay with the pagan religion.

Rollo neither believed nor disbelieved the rumour. He had merely stored it away for future reference.

He turned his mind back to the events of the evening. The pale boy was closeted away in Ely abbey and, although Rollo had not seen them, there would undoubtedly be very efficient and capable men posted to guard over him. Tomorrow he would find out how many men formed this guard and what sort of threat they posed. They would, however, be mere henchmen, engaged for their strength and their ability to carry out orders without question. The driving force behind this affair would lie elsewhere. The king had told Rollo where he thought this force originated; part of Rollo's commission was to ascertain whether he was right.

He drained the goblet and set it down on the small table beside him. The he sat quite still, formulating in his mind what he would do in the morning. He was aware as he did so of a troubling, turbulent and insistent image that battered against the place where he had penned it. Deliberately, he fortified his defence against it. He sat for some time, making the careful, painstaking plans that were typical of him. Then, when he was satisfied, he left his chair by the fire and went into the next room, where a bed with a feather mattress and fine wool covers awaited him.

It was only with the relaxation of sleep that the image broke out of its prison. Rollo lay dreaming, and his dreams were full of a boy who turned into a girl, whom his dreaming mind seemed to recognize as if he had known her all his life and whom he had kissed with a passion that had exploded like a new sun.

Gewis was very afraid. He sensed that something was about to happen and, although he did not know exactly what, instinctively he sensed danger.

His four guardians had moved him from his bed in the dormitory, and now he occupied a tiny cell, furnished with a hard, narrow cot, a low wooden stool and with nothing to relieve the bare stone walls except a stark wooden crucifix. Food and small beer were brought regularly – whatever his fate might turn out to be, it did not appear that they were going to starve him – and several times a day he was taken out to pray with the brethren. On those occasions he was escorted by no less than two and sometimes all four of his guards.

He had heard them muttering among themselves. They spoke of someone called Lord Edmund the Exile; they spoke of him with respect and awe, and it appeared that this Lord Edmund was coming out of hiding somewhere abroad and returning to England. He was making for Ely. Gewis had no idea who this great lord was, but the fact that he inspired something quite close to fear in Gewis's tough, brawny guardians was quite alarming.

He did not think there would be many more chances to evade the eyes always on him and slip away to the site of the old Saxon church. He was both drawn to and repelled by it, and in a way it was a relief to have the option taken from him. He thought back to the visit he had tried to make a few hours ago. It had called out to him as it so often did, and he had crept along the dark passageways until he'd emerged in the vast space where the new cathedral was going up. He had been about to cross over to the ancient wall when he saw a figure. At first glance it had appeared to be a boy, but he'd caught a glimpse of the face and had recognized the young woman whom he had seen before dressed as a nun. He was about to hurry over to her – if nothing else, he was curious to know why she was back again and why she was now disguised as a boy – but he lost sight of her for a moment, and when he looked again she had gone.

He had seen something else. In the place where she had just been standing, right next to what remained of the old wall, the air was ... *shimmering*, was the only way he could describe it. He had approached the spot, already very afraid and suspecting what might be there, but it had felt as if he'd walked into a wall of ice and he had stopped.

It is here, he'd thought, his mind numb with panic.

For the length of a heartbeat it had materialized before him. He would have screamed but his throat had frozen, and he'd thought he was about to die.

Then the enchantment released him. He'd turned and run.

He could remember little of his terrified flight through the abbey. He'd become aware that one of his guardians was pounding along behind him, and it had taken all his self-control not to stop, turn and fling himself into the man's brawny embrace. The narrow corridor that led to his new quarters had never seemed so welcome and he'd thrown himself through the low door with a sob of relief.

Now, he lay face down on his hard bed. He had the palms of his hands pressed tightly against his closed eyes, but all the same he still saw flashes of the horror in the old church. Amid all the other ghastly aspects of its destroyed face and mutilated body, one thing stood out and, try as he might, he could not stop the image sliding again and again into his mind. *It is nothing*, he told himself. Nothing but the effects of age and long interment.

Slowly, the terror retreated, and Gewis came back to himself. He raised his head, quite surprised to find that his face was wet with his own tears. He heard a quiet cough, realizing only then that there was somebody else in the room. Expecting to see one of his guardians, wearily he sat up and met his visitor's eyes.

It was not one of the guards, although he saw two of them outside the room, standing in the dark passage.

It was the abbot's most senior prior.

Gewis shot to his feet. He might not be a monk, but during the short time he had been at Ely he had picked up the habit of reverence from the brethren. The man who now stood before him was second in seniority only to the abbot himself.

'Please, Gewis, sit down,' the prior said quietly.

He called me by my true name, Gewis thought. *Why, when everyone else here calls me Brother Ailred?* Slowly, he sank down on to his thin, hard mattress.

The prior drew up the wooden stool and sat down close to the cot. He studied Gewis intently for some moments without speaking.

Growing uneasy under the scrutiny, eventually Gewis said hesitantly, 'S–sir?' *Sir* was not right. He frowned, embarrassed, as he tried to remember if he should call the prior father or brother...

But the prior did not seem to have noticed. 'Are you unwell, Gewis?' he asked. His tone was gentle, kindly, but Gewis did not entirely trust him. He looked up into the prior's face. He was a man in the mid-thirties, dark-haired, sallow complexioned, and the intense, brown eyes were small and deep set, their steady gaze

235

unblinking and penetrating.

'I am quite well, thank you,' Gewis stammer-
ed.

'You look pale, my son,' said the prior. He shot
a look in the direction of the guards. 'Not
enough time out in the good, fresh air, I expect.
Tomorrow you shall have more.' He frowned,
his eyes appearing to take in every detail of
Gewis's face and body. 'You are thin, I see. Is
the food here not to your taste? Perhaps there is
some special dish you would like?'

Gewis could barely believe what he was hearing. The food was fine, he wanted to say, better
than he was used to. If he ate little of it that was
because he still had no idea why he had been
brought to Ely, he was very afraid that they
meant him harm, he was lonely, he missed his
mother and there was something within the
abbey that terrified him and which, despite the
rumours that now flew around freely between
the brethren, nobody seemed prepared to talk
about out loud.

He did not feel able to say any of this to the
prior.

'Er ... the food is very fine,' he managed.

'Good, good,' the prior said. 'And you are
comfortable here in this room?'

'Yes, but—' His nervousness overcame him.

'But?' the prior prompted.

'But I don't understand why I've been taken
away from the others,' he said in a rush. 'I was
quite happy in the dormitory with the brethren,
and—'

'You are not a monk, Gewis, and therefore you

do not belong with them,' the prior interrupted smoothly, his face twisted in a rictus of a smile. There was a moment of silence. Then Gewis heard himself say, 'Then why am I here?'

The prior sighed. Gewis stiffened in fear – surely he had just been unforgivably impertinent and he would receive some awful punishment? – but then to his amazement the prior stretched out a long, graceful hand and laid it on Gewis's wrist.

'You are here for your own safety,' he said. 'Your existence has long been known to – to the people who wish to safeguard you. You spent your childhood in Fulbourn, hidden away from the eyes of the world. Those who knew where you were did not know *who* you were; those who were aware of your identity did not know where to look for you. Nevertheless, you were not left unguarded. Those whose concern you are were kept informed regarding your progress as you grew out of boyhood towards manhood. When the time was right, you were brought here to the safety of Ely abbey.'

My mother knew they would come for me, Gewis thought suddenly. He remembered the night that the four burly men had sought him out. His mother, opening the door, had greeted them as if she had been expecting them. When he'd said goodbye to her, she had smiled through her tears and whispered words of encouragement. It had always puzzled him because in that emotional moment of farewell she had seemed so very *proud* of him...

Gewis straightened his back, raised his chin

and stared the prior in the eyes. 'What do you want of me?' he demanded. He was gratified to find that his voice sounded strong and firm.

The prior sensed the change in him; Gewis knew it for he saw it in the man's expression. But, instead of frowning at his impudence, the prior nodded slowly, and Gewis saw some strong emotion flash briefly in the dark eyes. For a moment he thought it might have been respect.

'We wish to protect you from those who would do you harm,' the prior said.

Gewis laughed, a short, sharp, humourless sound. 'Who might that be?' he demanded.

The prior shook his head. 'It is not for me to say,' he replied smoothly, 'but you must trust me when I say you have not been brought here without very good reason.'

'If not you, then who will tell me?' Gewis persisted. The night was becoming more unreal with every moment that passed. Being permitted to speak his mind to the second most senior figure in the abbey was an unexpected indulgence, and he intended to make the most of it.

The prior was watching him closely as if assessing his mood. Then he said, 'One is on his way here who will supply all the answers. He is—'

'He is Lord Edmund the Exile,' Gewis interrupted. 'Yes, I know.'

The prior had gone pale. 'How do you know this?' His voice came in a low, angry whisper in which Gewis detected anxiety and, watching him closely, Gewis saw him shoot a furious, accusatory look at the guardians out in the passage.

Gewis had no wish to make trouble for his four guards. They might have taken him from his home and brought him to the abbey without a word of explanation but they were only following orders. Besides, they had treated him well; apart from the one incident just outside the abbey walls, when he had cried out and they had silenced him, none had raised a hand to him, and they had always seen to it that he had warm clothing, blankets on the bed and enough to eat and drink. There were worse gaolers, Gewis was sure.

He thought rapidly. 'I heard some monks talking,' he said. 'They said an important visitor was expected, and one of them mentioned the name.'

The prior looked sceptical. Gewis, risking a quick look at the guardians, saw relief on their faces. One even gave him a short, tight smile.

'Hmm,' said the prior.

Gewis met his gaze, trying to make his expression innocent. 'Who is this lord?' he asked. 'Is it true that he's important?'

The prior managed a smile. 'He is important to some,' he said evasively. 'As to who he is, he will explain all of that to you when he arrives.'

'Has he far to come?' Gewis asked.

The prior did not answer for some moments. Then he said, 'Oh, yes.'

He said something else, but Gewis could not have heard right for it made no sense. After the prior left and the door of the little room was quietly closed, Gewis was left alone in the dark with his thoughts.

He had much to think about, but his mind returned again and again to the prior's final words. Because what Gewis thought he had said was, 'The blood calls out to him.'

SEVENTEEN

It took me a long time to get to sleep, and in the morning I felt groggy and listless. I recognized that I had suffered a shock last night; more than one, for I had seen a ghost and been kissed hard by a stranger. Stranger ... no, that was not the right word for him, for something inside me had known him, recognized him ... With an effort I pulled myself back from the indulgence of thinking about him and instead addressed myself to the day ahead.

Although I felt I ought to hurry out to pursue my investigations, I knew I was in no fit state. I made myself a calming brew, the main constituents of which were chamomile, clover and honey, and then I ate some bread and more of the honey for my breakfast. I barely tasted the food, but I did feel better after it had gone down.

Then I tidied the room, folding my borrowed garments and stowing them back in Sibert's pack, and tried to see my way through the misty maze that appeared to surround me. I sat in thought for some time, and I got absolutely nowhere. I began to wonder what I was doing in Ely, for surely I was no good to anyone here and I'd be better off at home pursuing my studies and helping my aunt with her patients? But I knew that I would stay; for one thing, Sibert was still absent, and although Hrype was on his trail it was by no means certain that he would find Sibert if Sibert didn't want to be found. Some instinct told me that, if ever Sibert was going to ask for anyone's help in finding the answers about his own past that he so badly wanted, it would not be Hrype he approached but me.

I could not therefore leave Ely and desert my friend. There was something else: when I thought back to the previous evening and managed to see beyond the terrifying vision in the old church, I remembered the pale youth. He had recognized me and he had been about to hurry over and speak to me, of that I was sure. He needed my help, and I wasn't going to let him down.

Although I told myself it was on account of these selfless reasons that I resolved to stay in Ely, even in my own head that was a lie – or, if not exactly that, then a fudging of the truth. I stayed because my dark-eyed stranger was on the island, and I wasn't going to leave all the time there was a chance I would see him again.

I swung my cloak round me, pulled up the hood and went out into the morning. I was not at all sure where I was going but, as I paced up the narrow alley, I was filled with the sense that something was about to happen. The foreboding was at the same time both exciting and vaguely threatening.

Hrype had woken at dawn stiff and cold. After parting from Lassair the previous day he had

242

looked for Sibert all along the Ely quays, asking if anyone had seen him or ferried him across the water. Nobody had or, if they had, they weren't prepared to reveal the fact to a nosy stranger. As the light failed he had found a waterside tavern and ordered food and beer while he'd decided what to do. The obvious answer had been to return to the room, have a good night's sleep and start again in the morning, but he could not face Lassair just then – or now. She surely must know from Sibert that he had welcomed the visit to Ely because it gave him an opportunity to discover more about his past, and Hrype perceived that she was very curious about what exactly was going on between him and Sibert. With good reason, he thought ruefully, but that did not mean he was ready to explain. He was not at all sure that the day when he *was* ready would ever come...

So he'd paid for a bed in the tavern, but the space that his coins bought him was narrow, smelly, bug-ridden and he'd had to share it with other men. He had opted to sit on the bench in the corner, where he'd managed to doze on and off through the long night. It had been a relief when morning had come.

A wakeful night had, however, given him time to think and he had resolved to find Sibert, whatever it took and no matter how far he had to travel in the search. Hrype was not like other men, and he had an aid in his search that was not available to many; after he had taken a fairly unappetizing breakfast in the inn, he'd set off along the quay until he found a quiet spot where

243

the track gave out and low-lying, waterlogged fields began.

He went in under the thin shelter of some winter-bare alders and crouched with his back against the trunk of the largest. It was not ideal; even his skill could not light a fire on the sodden ground. Also, although it was a desolate and deserted place, the town was quite near, and there was always the possibility that he would be disturbed. Nevertheless, he closed his eyes, drew deep on his reserves for the necessary concentration and, when he had put himself in the light trance state, summoned the guardian spirits and asked his animal guide for help. He opened his eyes and thought he glimpsed a large presence beside him, its thick brown fur brushing against him. His bear was there. He smiled faintly, then he shook the runes on to their cloth.

He looked for a long time. What he saw both reassured and deeply disturbed him, for the stones told him how and where he would find Sibert but also that there was a great disturbance hanging over the young man and grave danger hovered very close.

Hrype thanked the spirits, asked his guide to stay close and, his hands moving deftly but reverently, packed the runes away in their leather bag. Then he stood, straightened his cramped spine and set out back the way he had come.

He found a boatman to row him across to March. Almost in a daze, he headed off for the place where the causeway to Bearton branched away into the misty distance. He had almost

244

reached it when he felt a hand on his sleeve. He turned to see Aetha.

'I have been awaiting you, Magic Man,' she said very quietly. There were people about, hurrying to and fro about the morning's business. Aetha looked around quickly, and then she climbed the low wall and walked a few paces down the causeway to a place where a stand of willows stood with the bases of their trunks in water. She hopped nimbly up on to the top of a low rise where the ground was relatively dry and beckoned him to join her.

He stood staring down at her, waiting for her to speak. He read guilt and distress in her expression, and he believed he knew what she had done. The stones had spoken true.

Finally, she said, 'I have betrayed you, Hrype. I told you when you came to me before that I believed some things are best left in the past, and when the youth came looking for me the first time I played on his fears and made sure he stayed away.'

'But he came back,' Hrype said dully.

'He did.' Her voice was barely audible.

'So what changed?' Hrype burst out. 'Why did you allow him to reach you when before you had kept him away?'

'He was desperate!' she cried. He saw clearly that she was as angry as he was. 'I had no wish to be involved in your anguish, Magic Man, for I know what you are and I fear you. It was through no invitation of mine that the boy came to seek me out with you hot on his heels!'

It was a fair comment, and Hrype waited until

245

the blaze of his fury had cooled. Then he said, 'You sensed his despair then, and this time you allowed him across.'

She smiled grimly. 'It was not a question of allowing him, for his despair fed his courage and he mastered his fear. Before I could prevent it, he was on the island knocking at my door.'

Very slowly Hrype nodded. 'And you told him.' He knew it; there was no doubt in his mind, for the stones had hinted at it in their own enigmatic way and now he read it in the old woman who stood before him.

She gritted her teeth, looked him in the eye and said, 'I did.' Then she closed her eyes and added, 'Do what you will with me, Hrype. I deserve it, and life holds little sweetness for me any more.'

He stood rock-still beside her, bending his whole concentration on controlling the fury and the malice that threatened to pour out of him. He would not hurt her, though, for this was no fault of hers. He asked himself what he would have done had the positions been reversed and it was he to whom a deeply disturbed, suspicious young man had come seeking answers. He had an idea he would have acted no differently.

'Aetha, I do not blame you,' he said wearily. 'I have been praying that Sibert would not reach you, but it was ever a feeble hope. He is more determined than I give him credit for.'

'He has courage, but he does not realize it,' she said. He had heard her sigh of relief at what he had just said, and now he observed, amused, that with her fear gone she was now trying to be as helpful as she could to make up for her betrayal.

'I see a stout heart in him, yet he does not believe in his own abilities.'

'He saved a young woman's life once,' Hrype said. 'It took courage, for to prevent her death he had to kill a man.'

Aetha nodded. 'He is from warrior stock,' she said. 'It is—' She stopped, her expression revealing embarrassment.

'Go on.'

She eyed him cautiously; then, apparently deciding that she had nothing to lose, she said, 'He was with me for some time, and we talked much, or rather he talked and I listened.'

'That was ever your skill,' he remarked.

Her face softened in a gentle, reminiscent smile. Then she went on, 'He spoke to me about his mother. I remember her, Hrype, and from what the boy says it appears she has continued along the path that I foresaw for her.'

He believed he understood what she was saying. 'Froya is not strong,' he said. 'She ... many things disturb her equanimity, and she lives in a state of fear even when there is nothing to be afraid of.'

'She requires a lot of love and a lot of care, I imagine,' Aetha said. 'Like her son, she has courage but does not see it.'

'Courage?' he echoed. It was not a word he associated with his brother's widow.

'She took her man away to safety, making the crossing of the fenland under the most difficult and dangerous circumstances,' Aetha reminded him. 'That was not the action of a coward.'

'No indeed, but—' But what? It was not the

moment to discuss Froya's fragile emotional state with someone he had not been close to in almost twenty years. And, indeed, what would he say?

He became aware that Aetha was watching him. He met her eyes. 'Be careful, Hrype,' she warned. 'There is a great anger in him.'

'Directed at me, no doubt,' Hrype said lightly. Despite everything, he found that it was difficult to be apprehensive about Sibert.

'Do not underestimate him,' Aetha said darkly. Then, starkly, 'He wants to kill you.'

Hrype had no memory of leaving the causeway, but he must have done for he found himself down by the waterside at the southern end of March island, waiting for a ferry to take him back to Ely. As he returned to himself he realized that he did not in fact wish to go back, for he knew that Sibert was not there. *I must find him and face him*, he thought.

Moving almost like a sleepwalker, he turned away from the quay and the busy scene of people, animals, boats of all sizes and shouting, sweating boatmen and, taking a narrow path that turned and twined away inland, he set off to look for Sibert.

It was late in the day when he found him. It was, he thought, more a question of allowing Sibert to find *him*, for he sensed the young man's presence before he saw him. He was on a path that led between water meadows; there was a cluster of dwellings in the distance, but nobody was about. Hrype felt fear; turning, he saw

Sibert sliding down a low bank. He reached the path and leapt forward, straight for his uncle.

He had a long knife in his hand.

Hrype stood quite still. There was nothing he could say or do and he knew it.

Sibert's face was working, and he had tears in his eyes. More than anything, Hrype wanted to comfort him, but he knew he could not, either now or perhaps ever.

He waited.

'How could you do it?' Sibert shouted. 'It was betrayal, of the worst kind!'

Betrayal. That word again, Hrype reflected. What a terrible word it was ... Still he did not speak, for the words he longed to utter would sound like the most insubstantial excuse. Rather than be misunderstood, he preferred to keep silent.

Sibert wanted him to speak and now he goaded him, accusing him of terrible things from which Hrype flinched, despite himself. Still he would not speak in his own defence, and he had to listen as all the hurt and distress poured out of the young man who stood, tears in his eyes, trembling with tense emotion and brandishing his blade, on the path in front of him.

That it was Sibert who so accused him made it all but impossible to endure. We do not care what our enemies and those we despise may think of us, Hrype thought as he lowered his eyes before the onslaught. What rips us apart is when we are attacked by those we love.

He gathered his courage and raised his head. He tried to put his heart into his expression. He tried silently to tell Sibert that he understood.

He got it wrong. He who thought he could read people so well, predict what they would say and do and be busy working out how to react even before they had moved a muscle, made a mistake so grave that it threatened his life.

For where he intended love and compassion, Sibert read something very different. Perhaps he read pride; perhaps he believed Hrype was demonstrating by his apparent lack of emotion that, complacent in his power, he did not fear Sibert and was not disconcerted by his fury. There was no time to think it through. There was no time for Hyrpe to defend himself, even had he wanted to.

With an animal howl of anguish that ripped at Hrype's heart, Sibert swung his knife high in the air and, leaping forward, brought it down in a wide, whistling arc that was aimed at Hrype's head. But his toe struck a tree root that snaked across the path and, stumbling, his swing went off course. Hrype, still as a statue and with his eyes closed, was aware of a very hard blow that knocked him off his feet.

He heard another cry – a very different cry now – and there was a thump as Sibert's blade hit the damp ground. He heard footsteps pounding off down the path, the sound steadily receding until he could not detect it any more.

He was lying on something wet and warm. He turned his head slightly and saw that it was his own blood.

Then the pain began.

* * *

I frittered away most of the entire day. I was still beset by the weird sense that something was approaching but as the hours went by, and the daylight began to fade, nothing revealed itself. I wondered if I ought to try again to go inside the abbey that evening. I could dress myself in Sibert's clothes and get in as I had late the previous afternoon; it had worked once, and there was no reason it wouldn't do so again.

I wondered if I could locate the place where my dark-eyed stranger had helped me over the abbey wall last night. After a few dead ends and false trails, I found it. Not that it helped me much for, although there had been a convenient compost heap to climb on the inside, out here the wall reared unbroken high above my own height, and there was no way I could climb it unless someone gave me a leg up.

I stood staring up at the top of the wall. Last night I had jumped down from there into someone's arms and that someone had kissed me...

I admitted to myself that all day I had been hoping I would bump into my stranger. Now, faced with the fact that I had failed, I felt both crushingly disappointed and also cross with myself for mooning after someone who probably hadn't spared me a single thought.

Dejected and miserable, I went back to the little room.

I'd forced myself to eat a bite of supper and was just clearing away the remains when I heard a noise outside. I thought I heard footsteps – slow, irregular footsteps – and there was a sound as if someone was dragging something heavy along the alley.

At first I took little notice. The dwellings around ours housed workmen engaged on the new cathedral, and when they had money in their pockets some of them were apt to stay too long in the tavern so that their progress home was haphazard, to put it mildly.

The steps grew closer. They paused – I thought whoever it was had reached his own house – then after some time they started again. There were several in quite quick succession, and then there was a heavy, dull thud on my door.

I froze. Who could it be? Was it one of the burly monks? Had they seen me last night and taken note of where I lived so that now, when it was dark and I was all alone, they were taking their chance to come and kill me?

Oh! They had attacked that nun who they'd thought was me. Now they had come for me...

I stood in the middle of the room, weakened by terror and emitting soft little moans of distress. I was too scared even to reach for my knife.

Then I heard someone whisper my name.

It's a ruse, I thought, *they're pretending to be someone I know who is calling me outside, and when I go out there they'll jump me and slit my throat.*

Even in my panic I realized how silly that was. If anyone wanted to kill me then surely they would slip inside to do it behind a closed door rather than summoning me out into the alley? As my terror receded I realized something else: it was becoming known that I was a healer, so it was just possible that someone had come to me sick or injured for help.

I gathered my courage, made sure my knife was on my belt and opened the door. There was a body slumped against it; the thump had been the sound of it falling. I detected the metallic smell of blood and, as instinctively I put out my hands to my patient, I felt it, warm and wet on my skin.

I pushed aside the heavy cloak and got hold of the tunic underneath – my patient, it seemed, was a man – and slowly dragged him inside. The hood had fallen across his face and from beneath it I could hear ragged, uneven breathing. He was still alive then. I got him on to my mattress and tucked his cloak around him – even through it I could feel how cold he was – then knelt to build the fire and blow it up into a good blaze, setting water on to boil as I did so.

Then I lowered the hood, unfastened the neck of the cloak and set about discovering where he was injured and how bad it was. The blood was welling up from where his left arm met his chest and the cut was long and deep. I stifled my groan of despair, for Edild always presses upon me the need to reassure rather than alarm a patient. But in my heart I doubted my ability to save him. He seemed to have been bleeding for some time, and even if I managed to stitch him up and stop the flow now it could well be too late.

I was going over in my head Edild's lessons in stitching, recalling what I had done for Morcar and mentally checking that I had everything I would need, when my patient spoke.

'I think,' he said in a husky voice that was barely audible, 'that it may look worse than it is.'

I looked up into his face. It was Hrype.

I bathed and stitched for what seemed like most of the night. I had never treated such a grave injury without the steadying presence of my aunt, and I knew in my heart that I was not ready for anything like this. I must have caused him so much pain, and when he managed to unclench his teeth sufficiently to suggest some of the poppy draught I could have kicked myself for not having thought of it straight away.

Once the sedative took effect I managed better. Hrype relaxed, and I think he lost consciousness. A new dread filled me – that I had put too many drops of the draught into the cup of water and he would never wake up – but it made it much easier to force his sliced flesh together and insert the stitches. At long last, the bleeding slowed and eventually stopped. I sat back on my heels and all but wept with relief.

I checked that my patient was warm and then carefully covered him, piling on his cloak, my blanket and two of Sibert's. Edild had told me that it's no use tucking up a cold person because the covers merely hold the chill in and that she advocated warming a patient with your own body if that is the only means available. I was quite glad it had not been necessary. I was not sure how I would have felt about snuggling up to Hrype, even if he had been unconscious.

I watched him for some time. He was restless,

twisting and turning so much that I had to keep putting the covers back. I put my hand on his forehead and found that he was burning. I did not know what to do.

It is indicative of my state of mind that I did not even think to wonder where Sibert was until, shortly after dawn, the door opened quietly and he slipped inside. I was so glad to see him that I leapt up and threw myself into his arms.

He did not respond and I was instantly cross with myself for not realizing how shocked he must be at the sight of Hrype lying there heavily bandaged and pale with fever. 'He's strong and he's fighting it,' I said, trying to sound reassuring, 'but I'm worried because he's so hot. What should we do, Sibert? Do you think we ought to—?'

'Don't ask me, you're the healer!' he interrupted angrily. He did not sound like himself. His voice was high and strained.

I stroked his arm, trying to calm him. 'I wasn't going to ask for your professional advice,' I said gently. 'I just wondered if you thought we should summon the infirmarer from the abbey. This is really beyond my skill and—'

'No,' he said, 'not the monks,' and even though he was whispering there was no ignoring the emphasis.

'But—' I began, then stopped. This dreadful injury to his uncle seemed to have unhinged poor Sibert, and if I insisted on involving the abbey infirmarer it might make matters worse. There was, in any case, an alternative.

I took Sibert's hand and led him over to his

own mattress, where I gently pushed him down and then sat beside him.

'Very well then,' I said, keeping my voice level and steady, 'we won't ask the monks.' I felt him slump with relief. 'But I do need aid from someone, Sibert. I can't manage this by myself, and I won't risk your uncle's life.'

He turned to look at me, and I was horrified by his expression. 'What must we do?' he whispered.

'I will stay here with Hrype,' I said firmly, 'and I want you to go for help. You remember the boat you borrowed when you took Morcar off the island?' He nodded. 'Well, you must borrow it again. The water's not quite as high as it was then but it's not far off. Go back to Aelf Fen and fetch my aunt Edild.' Just saying her name calmed and reassured me.

'Your aunt Edild,' Sibert echoed.

'Yes, that's right. Tell her that Hrype has what looks like a deep sword cut and, although I've stitched it and the bleeding has stopped, I'm worried because his skin is burning and there must be some bad infection.'

He repeated my instructions back to me, almost word for word. I knew then that, despite his shock, I could trust him. 'Will she save him?' he asked, his eyes full of pleading.

'She will do her very best,' I said staunchly.

He got up and headed for the door. I noticed that he could not make himself look at Hrype. He stopped, his hand on the latch, and said softly, 'Should I bring my mother?'

Why should he ask that? I had no idea. In fact,

256

Froya was pretty much the last person I wanted in the little room. She might once have been Hrype's pupil, and had worked side by side with him as they'd tried to save Edmer, but I guessed she had changed since then, or perhaps life had changed her. I judged her to be easily frightened and someone who would lose her head in a crisis.

But she was Sibert's mother, and it would have been unkind to say so. I smiled at him and said, in what I hoped sounded a reassuring tone, 'No, I shouldn't – just bring Edild.' He still looked anxious so I added, trying to make a joke, 'I don't suppose that leaky old boat would hold three of you!'

He tried to smile back, but it was a poor attempt. Then he opened the door just enough to get through the gap, quickly closing it behind him.

Alone with my patient again, I knelt beside Hrype and tried not to think how long it was going to be before my aunt Edild arrived.

EIGHTEEN

They came for Gewis at dusk. All four of his guardians stepped into his cell, and in the first anxious moment he had the impression that they had taken pains to smarten themselves up. The dark robes had been brushed free of dust and food stains, and the men had washed their faces and hands. One of them still had damp hair.

The largest of the quartet indicated to Gewis to get up off his bed, then said, 'Come with us.'

'Where are we going?' Gewis's voice was little more than a squeak.

There was no answer. The four men fell into step around him and as they marched him along – he noticed with a hysterical desire to giggle that, walking two abreast, their broad shoulders brushed against the walls of the narrow passage – he heard the clink of metal.

His guardians were armed. In what must surely be a brazen flouting of the rules of the abbey, all four wore swords.

Gewis's fear increased.

They emerged from the maze of passages and into the huge open space where the new cathedral was being built. Gewis risked a quick look. His eyes fastened on the ancient wall and from out of nowhere he felt a sudden surge of strength, as if someone had slipped in beside him and silently offered their support. It was a heartening sensation, and he welcomed it.

The guards escorted him through the abbey gate, the one in the lead giving a brief nod to the monk on duty there. Then they were out in the marketplace, quiet now with the day's business over and only a few people still about, and they set off down a street leading off it.

Gewis suddenly remembered what the prior had said about the need for him to have more exercise out in the fresh air. *So that is the explanation for this excursion*, he thought. *They have waited until now, when the town is settling for the night, to minimize the risk of my calling out to someone for help and...*

But he had guessed wrongly, for the guardian on his right had stopped in front of a stoutly built and well-maintained house a few yards along the street. He knocked on the door, which was opened almost immediately by a manservant dressed in good wool hose and a fine tunic. The servant inspected the four guardians, and then his glance fell on Gewis. His eyes widened, and then he looked away. With a jerk of his head he ushered them inside and firmly closed the door, putting a bar in place to secure it. Then he said, 'Follow me, please.'

He led the way across a stone-flagged hall and then into a small room that led off it. A fire blazed in the hearth, and there were torches set in brackets on the walls. Two elaborately carved wooden chairs stood either side of the hearth. One was unoccupied and in the other sat a thin man dressed in a flowing gown of deep-red velvet that must once have been beautiful but now showed signs of long wear. He had grey hair that reached his shoulders and pale blue eyes. The flesh of his face was drawn tightly over the bones of his skull, and his hands on the arms of his chair were as skinny as claws. On the middle finger of his right hand was a heavy gold ring that bore a huge red stone. He sat straining forward as he stared at Gewis, giving him the air of a hungry bird of prey.

Gewis did not know who he was, although he thought he could guess. Instinctively, he feared him.

'Gewis, how good it is to welcome you to this house,' the man said, in a voice that tried too hard to cover desperate need with feigned friendship. 'Come, sit by the fire' – he indicated the other chair – 'and let us offer you food and drink. What will you take? Are you hungry? Do you prefer beer or wine?'

Gewis did not really want a drink, and he did not think he could have forced food down his dry, contracted throat. He noticed a pewter jug set down by the hearth and, from the steam rising from it and the delicious smell, thought it must be hot, spiced wine. 'Is that wine?' he asked.

'Yes indeed,' said the man, beaming, 'fine red wine from France, sweet and spicy! Will you have some with me?'

'All right.'

The man snapped his fingers and a servant appeared. He was a different man from the one

260

who had opened the door. He bore a tray on which there were two silver goblets, which he filled from the jug and handed to his master and Gewis. Gewis looked at the goblet. It was old, and the lively, swirling decoration of stylized animals was, although worn, still quite clearly the work of a true artist. Gewis sipped the wine. He tasted ginger, cloves, cinnamon, honey. It was delicious. He took a second, larger sip and gulped it down, the sound of his swallow too loud in the room. He felt the heat rush into his face and dropped his head, embarrassed.

'Drink, drink, my young friend!' the man encouraged him. 'The night is cold, and you have lived for many days on the adequate but basic fare of the monks.'

'I have no complaints,' Gewis said stiffly.

'Good, that is good, but nevertheless I must apologize for the fact that we had to lodge you there.' The man's face wore an expression of regret that was like a parody. 'Our only concern was for your safety, and—'

Emboldened by the wine, Gewis burst out, 'Why must I be kept in safety? Who is it that threatens me?'

The man studied him for a long moment. Then he said, 'Yes, it is time, I think for explanations.' He glanced at the four guardians, who shuffled outside the room and closed the door. 'Now then. First, allow me to introduce myself. My name is Edmund. I am known as Lord Edmund the Exile, for I have spent much of my life far from this land where my ancestors long lived and flourished.' His face clouded as if with some

261

bitter memory. 'From afar my kinsmen and I have been forced to witness the rape of our homeland by our enemy. Always our minds and our hearts have bent towards England, but we are few, our bloodlines weak and diluted by time and ill fortune.' He sighed, running a hand over his lean face. 'We have maintained our purpose by our hope in the future. We prayed to the gods and to our forefathers that the day would come when one would step out of the shadows and lead us back to our rightful place. We observed, we recorded the crucial events, we saw our hopes raised and then dashed. Now the moment has come at last, and everything is being set in place for our triumphant return to glory.' He beamed at Gewis.

I have no idea what he is talking about, Gewis thought wildly. *Is all that supposed to mean something to me?* He frowned in concentration, for the man – Lord Edmund – clearly expected him to comment. And slowly, emerging like a distant figure approaching out of the mist, Gewis remembered something.

He thought of his father, embittered, angry, struggling to complete a difficult piece of carpentry. He saw him throw down the tool, an expression of frustration on his face as he shouted at his wife cowering in the corner. Gewis saw the long days of his childhood and recognized the fear that had always hung about the house. He remembered his feeble, unsatisfactory conclusion: that somewhere, at some time, somebody had cheated his father, robbing him of something that would have allowed him and his family to lead a better, happier, wealthier, easier life...

Was that what this was all about? Was this man, this Lord Edmund, at last going to reveal to Gewis the secret of his past?

Praying that he had guessed right, Gewis said, 'What has this to do with me?'

Lord Edmund looked at him with an indulgent smile. 'Patience, Gewis, for soon you shall know. For the moment, I must ask you some questions – oh, they are not difficult! Do not look so alarmed! – and, according to how you answer me, I shall reveal the truth.'

'I don't know anything!' Gewis cried, not in the least reassured by Lord Edmund's words. 'I'm just a carpenter's son, and until recently I've never left the village where I was born!'

'You were not, in fact, born there,' Lord Edmund corrected him, 'but let us not bother with that just now.'

Not born there? How did he know? Gewis felt his heart beating fast, although he could not have said whether it was in alarm or in sudden excitement. 'I don't—' he began, but Lord Edmund held up a thin hand. It was his right hand and the jewel in the gold ring flashed like fire as the torchlight caught it.

'You tell me you are a carpenter's son,' he said. 'What is your father's name?'

Gewis shot him a quick glance. Was this a trick question? Did he not know that Gewis's father was dead? 'My father's name was Edulf,' he said boldly, 'and he died four years ago.'

'How did he die?' Lord Edmund was leaning

263

forward again as if he could barely wait for the answer.

'He was summoned to work on an important new building in some nearby settlement,' Gewis said, 'and while he was there he was busy on a carving when he slipped and fell, breaking his neck.'

'His body was brought home for burial?'

That was the strange thing, Gewis reflected; it had puzzled him at the time, but, in his shocked and grieving state, he had not thought to question the voice of authority ... 'No. The priest came to see my mother and he told her that my father had been buried in the place where he died. It was summer,' he added, as if trying to excuse the actions of others, 'and the priest said the burial had to be done quickly before ... er, before—'

'Yes, yes, quite so,' Lord Edmund said quickly. 'And you have visited your father's grave?'

'No.' Gewis hung his head. 'My mother tells me repeatedly that we shall make the journey soon.'

'But the day has not yet come?' Lord Edmund persisted.

'No.'

There was a short silence. Gewis felt deeply ashamed for, although he could not honestly say that he had loved his father, what sort of son was he that he had never knelt at the graveside and offered prayers to speed his father into heaven?

Lord Edmund seemed to read his thoughts. 'Do not berate yourself,' he murmured. 'Try as you might you would not find the place where your father lies buried, for it is not there to be found.'

'Not ... What do you mean?' Gewis was half out of his chair, horrified. How could there be no grave?

'Calm yourself,' Lord Edmund said soothingly. 'There is no grave because those who murdered your father wanted no place where his supporters might make a shrine. They would have no hallowed spot where people would flock to uphold his memory.'

Gewis slowly shook his head, his incomprehension rendering him dumb.

'Tell me, Gewis, was your father a good carpenter?'

'No. He only got the plain work that other men didn't want.'

'Quite so. And—'

'When he was called away for that special job he forgot his tools, and my mother had to go after him with them,' Gewis added. 'He'd only gone a couple of miles down the road, which was just as well because Mother didn't know where he was bound, and if he'd got any further she might not have found him.'

'I see,' said Lord Edmund. 'And just why, Gewis, do you think that a carpenter of your father's standard would have been chosen to work on that grand new structure?'

'I don't know,' Gewis admitted. 'It makes no sense.'

'It makes no sense because it did not happen,' Lord Edmund said gently. 'Your father was tricked, Gewis. His enemies needed to draw him away from his family and his village, for they wanted no witnesses. They made up this fiction of the new building as an excuse for your father to go with them, but all along they had told him a different tale.'

'What was it?' Gewis whispered.

'Ah, Gewis, this is so sad,' Lord Edmund sighed, 'for they were clever and they played on your poor father's secret dreams of glory. They told him they had come to restore him to his rightful place, but that in order to do so he must travel with them to some unspecified destination. That, of course, is why he did not take his tools when he left; he believed that, far from going to work on a building, he was at last going to receive the honour he had always known was his due.'

Oh, but it makes such sense! Gewis thought. His father's lifelong resentment and barely suppressed anger at his lowly station in life would be explained perfectly if, all along, he had believed he deserved something far better.

Was it true? Could it really be that his father had been an important man? Somebody had wanted him dead, it seemed, and that somebody had succeeded. 'Who killed him?' Gewis demanded. 'Why did he have to die?'

'He was killed by his enemies,' Lord Edmund repeated. 'They had grabbed power in the land and a man such as your father threatened them, for while he lived there was always the chance that men would rally to his cause.'

'*Who was he?*' Gewis shouted.

But Lord Edmund shook his head. 'Not yet,

Gewis. First, I must explain my involvement in your affairs.' He paused, his eyes unfocused. Then he said, 'I have, as I told you, lived most of my life abroad, for my father served in the household of a prince in exile who, with his brother, was sent out of England apparently for his own safety but in reality so that he could be quietly killed. He received help, however, from an unexpected source and, by a circuitous route and through the kindness of strangers, eventually he and his brother settled in Hungary. His brother left no descendants, but my father's prince married and had a son. This boy was still a child when my prince made his attempt to take the inheritance that was his due; an attempt that led to his death.' Lord Edmund paused, momentarily covering his face with his hand. Then, with an obvious effort, he continued. 'The prince's son grew to manhood, and we had high hopes of him, for he was of the blood and he was ambitious. However, he failed us. Instead of accepting his part in the continuing struggle, he threw in his lot with the enemy. He is lost to us.'

'Is he dead?' Gewis was absorbed in the tale.

'No, he lives, as far as we know. He supported Duke Robert of Normandy in the attempt to take England from King William, and when it failed he fled to Scotland, where his sister is wed to the king. Now they say he plans to fight abroad.' Lord Edmund shrugged. 'He is, as I say, no more a concern of ours.' His look of disdain said more than his words.

'So...' Gewis let his mind run back over all that he had just heard. 'You lead a faction that opposes the Normans and that—'

'Hush!' Lord Edmund hissed urgently, looking around him anxiously. 'Do not speak such things, even in private, for there are spies everywhere and they are ruthless!' Leaning closer, he murmured, his voice barely audible, 'Agents of the Conqueror killed your father, and they will not rest until they have killed you too.'

'Me?' Gewis cried. 'What have I to do with this?'

'You are your father's son,' Lord Edmund replied. 'The role that was planned for him is now for you to fulfil. How old are you?'

'Fifteen, I believe.'

'Fifteen. Yes, yes, quite old enough.' Lord Edmund was beaming again. 'We shall take you from here to the secure place where our supporters will be gathering, and there we shall reveal to you the full story.'

I do not want to go, Gewis thought. He did not understand – how could he, when this wily, devious man with his insincere smile and the hunger in his eyes refused to explain? – but every instinct was commanding Gewis to have nothing to do with him.

I must escape, he decided. He stitched on an eager smile and said, 'That is wonderful news, and I am in your debt for all that you are doing for me.' Lord Edmund inclined his head in acknowledgement, his face full of smug satisfaction. Gewis put his goblet to his lips and pretended to take a long pull of wine. Then, carefully placing it on then floor, he put a hand to his stomach and muttered, 'Oh dear.'

'What is the matter?' Lord Edmund demanded.

Gewis made a rueful face. 'I am not used to such excellent wine,' he admitted. 'I apologize, my lord, for I have been a glutton and supped far too freely.' He gulped air and then burped loudly. 'Sorry.'

Lord Edmund was watching him warily. 'Are you not well?'

'I'm fine, I ... Oh, no!' Now he was retching, his hands up to his mouth.

'Do not throw up here!' Lord Edmund exclaimed, distaste evident in his tone. 'The privy is in the yard – down the passage and straight in front of you.' He waved a hand.

Gewis retched again, more violently. 'Thank you, my lord ... Oh, *oh!*'

'Hurry, lad!' Lord Edmund urged.

Gewis leapt up and lurched for the door, flinging it open and pulling it to behind him. He heard voices from down the passage. That way, presumably, was the kitchen area and beyond it the yard. There was no sign of either his guardians or either of the servants. With any luck the voices were theirs and all six men were ensconced in the kitchen grabbing a bite of supper.

On light feet Gewis raced the other way, across the hall to the door. He shoved the bar out of the way and opened the door just enough to slip through the gap. He emerged into the darkness, closing the door as soon as he was clear. The longer they thought he was still in the house, the better.

He ran along the alley to the market square. There was the abbey, directly in front of him.

Torches flared high in their brackets either side of the gate. Careful to keep in the shadows, Gewis crept around the square until he was on the opposite side to the street where the guardians had taken him. A series of narrow, dark alleys led off in a generally downhill direction, presumably towards the water. Gewis knew he had to get away, and the only way was by water. He set off down the alley that crouched beneath the abbey wall.

He ran down its full length and at the end found that he could go no further. The water was lapping at his feet, and there was no way across. In the darkness, the scene lit only by the moon, he probably would not have made out any sign of a causeway, even had there been one.

I must wait for the daylight, he decided. He looked around for somewhere to hide, but nothing suitable offered itself. He was resolving to creep back to the abbey wall and crouch against it when he heard the sound.

At first in his panic he thought they were chasing after him. Then he realized that the sounds were coming from the wrong direction and that they were not running footfalls but faint splashes.

Somebody was approaching by water, carefully working the oars to make as little noise as possible.

Gewis stood in the shadows and waited.

Presently, a dilapidated boat appeared. It was quite small and in the stern there was a rough framework that supported a tattered awning. A young man was rowing and there was one passenger, a woman dressed in a dark cloak, the hood pushed back to reveal reddish-gold hair closely braided. She was tense with anxiety, biting her lips incessantly. A frown creased her high forehead.

The young man deftly manoeuvred the boat until it bumped gently against the bank, then leapt out and secured the painter to a post. He leaned down and held out his hand to the woman, who took it and followed him out on to the land. She carried a large leather satchel that appeared to be heavy. The young man offered to take it from her but she shook her head, clutching it to her.

Gewis had been craning forward to watch the pair and, although he did not realize it, his head and shoulders were out of the shadows and the moon fell on his bright hair. The young man looked up – he seemed to be searching for the track – and caught sight of Gewis. With a soft exclamation, he hurried forward.

Gewis cursed himself for his carelessness. He turned, about to flee, but – his voice low and urgent – the young man called out to him.

Gewis stopped. Slowly, he turned round.

The young man was right behind him. He was slim, quite tall and had long fair hair. The flash of recognition came swiftly. 'I've seen you before,' Gewis whispered. 'You came into the abbey looking for rats.'

The young man's face was haggard as if from some deep, abiding sorrow, but now he grinned briefly and said, 'Yes. I was actually looking for you.'

Gewis studied him. The woman had come up to stand behind the young man, and Gewis was aware of her watchful presence. He felt no threat from either of them; besides, what choice did he have? He could try to row away in their boat, but he had no idea which way to go and would probably end up drowned. If he stayed where he was then Lord Edmund's men might find him.

He stared into the young man's eyes. 'Have you somewhere to stay?' he asked.

'Yes, we are on our way to ... Yes,' he replied. Gewis noticed the quick glance he exchanged with the woman.

'I am being followed by men whom I do not trust,' Gewis said. 'If I come with you will you hide me?'

The young man reached out a tentative hand and Gewis took it. 'We will,' he said. 'I am called Sibert, and this is Edild.' The woman nodded to him. 'Come with us,' Sibert added, 'and we will help you.' Still grasping Gewis's hand, he led the way along the bank and then up a narrow alley. He turned, grinned at Gewis and said, 'We have, as I just told you, been looking for you. We will not let you down.'

NINETEEN

I was so relieved to see Edild that it was a moment before I noticed who else Sibert had brought with him. When I realized it was the pale youth, I thought I must be dreaming and that his unexpected appearance was just one more facet of this extraordinary night.

Edild was already on her knees beside Hrype, her anxious eyes taking in every aspect of his condition, one hand on his forehead. She uncovered the wound on his chest and, calling to me for a light, inspected the stitches. She glanced up at me, and I saw from her expression that I had done all right. Then she said, 'Is there water boiling?'

'Yes,' I replied.

'Good.' She reached out for her satchel, unfastening the straps and quickly laying out ingredients.

I could not contain myself any longer. 'Is he going to live?' I whispered.

'I will do my best to make sure he does,' my aunt replied. 'Now, stop hovering over me, Lassair. You keep getting your head between me and the light.'

I was, for the time being, dismissed. I turned to where Sibert stood with the pale youth. 'Where on earth did you find him?' I asked.

Sibert tore his eyes away from his uncle – he looked sickened by the sight of the huge wound – and looked at me. 'He was down by the water when we got back just now. I recognized him initially by his hair. I don't know what he was doing out there, but he asked if we'd shelter him.'

'I can talk for myself, you know,' the pale boy said.

I turned to him. I could think only that his mother was dead and he probably didn't know, but it was hardly the moment to blurt out the news. 'Who are you?' I said instead.

'My name's Gewis.'

I knew that already, and more. 'You're a carpenter's son from Fulbourn.' I remembered his exact words. 'You said you were a monk, but—'

'No, I'm not, for I've taken no vows,' the boy protested. 'I said they'd turned me into one, but I only meant they'd shaved my head and put me in a robe, and I don't think that's binding.'

'I'm sure it's not.' I smiled at him and after a moment he grinned back. 'So, you've managed to get away from them, and now you're trying to get off the island?'

He frowned. 'That's right, but there's much more to it than that.' The frown deepened. 'They seem to think my father belonged to some ancient family, and they wanted to make him a figurehead for men to rally round, only his enemies tricked him and they killed him.'

He appeared to recount that terrible fact with

equanimity. I wondered how he would react when I told him about his mother. 'And now, in the absence of your father, they plan to use you as a rallying point?' I asked.

'Yes,' he said slowly, 'I reckon they do.'

I had no idea who these ambitious men might be. The important thing was that, to judge by his face, this boy wanted no part of their scheming. Besides, hadn't he just run away from them? But it seemed wise to make sure. I hesitated, choosing my words, and then said, 'Do you wish to join them and lead this faction?'

He said simply, 'No.' Then, watching me closely, he added, 'Why? Do you know anything about them? There's something, I can see it in your face.'

So I told him as gently as I could what these men who wanted so badly to advance him into prominence had done to his mother.

He went even paler, if that was possible, and he would have slumped to the ground had it not been for Sibert's support. His eyes anguished, he said, 'Are you sure?'

'I found her body, and I went back to the village for help,' I said, pity for him threatening to make my voice unsteady. 'A man from the village identified her. There was no doubt.'

'Why?' he asked. The word was a sob.

'I think it was because she knew the secret of why you had been taken to Ely and they feared what would happen if the truth got out,' I said. The four guards had killed, or tried to kill, all those who had witnessed their actions, and I could not help but think they would have killed me, too, if they discovered that I knew about Gewis; after all, a young nun had been attacked because they thought she was me and she might very well have died had not her sisters woken up. If anyone from Ely had sought out Asfrior, as indeed I had tried to, there would always have been the danger she would tell them too much.

I had gone to find her. It was quite likely that I had precipitated her death. I did not tell the boy that. I was barely able to deal with it myself.

Slowly, he nodded. 'I must go back to where they have buried her and tell her I am sorry that I abandoned her,' he said slowly. 'I will do so as soon as it is safe. And then...' His words trailed off.

'What will you do?' I asked him. 'Where will you go?'

With a visible effort he brought himself back to the present. 'I must get away from here,' he said. 'Now that you have told me what they have done, that makes them my enemies. They will cut me down as my father and mother were cut down if they know I am against them.'

'You must—' I began.

But just then there was a soft exclamation from Edild. 'He is stirring,' she said. 'Lassair, come here – I need your help, for he must not twist and turn or he will tear the stitches.'

I hurried over to kneel beside her. Hrype's eyelids were fluttering; she was right, he was about to wake up. 'He'll be able to tell us who attacked him!' I murmured to Edild. 'He hasn't said a word so far, but—'

I heard Sibert speaking urgently to the boy.

Then he was right beside me, whispering in my ear and speaking so fast that it was quite hard to make out what he was saying.

'Sibert, slow down!' I protested. 'What did you say?'

'I'm taking Gewis to Aelf Fen,' he repeated. 'He'll be safe there, and he can hide out till he decides what to do.'

'Where *is* this Aelf Fen?' said Gewis plaintively from the door. 'Where are you taking me?'

'It's where we live,' I said, turning to look at him. 'We all have family there, and Sibert will make sure you are well looked after. Sibert, are you sure you want to go?' I added in a low voice. 'Hrype's just about to come round – don't you want to stay and talk to him, just to reassure yourself he's all right?'

Sibert muttered something but I didn't catch it. He had gone white again, and there was sweat on his brow – was he really that squeamish? – so I thought it best to let him be. Besides, Hrype was starting to struggle, as Edild had predicted, and I had work to do.

I was only vaguely aware of the door closing behind them as Sibert and Gewis went out into the night.

My aunt and I worked over Hrype as he lay there on the straw mattress. Edild always stresses that a healer must be detached, with all their concentration fixed upon the needs of the patient, and that this is hardest to achieve when the patient is a friend or a relation. I had never appreciated until that night how difficult this could

277

be. We worked so hard, Edild and I, and once when the wound started bleeding again and she couldn't stop it she called out in anguish to her spirit guide and I really thought I could see her silvery wolf in the little room with us. I was tired and overwrought, however, and so perhaps it was just my imagination.

When we had done all that we could, we sat down on either side of him and Edild held his hand. He was calm now, the hectic flush of heat gradually lessening, and he was slipping in and out of sleep. I stared at him for a long time, and then I looked up at my aunt. She was not aware of my eyes on her and the expression on her face took me by surprise.

I realized, at last, something I had known deep down for some time: Edild loved Hrype.

I dropped my gaze. She had never breathed a word about what she felt for him, and presumably this meant she preferred to keep it to herself. Well, that was her choice. I would make sure she didn't know I knew.

I got up and stretched, then slipped outside to the privy. I stood for a while in the quiet alley looking into the eastern sky. There was the suggestion of a lightening of the darkness; dawn was near. I wondered what the new day would bring. I was shivering – it was a cold night – and went back inside.

Hrype was awake. Edild held a cup to his lips, and he was sipping at the contents. She was speaking softly to him, and something she said made him smile. It was only a slight smile, but I took it as a good sign. I went to kneel at his other side. 'How are you?' I asked.

'I will live, Lassair.'

I wasn't sure how to reply, so I just said lamely, 'Oh, good.'

His smile widened. Then he said, 'Edild tells me I have you to thank for the fact that I am still here.'

Now I felt embarrassed and the hot blood rose in my face. 'The stitches are a bit rough,' I muttered. I knew I had hurt him terribly – the memory of how he had howled with pain before, at his own suggestion, I'd thought to give him the pain-deadening poppy draught was all too vivid – and to have him express gratitude was hard to take.

'Rough or not, they stemmed the blood and stopped my life force running out of me,' he said. 'Lassair, I thank you.'

He and Edild were both staring at me, grey eyes and green eyes carrying the exact same expression. It was too much; I dropped my head, unable to look at them. The mood in the little room was full of tension, and I felt an urgent need to dilute it. I said, 'Hrype, who attacked you? Did you see his face? Should we try to bring him to justice?'

There was a long silence, and I sensed something quite dreadful. Edild looked at Hrype and, all but imperceptibly, he nodded. Then he looked at me and said, 'Sibert.'

I didn't understand. Did he mean Sibert was to seek out the attacker and have him arrested? Or...

Edild must have noticed my confusion. 'Sibert

attacked Hrype,' she said. 'Hrype went back to see Aetha again, and then he went searching for Sibert on March island. Sibert was waiting for him and attacked him with a large knife.'

I said stupidly, 'I didn't know he had a large knife.'

Edild gave a short sound of irritation at the irrelevance of my remark, but Hrype, who seemed to understand better what I was feeling, said, 'It was an old blade, and I think he must have stolen it, perhaps from Aetha.'

I tried to take it in. I looked from one to the other of them and read such a complex mix of emotions that I felt totally confused. Eventually, I said, 'Why?'

Hrype sighed deeply, wincing as the movement tugged at his wound. The wound that his own nephew had inflicted ... Then he said, 'It is a long story. I will begin the tale, for it is mine to tell, and if I grow weary Edild will take over.'

I waited.

After what seemed like an age, he began. 'You have heard, Lassair, of how my mother, my brother, my brother's wife and I were together here on the Isle of Ely at the time of Hereward's rebellion against the Conqueror's rule.'

'Yes, of course.'

'You know that Edmer my brother was gravely wounded and that, although Froya and I did all we could, in the end there was no alternative and I had to amputate his leg.'

'Yes, and then she got him away because his enemies here wanted to kill him, and she took him to Aelf Fen while you stayed here pretending you were still looking after him, and she was pregnant with Sibert and he was born later, after your brother was dead.'

'You know the story well,' he remarked. 'Yes, all that is true.' Something flashed across his face – I thought he was reacting to a stab of pain – and then he said, 'Lassair, consider this: Sibert was born a little less than nine months after Edmer was struck by the arrow that eventually took his life.'

'Yes I know,' I said, 'I just said that.'

Hrype seemed to be waiting for me to go on. When I didn't he sighed again and then said, 'Let me tell you about Froya. What do you think of her, Lassair? What sort of a woman would you say she is?'

I felt very awkward. It was not for me to judge my elders or, even if I did, it would be disrespectful to reveal my thoughts. 'She's ... er, she's very nice,' I said.

Hrype smiled, the expression there and gone swiftly. 'You may speak freely,' he said.

'Oh.' I arranged my thoughts. 'She is an unhappy person. She finds life hard, and she is easily cast down by problems.' I recalled how, when Sibert had gone to fetch Edild – *oh, Sibert!* – he had asked if he should also fetch Froya, and my instinctive reaction was that she would be the last person I'd want in a crisis. 'She panics readily and she is not strong,' I finished. I hoped it was enough – it felt like much more than enough to me.

Hrype nodded. 'All that you observe is true,' he said. 'However, I must tell you that she was

281

not always as you see her today. She was my pupil – it was I who introduced her to my brother – and as a young woman she was spirited and a quick learner. We achieved much working side by side and never more so than when we tended the wounded and the sick during the rebellion here.'

'She fell in love with your brother,' I said dreamily, 'and they were wed.'

'They were,' he agreed. 'They made a good couple, for Edmer loved her dearly, and it moved many people to see that big, tough, strong man side by side with a fair, fragile woman like Froya. Her looks were an illusion, back then, for she, too, was strong, in her own way.'

'I have never doubted it,' I said. 'No weakling wife could have got her gravely wounded husband across the fens the way she did. It must have been dreadful, *and* she was pregnant so she must have worried about the child she carried as well as poor Edmer.'

The child she carried ... Something was nagging at me, trying to claim my attention.

Hrype was speaking, and I made myself listen. 'What she achieved was remarkable,' he said, 'and in many ways it was an event that she has never truly got over.'

I tried to work out what he meant. 'You mean she injured herself in some way?' That made sense. 'Was it something to do with the baby? Did her efforts to take Edmer to safety damage her body so that the birth was more difficult than it should have been?' I was quite sure I was on the right track; after all, Froya had borne no more babies after Sibert. But then, cross with myself, I thought, of course she hadn't! She couldn't have, because her husband was dead.

Hrype was staring at me, almost as if he was willing me to go on. Helplessly, I shook my head. I didn't know what to say.

'You ask if it was something to do with the baby,' he said. 'You are right, but not in the way you think.' He paused, frowning. Then he said, 'Let me tell you about what happened yesterday, Lassair. I went back to Aetha, Yorath's old mother, believing that I would find either that Sibert was with her or that he had recently visited. Aetha, you see, worked with Froya and me during the rebellion. She has sharp eyes and a long memory. She knew what happened, and she has not forgotten. When Sibert finally nerved himself to go to her on her island, she told him.'

'And that's why he attacked you?' I whispered.

'Yes.'

I knew then, although I shied away from accepting it. To have everything I had always believed turned upside down at a stroke was like a blow to the head. If I felt as if I had just been stunned, however must Sibert have reacted?

Now Edild held Hrype's hand in both of hers. She was gazing anxiously down at him, her full attention focused on him. He looked up at me. Then he said simply, 'Sibert is my son.'

I don't know how long I sat there in silence. It was probably only a few moments, but it felt like an age. Hrype was Sibert's father. He had lain with his brother's wife – his gravely wounded brother's wife – and she had conceived his child. Nobody knew, for she had fled from Ely and taken the dying Edmer to Aelf Fen. Had he known his wife was pregnant? Oh, poor, poor man – he must have realized it was not his child, for a man with an infected wound in his thigh that leads to amputation could surely not be in any state to make love.

Hrype was still looking at me. Belatedly, I remembered his uncanny ability to read other people's thoughts, although I dare say mine were fairly obvious just then.

'He did not know, Lassair,' he said softly. 'Froya was a slender woman even then, and the swelling in her belly was easily disguised beneath her garments.'

And a fatally sick husband would not be likely to see or touch his wife's naked body...

I was trying so hard to understand. I was trying not to hate Hrype and Froya for what they had done. Again, he knew what I was thinking. 'It was done from compassion,' he said. 'I know it sounds as if I am trying to excuse a base action and disguise it as something less wicked, but when I took her in my arms it was with no wish but to comfort her.' He twisted on the mattress and a moan of pain broke out of him. 'My mother had recently died – my mother, whom Froya had grown to love, whom she had cared for during the flight across the fenlands and those terrible days in Ely – and her husband was so badly wounded that we knew, if we were honest with each other, that there was little hope for him.' He stopped, took a deep breath and then, his eyes now fixed on a point on the wall as if he could no longer bear to look at me, he said, 'I was asleep. She came to my bed, and she was weeping. She said, "Hold me, Hrype, hold me, for I am so afraid," and I moved over so that she could lie beside me. She was cold, so very cold, and her face was wet with her tears.' His voice broke. Recovering, he went on, 'I held her, trying to warm her with my body, and I wiped away the tears with my fingers. She pressed herself to me and we clung to each other, both of us desperate for comfort, for she was forced to witness the sufferings of a treasured husband and I of a dearly loved brother.'

He paused again, this time for a long moment. Then he said, 'It should not have happened, and we both knew it; we both know it to this day. But human flesh is weak, and in that brief time we gave each other the only thing we had to give. In the morning she was up and dressed before I woke. We did not speak of it, and I believe both of us pretended to ourselves that it had not happened.'

'Then she discovered she was pregnant,' I said dully.

'Yes. She bore her shame and her pain all by herself. I told you just now that Edmer never knew she carried a child; I did not know either, not until a month or so before Sibert was born. I had joined her at Aelf Fen that summer, in time to be with my brother during his last days, and Froya kept her distance from me. When finally she had to tell me, I thought that the child was

Edmer's. Against all sense, I believed my dying brother had impregnated his wife.' Slowly, he shook his head. 'Such is our ability to fool ourselves. I believed what I wanted – *needed* – to be the truth.'

'When did you find out?' I whispered.

He smiled crookedly. 'I saw the baby soon after he was born, and I knew him for a full-term baby. I thought back to where we had all been nine months ago and I knew. I asked her if he was mine and she said yes.' There were tears in his eyes, but he ignored them and slowly they spilled out and ran down his face. 'She said she and Edmer had not lain together as man and wife since before he had gone off to fight, and that was ten, perhaps eleven months back. There was no doubt in her mind, and there has never been any in mine.'

We sat there, the three of us, and I tried to take in what he had told me. Had Sibert suspected something? Had he wondered about that time in Ely, when his badly wounded father and his desperate mother had apparently started a child? Had he understood that the timing was wrong? He must have had his doubts, I realized, for given the opportunity to visit the place where his life had begun he had not hesitated. And, once there, he had set about discovering the truth with a dedication that bordered on obsessive.

Yes, I thought. Sibert had suspected. But now he knew, and that was something very different.

I sent my thoughts his way, telling him I was thinking about him and that I would help him bear this huge blow in any way I could. I didn't

286

know if he heard; I hoped so. I realized then why he had looked so sick when he'd seen Hrype's wound: because he had inflicted it. *Sibert, Sibert,* I thought, *why did you want to kill him? Was it that terrible, to be told that your uncle is really your father? He is still Hrype, whatever his relationship to you.*

I tried to put myself in Sibert's boots. How would I feel if suddenly they told me that, instead of the man married to my mother, my uncle Ordic or my uncle Alwyn had fathered me? I had no idea. Would I want to kill my true father? Again, I didn't know. It was possible, I supposed. Then I thought, but it is not quite the same, because Sibert never knew Edmer whereas I have known and loved my father all my life.

It was beyond me. All I could think was that Sibert was suffering and I could not help him. Would he come back to Ely once Gewis was safe at Aelf Fen? Or would the desire to put as much distance as possible between him and Hrype drive him far away?

I looked up to find Hrype staring at me.

'What are you going to do?' I asked.

He just shrugged.

Edild murmured something – it appeared she wanted to check his wound – and I watched as her gentle hands tended him. Did he care for her as she did for him? I studied his face as he looked up at her. He said something that I did not catch, and her face broke out in a lovely smile. He reached up and touched her cheek, and she folded his hand in hers and drew it to her lips.

The love between them seemed to envelop them in a soft little cloud. I had my answer.

I was young and still to experience love between man and woman. Nevertheless, I understood something about Hrype and my aunt Edild that night, something that moved me profoundly and made me ache for them. It was this: by the well-intentioned actions of one night nineteen years ago, Hrype had tied himself to a woman whom he did not love. Well, he might love her as a brother loves a sister, but she was not his soul mate and, I guessed, did not share his bed and had never done so, apart from that one fateful occasion. He could not leave her, for together they had betrayed his brother and her husband and she had borne their child. Froya was slowly destroying herself with guilt – now I recognized exactly what ailed her and why – and Hrype, who shared that guilt with her, felt far too much responsibility for her to leave her and go where his heart led him. She was frail. She would not manage life without him.

I was so sad for them, all three of them, that I knew I was going to weep. Edild and Hrype were wrapped up in each other – this was, I realized, a rare opportunity for them to be alone together – and they did not need a third.

Quietly, I picked up my cloak, tiptoed across the room and let myself out into the pale light of early morning.

TWENTY

The morning was chilly, and it was as yet too early for any of the food stalls to be serving. A few workmen were queuing up waiting for the abbey gates to open. The men were huddled inside their heavy garments, preoccupied and not interested in a young woman pacing the streets. I was alone with my thoughts.

I crossed the marketplace and headed off to the east, towards the rising sun, keeping level with the high wall that bordered the abbey on its north side. I passed a gatehouse and noticed a clutch of low buildings beside it. This gate, too, was still fast closed. I imagined that somewhere within the monks were at prayer, perhaps seeking strength for the vagaries of the day ahead.

It was very quiet. There was no wind and, although heavy clouds were massing in the western sky, as yet it was fine. The pale sun made the green grass glow. I walked on, presently coming to a meadow that sloped gently down to the water. There was a stand of trees over to the left, and I noticed absently that the water level reached well up their trunks.

There was a ruined building behind me – it looked as if it had once been a cow byre – and I went to sit on a low wall, lifting my feet out of the wet grass and resting them on a stone. I put my elbows on my knees and dropped my chin in my hands. Then I gave myself up to the whirl of thoughts, impressions and recent memories flying around inside my head.

She did not know he was there until he was standing just behind her. He had been watching her for some time, impressed by her utter stillness and wondering what she was doing out there all by herself. He had approached slowly, expecting that at any moment she would hear him and spin round. He only saw the tears on her face when he was close enough to touch her.

He said the first thing that came into his head: 'What's the matter?'

She did not turn; it seemed she knew who he was without looking. 'I've just been told something so sad,' she said.

'Ah.' He sat down beside her on her wall. 'Is there anything you can do to help?'

'No, I don't think there is. It's to do with something two people did here on the island nineteen years ago. They are still living with the consequences – someone else is as well – and nothing's going to change what's happened.'

'I see.' This, then, seemed to be nothing to do with the boy in the abbey. To be sure, he said, 'It concerns friends of yours?'

She nodded. 'Yes. Well, one of them's actually my aunt. The other two are my friend's mother and father, only up until yesterday he thought he was his uncle.'

He worked out what she meant. She could not

be speaking of the pale youth, and he was surprised at the relief that flooded through him. He had found her, by the purest chance, and it seemed they had been given an opportunity to talk of matters far removed from the business that had brought him to Ely. That still must be resolved, and he knew it. He knew, too, that soon he would have to ask her why she had been in the abbey and what her interest was in the pale youth. For now, she was distressed because of something that had nothing to do with him. Perhaps he could comfort her. He intended to enjoy this moment out of time to the full.

He leaned closer to her. He caught her scent – she smelled of rosemary and lavender, among other things, and he guessed she was a healer. The scent awoke memories of how it had felt to kiss her.

'I'm sorry you are sad,' he said softly. He put his arm around her and she snuggled against him. 'Would it help to talk about it?'

'No,' she replied, then immediately added, 'That was rude and I apologize. I know you're trying to be kind.'

I would always wish to be kind to you, he thought.

They sat close together, not speaking. Presently, he raised a hand and, gently cupping her face, turned her so that he could kiss her. She kissed him back.

After an embrace that had lasted quite a long time, he said, 'What's your name?'

'Lassair.'

'Do you live here on Ely?'

'No.'

He did not ask her where she did live; he sensed she would not answer.

'What are you called?' she asked.

'Rollo.'

'And you don't come from here either.' It was a statement, not a question.

He said simply, 'No. I was born a long way away.'

'You sound foreign,' she remarked. 'You don't talk like other people round here.'

He smiled. 'I speak several languages. This is one of them.'

She reached up and ran a finger the length of the scar that bisected his eyebrow. She said softly, 'Rollo.' Then she grabbed hold of his face and kissed him with an intensity that took his breath away.

She was warm in his arms, her smooth hair soft under his hands. It was long – so long – since he had held a woman. She was arousing sensations and emotions in him which he had believed he had put aside. For now, anyway, when there was a job to be done.

But the job was as yet incomplete. Gently and reluctantly he broke away from her and, still holding hands, they sat for some moments, the silence broken only by their fast breathing that slowly returned to normal. Then he said, 'The boy in the abbey; did you get inside specifically to try to see him?'

'Yes.' Her answer was instant and, if she regretted the intrusion of the real world, she gave no sign. Perhaps she too recognized that this was not the time to indulge whatever it was that had so suddenly sprung into existence between them.

He forced himself to concentrate. 'Why?'

'Because my cousin witnessed those four big men who guard him bundling him in through the gate. Then someone tried to kill him – my cousin, I mean – but they didn't because they thought he had drowned, but he managed to hold his breath and evade them, only he managed to stick an eel gleeve in his foot and the wound went putrid. Then two other eel catchers dressed in cloaks exactly like my cousin's were murdered, and we guessed the men were trying to get rid of Morcar – my cousin – because he'd witnessed them manhandling the boy.'

He digested the rush of words. Then: 'So you thought you should help the pale boy in case he had been taken inside the abbey against his will?'

'Yes, but it wasn't only that. They had tried to kill my cousin, and there was always the possibility they'd make another attempt and succeed – well, they won't now because he's not here any more and he's well hidden somewhere they won't find him – and we thought it might help if we had some idea of what this was all about.'

Slowly, he nodded. 'When you say *we*?' he said, turning it into a question.

'Sibert and me, mainly. He's my friend who I told you about. The one who has just discovered that his uncle is his father.'

'I see.' He wanted to smile, for her life seemed

full of tangles and he was enchanted by the way she had no hesitation in sharing them with him. Except, he noted, she had told him neither where her home was nor where she and her friend had hidden the cousin; in all likelihood the places were one and the same. He did not blame her for being careful. She might have opened her heart to him – he was still staggered by what was happening between them – but she was sufficiently cautious to watch her tongue where others were concerned. Since he intended to do the same, he was in no position to criticize.

He said, 'Do you know who the pale boy is?'

She hesitated only for a moment. Then she said, 'His name is Gewis. He's the son of a carpenter called Edulf, who died four years ago, and a woman called Asfrior, who died the day before yesterday.'

The boy's mother was dead. It was as he had thought. The woman knew the whole story, and, knowing he had closed in, they would not have risked letting her stay alive. The secret had died with her. Except that of course it hadn't, for it was known to a select few of her own people. He knew it too. He was her enemy.

How much did Lassair know?

Knowledge such as this was dangerous. He knew then that he would protect her, whatever happened.

He said, carefully choosing his words, 'He is someone of great importance, although he does not know it.'

'He does, and I'd already guessed as much,' she said. He detected a hint of irony. 'People don't normally make such a fuss about a carpenter's son from a small fenland village.' She turned to stare at him. Her eyes looked green in the bright light. 'He has gone, Rollo. Whatever you, or they, want him to be a part of, he will not do it. I told him they killed his mother, and even if he hadn't made up his mind before he did then.'

He sighed. 'I had nothing to do with the death of his mother,' he said. 'It is true that the slaying of his father was the work of the faction to which I belong' – was that right? Did he belong with the king's party? Just then he did not know – 'but I was not involved. Four years ago I was a thousand and more miles away from eastern England.'

She nodded quickly. 'I believe you.' He was surprised at how much pleasure those three words gave him. 'Why did your people kill Gewis's father?'

He paused. Should he tell her? This was the most dangerous part of the secret, but then she knew so much already and he did not think she would rest until she had uncovered the whole story. 'Because the blood of kings ran in his veins. He was of the bloodline of the House of Wessex, and from that house came Edward the Confessor, the last Wessex king. Many men who support the old regime want to see a Wessex king back on the throne of England.'

She did not speak for some time. She whispered, almost to herself, 'My kinsmen fought and died for the old regime.' Then aloud she said, 'Gewis, too, must be of the bloodline.'

'He is.'

'He's aware that he belongs to some ancient family, but does he know what an elevated one it was?'

'No. Or, rather, he did not know yesterday, although I have reason to believe he was taken to see someone last evening who was in a position to enlighten him.'

She frowned. 'He did see someone last night. He ran away from whoever it was, and he found his way to us.' Her frown deepened. 'I'm quite sure he didn't mention the House of Wessex.'

Then, he thought, they probably didn't tell him.

She was very quiet, and he knew she was thinking hard. Then she said, 'Why is your faction so determined that the House of Wessex shall not rise again?'

He sighed, for the answer was complex. 'The old kings made this country,' he said, 'but they had their time and now it is over. The Normans are not universally popular' – her snort of derision suggested she agreed – 'but they are strong, and they will make England march according to their rules. They are fair, in their way, and they have the might to stamp out rebellion before it takes hold and tears the country in two. That is why they will not permit the existence of a figurehead out of the elder days to whom men could rally.' She did not answer. He leaned closer and said, 'Lassair, does anybody truly want another battle like Hastings?'

She winced, and he knew he had hit home. 'No,' she whispered.

'Did you lose many of your kin?'

'Yes.'

She could not have been born then, he thought, but no doubt the memory of the fallen was kept alive and vibrant by the family story tellers. Not that there was anything wrong with that; the living ought to sing the praises of their dead warriors, no matter on which side they had fought.

He waited to see if she would elaborate. Eventually, she sighed, but when finally she spoke it was not what he had expected. She said, 'You can't kill Gewis. He hasn't done anything, and he doesn't want to lead anybody, let alone some resurgent Wessex faction. He's just not the type.'

'He looks like his forebears,' Rollo said. It had been the boy's cream-coloured hair that had been his chief identifying feature.

'He may well do,' she retorted, 'but that's no reason to say he'll agree to be a new Wessex king.'

Rollo sensed she was right. The boy might have the right blood in his veins, but that alone did not make him a leader of men. And, anyway, how could anybody promote him to such an exalted role when he had disappeared? He wondered where the boy had gone. Was he in the same place as her cousin Morcar? And was this place...

He was struck by such a horrible thought that he felt a chill run through his body, and instinctively he clutched her closer to him. 'What is it?' she asked, and he knew from her voice that she had picked up his alarm.

He rested his chin on the top of her head. Her

297

hair smelled sweet. He had known her such a short while, but already she was infinitely precious ... He realized he could not tell her what he had just thought. It was bad enough for him to know, and if he told her he did not know how she would react.

No. He would bear the responsibility. He would not let anything happen to her.

He hugged her close. 'It's nothing,' he said. 'I'm cold – let's go and find something hot to eat to warm us up.'

There were so many things I ought to have been worrying about and for which I should have been busy making plans but just then, walking along beside him in the watery sunshine, I could think of nothing but him. Rollo. His name was Rollo and he came from somewhere a thousand miles away. He was tough and strong – when I had leaned against him the muscles of his chest and shoulder had felt like iron – and when he'd kissed me and I'd responded, it had felt as if we had been doing it forever. *I shall enjoy this day,* I told myself, *for I am with him and it may be the only time we shall have.*

I don't know why I thought that.

The workmen were now pouring through the abbey gates in a flood, and appetizing smells snaked out on curls and swirls of steam from the food stalls. I remembered that I had been up all night and for most of that time full of anxiety, mainly for Hrype but also for Gewis and, of course, for my poor friend Sibert. I was, I realized, aching with hunger.

We bought fresh bread, delicious little patties made of spiced, ground pork bound with egg, honey-apple sweet cakes, all washed down with ale. It was a better breakfast than I had enjoyed in a long time – certainly a more costly one – and I wolfed down the food quite undeterred by Rollo's amused presence beside me. When we had finished we found a quiet corner beneath the abbey walls and stood side by side, our hands linked, both of us lost in our thoughts.

Eventually, he said, 'I must go, Lassair. I am here to do a job, and I am answerable to those who sent me.'

I thought I knew what he meant. He was a Norman – or, at any rate, he supported their rule. I guessed that somehow word of this threat posed by the House of Wessex had reached the ears of the king's advisers and they had dispatched Rollo to come to Ely and find out if it was true, if it really was a threat and, if so, what should be done about it. The obvious conclusion was that Rollo had orders quietly to remove Gewis if he endangered the king, but I baulked at thinking about that.

'You must tell them that Gewis presents no danger,' I said, keeping my voice low. 'He doesn't. I give you my word.'

He smiled, as well he might. 'You do, do you? I'll remember to tell King William. I'm sure he'll believe you.'

I thought he was joking and I laughed. 'Seriously, he's the last person to lead men in a rebellion.' Something occurred to me. 'Are you absolutely sure he is who you all think he is? It's not very likely, surely, that the House of Wessex survives only in a tiny cottage in a forgotten village in the fens?'

He acknowledged that with a wry grin. 'It's not likely, no, but I am assured by those who make it their business to know such things that it is true.' Suddenly, he looked surprised, his eyes wide, as if something had just struck him. But before I could ask, he went on, 'As to his being the only surviving person of the Wessex blood, there is another, but he has abandoned the ties of kinship and thrown in his lot with the Normans.'

I barely heard that. I was still wondering what he had thought of that had so taken him aback.

'We must—' I began, but he put his lips to mine, very gently, and I was temporarily silenced.

'Stay here,' he said, and there was a new urgency in his voice. 'You have a place where you are lodging?'

'Yes, but—'

'Go back there,' he urged. 'Keep out of sight. Don't venture out, and certainly not by yourself.'

'Why?' His alarm was infectious and I was afraid. 'Why is it dangerous all of a sudden?'

His face twisted. 'It has always been dangerous, for so much is at stake.' He looked me full in the eyes. 'The difference is that now there is you.'

I didn't know what to say. My heart was singing *he cares about me!* but the image of myself meekly waiting in the little room while some looming, unspecified and highly dangerous threat rose up to shadow me and pounce on me was not one I could readily believe in.

'Where are you going?' I whispered. He was holding me close against his chest, and I could feel his heart thumping.

He hugged me. 'To make it safe.'

'How? What are you going to do?' Now it was I who feared for him. Other than the barest of facts, I had no idea who he was or what it was he did but I knew in my bones that it was dangerous.

'Don't worry.' He dropped a kiss on the top of my head. 'I've outwitted better enemies than these.'

He sounded strong and confident, sure of himself and what he was about to do. Why, then, did I feel so fearful? Why, when I looked up at him, did it seem as if a cloud had just obscured the sun?

Gently, he unwound my arms from around his neck, and he took a step back. Away from me. He raised a hand in farewell, and then he turned and hurried off. Although I stared after him, and tried as hard as I could to keep him in sight, within a couple of heartbeats he had melted into the crowd.

I wondered if I would ever see him again.

TWENTY-ONE

Gewis's sense of unease deepened steadily as the day went on. It was not that the people in the settlement were not being kind to him; they were. The young man, Sibert, had taken him to a small and well-kept cottage, which he said belonged to Lassair's family. It was soon after dawn when the two of them arrived, and a middle-aged man had come to the door in answer to Sibert's knock, rubbing at his tousled hair and staring out at them in puzzlement. Sibert had given only a sketchy explanation, but he had said at least twice that Lassair had said it would be all right and the family were to take Gewis in and look after him.

Gewis couldn't actually recall Lassair having given any such instructions, but now did not seem to be the time to point it out. Sibert had melted away, and the man, who had been introduced as Lassair's father, had ushered Gewis inside. The rest of the family had woken up – there was a woman with a long, fair plait who was the man's wife, an old grandmother, a young man of about Sibert's age, a lad and a child of around three. All six of them had stared at Gewis with round eyes, and then the lad said, 'Are you a monk?'

'No,' Gewis replied firmly. 'I've been living in an abbey, and they disguised me as a novice, but I've taken no vows.'

The woman with the plait got to her feet. 'Then we'd better find you some different clothes,' she said, eyeing him closely. 'Haward, we'll need something of yours – your garments will be a little generous because you're taller and broader than this lad here, but we can hitch up the tunic with a belt, and we'll find a cap to cover that shaven spot on the crown of your head.'

'Thank you,' Gewis said gravely.

The woman smiled kindly at him. 'I expect you're hungry,' she remarked.

'Yes. I am.'

'I hungry too!' piped up the little child; it was, on closer inspection, a boy.

'Hush, Leir, I'll see to you later,' his mother said softly. 'Go back to sleep – it's early yet.'

The child slipped his thumb into his mouth with a soft plop and, yawning, went obediently back to his cot in the corner. The young man went to rummage in a wooden box and emerged with a brown wool tunic, patched and darned but clean, a pair of woven hose and a floppy felt cap. Silently, he handed them to Gewis, who turned his back, stripped to his underlinen and put them on.

The grandmother gave a quiet cackle of laughter. 'Where's that monk gone then?' she said. 'Welcome to the family, lad. What did you say your name was?'

* * *

303

Gewis was moved by their kindness and their generosity. It was clear they did not have much, but what they had they shared willingly with him. He reckoned they must have a great deal of trust in their daughter to admit a total stranger into their cottage on her word alone. They must also love her very much, he realized; in the course of the day her mother, her father, her grandmother and her elder brother all found a quiet moment to ask if she was all right, and the young boy, whose name appeared to be Squeak, said that if Gewis saw her soon he was to give her his love and tell her the blackbird with the broken wing had died.

As the day passed he uncovered the source of his unease. His mother was dead, killed by the four tough men who had taken him to Ely and guarded him there. His memories of her were by no means universally happy – like his father, she had been deeply embittered, and her dissatisfaction with her life had been demonstrated with a hard right hand around her son's ear on far too many occasions. It had always been difficult, not to say impossible, to please her. She had once expressed the opinion that you must not praise your children because if you do they will become complacent and stop trying. For sure, she had never praised Gewis, so he wondered how she could have been quite so certain.

Yes. She had not been a caring, loving mother. She was nothing like this capable, brusque but devoted woman whom Lassair was lucky enough to have as a parent. But she was his mother, nevertheless, and now she was dead. He could not stay here in safety knowing how, and probably why, she had died. He did not have sufficient faith in himself to believe he could avenge her, but at the least he must go to Lord Edmund, who must surely have been behind the death, and register his protest. *I will report him to the sheriff,* Gewis thought, carried away. *He will be arrested and put on trial, and other men will judge him where I cannot.*

It was a good plan. It made him feel better.

Late in the afternoon, wishing he could explain to Lassair's nice family and say goodbye, he waited until he was unobserved and slipped away.

Rollo spent most of the day putting together everything he knew about Lord Edmund, known as the Exile. The king had briefed him well, revealing that he believed Lord Edmund was the power behind the Wessex faction and that it was he who would organize and lead the attempt to raise the Wessex banner and summon supporters to the cause. Rollo had verified that the king was right; he had also uncovered a great deal more about Lord Edmund than had been known to King William. Or more accurately, he thought with a private smile, that the king had known perfectly well but had chosen not to reveal. Well, it did not matter either way now. Rollo had found out what he needed to know, and, as always, he trusted discoveries that he had made himself far more than facts told to him by others, even – perhaps especially – if those others were kings.

In the comfort of his room, Rollo thought about the pale boy, Gewis. Was he who they claimed he was? Rollo still had not made up his mind. Logic suggested the boy was no more than a simple, unsophisticated village lad, the result of generations of people just like him. But there had been that moment in the old Saxon church, when Rollo had the extraordinary thought that a spectral hand from the past had reached out because it recognized its own.

That, however, was fanciful, and Rollo did not deal in fancy. The Wessex faction must surely be convinced of Gewis's identity, he thought instead, for they were going to a great deal of trouble on the lad's behalf. Rollo had been trying to keep thoughts of Lassair out of his head – it was not that he did not want to think about her, only that she was a distraction – but now he remembered how she had thought that Gewis's unwillingness to have anything to do with Lord Edmund and his scheme was the end of it. She was wrong, but then she did not move in circles where people like Lord Edmund operated. She did not know how ruthless and cruel a man like him would be. But then, he thought, she knows Edmund had Gewis's mother killed, so perhaps she does.

Contemplating Lord Edmund's nature was not something he ought to do at that moment. Against his will he recalled the moment early this morning when he had suddenly realized that Lassair knew where Gewis was and that, were so much of a whisper of that fact to reach Lord Edmund, he would find her and do whatever it took to make her tell him.

That did not bear thinking about.

And here I sit now, he thought bitterly, *doing what I know I must but wishing with all my heart that I could hurry to her side and take her away to somewhere they will never find her.*

That was impossible, and he knew it. Instead, he must remove the threat. That meant staying right where he was and preparing for every possible eventuality until he was ready.

Then he would act, and she truly would be safe.

He went out into the midday crowds milling around the marketplace and, by asking a few innocuous questions here and there, discovered where Lord Edmund was lodging. Then he found a place where, while hidden himself, he could observe the house and the comings and goings. He stood quite still, and he was all but sure that nobody spared him a glance. As he watched, he occupied his mind going over the alternatives. He could approach Lord Edmund and somehow convince him that Gewis was nothing to do with the House of Wessex. He believed he could achieve this, for the king had told him where, when and how the rumour that connected Gewis to his illustrious ancestors had originated and it would be possible to concoct a tale that questioned the connection. Would Lord Edmund allow himself to be convinced? Rollo had his doubts, for everything he had learned of the man suggested he was a fanatic, and fanatics were not normally renowned for being open to reason.

His thoughts ran on. The Wessex plot depended on both Lord Edmund, who was the driving force behind it and in addition its financier, and also, of course, on Gewis, and on the boy being who they said he was. If one or the other were to be removed then the plot would collapse. Rollo could not remove Gewis; for one thing he did not know where the lad was, and for another there was Lassair. If there was no other solution, he would just have to remove Lord Edmund.

He felt calm descend on him. It was always the way; all the time he was undecided, and several courses of action presented themselves, he felt as tightly stretched as a bowstring before the arrow flies. However, once he had made up his mind it was different. He had learned long ago to take all the time he needed to go through each and every possibility so that, once the decision was made, he knew it was the right one and he never undermined it by entertaining second thoughts.

In the middle of the afternoon, two of the big guards came hurrying along the street and were quickly admitted into the house where Lord Edmund was lodging. Rollo stiffened, his full attention fixed on the spot where the two men had just disappeared. They were worried. He had seen that in the way they moved and in the anxious glances they shot over their shoulders. Something had unnerved them; what was it? He ran over several possibilities. He would wait to see what happened next before he made up his mind.

Within a short time there was more activity outside the house. The two guards reappeared and checked up and down the street, then one beckoned behind him and from within the house a tall, thin, cloaked figure appeared, the hood drawn forward to conceal the head and face. The cloak, however, was of expensive material and the man's boots were of supple leather and polished to a shine; he was a man of wealth, and Rollo knew his identity. He watched as the other two guards fell into step behind him, one carrying a large bag, and the five of them set off hurriedly along the street.

Rollo emerged from his hiding place and followed them. They hastened across the marketplace, one of the guards swearing at a fat woman with a basket who got in the way and raising a hand to cuff her out of their path, and made straight for the abbey gates. The pair of guards in the lead summoned the monk on duty, and he came to speak to Lord Edmund. There was a muttered conversation, the monk nodded quickly a few times and then Lord Edmund was escorted inside.

Nobody was looking Rollo's way, but nevertheless it seemed wise to leave quickly. He was almost certain that the guards suspected the presence of an enemy within the town – which was why they had encouraged their lord to move inside the greater security of the abbey and its strong walls – but he doubted that they knew yet who this enemy was and what strength of men and arms threatened Lord Edmund and his faction.

Rollo smiled wryly. Unwittingly, Lord Edmund had, in seeking the safety of the abbey, done the very thing that Rollo wanted him to. *Out here I am one man alone*, he thought, *armed with my sword and my knife, and my strength is not in might but in stealth.* Inside the abbey, however, the situation would be different, for the odds would alter in his favour.

King William had explained the nature of the monks of Ely. Traditionally, the abbey had supported the House of Wessex. The last Wessex king, Edward, known as the Confessor, son of Aethelred, had spent his childhood in Ely and was educated by the monks; the link between the House of Wessex and the abbey of Ely was rumoured to endure still, although these days it was not safe to speak of it. King William, however, had eyes and ears in unlikely places, and he had told Rollo that Ely's prior was a Wessex man receptive to any plot that would bring back the old regime. However, the king's informants understood that many of the younger monks wanted no truck with the old ways. Feelings still ran high at the Conqueror's crippling reprisals against the abbey in the aftermath of the 1071 rebellion. Had the monks given away the secret of the safe ways on to the island sooner, the abbey would have held on to its vast wealth. The more worldly monks recognized that there was no point in fighting the might of the Normans and the surest route to a secure, peaceful life was to support the king. Moreover, the huge new church now soaring up within the abbey walls was without doubt an indication that Ely would rise to the heights, provided no further murmurs of rebellion reached the ears of the king...

King William had provided a name. *If you require support,* he'd said to Rollo, *seek out the master of novices, whom they call Brother Mark.*

Rollo silently repeated the name. Then he turned away and was swallowed by the crowds.

I spent much of the day shut up in our little room with Hrype and Edild. Hrype was very weak and still in pain – I told Edild the exact details of the draught I had given him, and she blanched and said he'd better not have any more pain relief for the time being – but he bore the agony bravely, and I did not hear him complain. Edild cared for him with a tenderness that spoke eloquently of her love for him. Now that I recognized what they felt for each other, I was amazed that I had never spotted it before. They must, I decided, have been very, very careful. In a little village like Aelf Fen, where everybody knows everyone else and we all watch one another like hawks over a cornfield, it was no mean feat to have been so discreet that not one word about them had ever been breathed.

It was left to me to prepare food and drink when Edild ordered it. She tried to make Hrype take a few mouthfuls to build up his strength but, although he tried, he barely ate a thing. He did, however, gulp down several cups of my honey mixture. Edild said it would do him good. I wished I had the wealth to go out and buy for him the sweetest, finest wine. It would have put heart in him far more effectively than warm water and honey.

He seemed better by twilight. Edild was sitting behind him, so that his head and shoulders rested in her lap. She held his hand in hers, and with her other hand she stroked his forehead. He was obviously enjoying it, and I had the distinct sense that she was putting her own strength into him to hasten his recovery.

It was hard to watch them. When, finally, Hrype muttered something to the effect that I must surely feel restless after a day closeted inside, I took the hint and announced I was going outside for some air and to stretch my legs.

I had told Rollo I would stay inside. While I appreciated that he had insisted on this because he was worried about me, it was not he who had been forced into the position of third party to a pair of lovers all day. As I pulled on my cloak and eased out of the little house, it was such a relief that I could have sung.

I didn't have anywhere to go. I wondered where Rollo was. He had implied he had some important task to do, and I believed he meant he was going to leave the town. It did not occur to me to go and look for him. I felt instinctively that I would not find him unless he wanted me to.

I thought about Gewis. My family would make him welcome, I knew that very well. They would be desperate to ask about Edild, Hrype and me but I thought – I hoped – they would be too polite to press him if he did not volunteer anything. I was far from ready to go home, but I did not like to think of my parents and my granny worrying about me. I reassured myself by remembering that they knew Edild was with me. They were not to know that, far from carefully watching over her niece, my aunt lay with her secret lover enjoying a rare moment alone with him. They would never find out from me either. Edild had kept many of my secrets in the past, and now it was time for me to do the same for her.

Poor Gewis. He would still be coming to terms with the death of his mother. I did not envy him. I hoped my mother was finding some way to comfort him. He was young still, and he had the look of someone who found the world a hard place.

That thought led me directly to Sibert.

My friend had been told something that devastated him. Yes, he had suspected that there was something odd about the time his parents and his uncle had spent in Ely together, but I was quite convinced that he had got nowhere near the truth, even with his wildest guesses. To learn after nearly nineteen years that his dead, hero father was no such thing – a hero, yes, but not his father – and that his mother had conceived him with her brother-in-law, Sibert's uncle, must have driven him to the verge of madness. He was, as I have so often thought, not really equipped to deal with too much reality.

I still did not understand why his reaction had been to attempt to kill Hrype. Why? Because for him to impregnate Froya had been a sin? Because it had been the worst possible betrayal of poor, wounded Edmer? Or because – and I thought this the most likely – Sibert had had to find out the truth for himself?

It would have taken a very brave man to say to the young Sibert, *There is something you must know. I slept with your mother as her husband lay dying, and you are my son, not his.* But Hrype *was* a brave man. Why had he kept silent?

Because of Froya, came the answer. I suppose I provided it myself, but at the time it sounded as if the words were spoken in another voice that could have been Hrype's.

I thought about that. Yes, it sounded believable. Froya was delicate, her equanimity readily shattered, and both Hrype and Sibert had to work hard to restore her calm when she got upset. If she had begged Hrype not to tell Sibert the truth, I thought he would have restrained himself, even if he thought it was wrong.

Froya. Oh, dear Lord, her secret was out now. Had Sibert gone to confront her? For a moment I was horrified that he had, but then I was suddenly quite sure he hadn't. He would not face her on her own. He loved her, I did not doubt it, and deep down that would not change, no matter what she had done. He was probably beside himself with fury at her now, but he would not attack until Hrype was there to protect her. It had, after all, been both of them who had done wrong.

They were his parents. I still found it all but impossible to believe, but Hrype and Froya were Sibert's parents.

That was something else I was going to have to keep from the inhabitants of Aelf Fen.

* * *

I found that my aimless wanderings as I thought about my friends had led me past the row of dwellings and towards where the water lapped at the foot of the track that bordered the lower edge of the meadow. Just along there was the place where Sibert had borrowed the boat. He had taken it three times now, and it was still missing. It was just as well that its rightful owner did not appear to have any use for it at the moment or we would all be in trouble.

I watched the dark water. It was still high, and I could smell rain on the air. The dark, heavy clouds in the west had been building up all day. Ely Island would soon be a little smaller as the water rose and...

There was a boat approaching. I heard it before I saw it, and as it emerged from the gloom I saw that it was the one Sibert had purloined.

One person rowed it. It looked like a boy, and he wore a worn tunic and a shapeless felt hat pulled well down so that it covered his hair. I thought I recognized that hat...

Clumsily, the boy shipped his oars and the boat slid alongside. I reached down and grabbed the rope, making it fast. The boy stood up, and I held out my hand to him.

'It's holed,' the boy said apologetically, shaking the water off his boots. 'I ran over a submerged branch, and I've been baling half the way back.'

Then Gewis took my hand and, with a sheepish smile, stepped out of the boat and on to the damp grass.

TWENTY-TWO

'What do you think you're doing?' I hissed furiously. 'Sibert took you away from here because it's not safe! Why on earth have you come back again?'

'They killed my mother!' he cried. Hastily, I shushed him, and he went on more quietly, 'I have to tell Lord Edmund I know what he's done. Then I'm going to get the sheriff and—'

It was a fine and noble idea but quite unrealistic. We were peasants, powerless, bound by invisible but unbreakable fetters. Lord Edmund was so far above us that there was nothing our feeble protests could do to touch him. 'You'll do no such thing,' I interrupted. Poor Gewis. How little he knew about the world. 'The four guardians will be hunting for you now. If they find you, they'll take you straight back to Lord Edmund—'

'That's what I want!' Gewis said passionately.

'*No you don't!*' Why wouldn't he see? 'If that happens, the outcome will be one of two things. Either they'll force you into the role they want you to play, which you already say you have refused—'

'I have! I won't do it, not for anything in the world!'

316

'—Or they'll kill you because you know about what they are trying to do and therefore you can't be left alive to tell anyone else.'

He was staring at me with his mouth open. Then, as I watched, slowly the terror left his eyes and he straightened up. When he spoke, there was a new note in his voice, and I knew that the time when I could boss him about had gone.

'I am going to the house where I was taken before Lord Edmund,' he said calmly. 'I do not expect you to come with me, for it is, as you say, perilous.'

I wanted to scream with frustration. I didn't. Someone would have heard. Instead, I just said, 'Come on then. Show me where it is.'

We kept in the shadows as we made our way up the dark, silent alley that led to the marketplace. We waited for our eyes to adjust to the sudden light of the torches flaring high up on the abbey walls, then hurried around the square, crouching low and staying right back against the encircling buildings. There was nobody about. Ely, it appeared, had retired for the night.

Gewis ran off along a wider street where the houses were large and prosperous-looking, stopping after only a few paces in front of a grand establishment that showed all the signs of wealth. Some gift of foresight, probably provided by my fear, permitted me to see what he was about to do; I grabbed at his arm, but I was too late. He was already banging on the door.

I didn't know whether to flee or prepare to

fight. My hand closed on the horn hilt of my knife, and I drew it out of its sheath. My heart was pounding in my chest, and I felt sick. Then the terror abated slightly, just enough for me to come to my senses and realize that, despite Gewis's forceful fist on the wooden door, no lights had come on and no cross servant had poked his head out to demand what we thought we were doing.

The house was empty.

I put my knife away and leaned forward, my hands on my knees, while my heartbeat and my breathing returned to normal. Then I looked up at Gewis and said, 'Now what?'

His face was thoughtful. 'Lord Edmund might have left the town,' he said slowly, 'but I don't think so. He wants me as a figurehead for this rebellion he's plotting, but he was never going to succeed with just me and my four guards. There must be many more supporters waiting for the word.'

He was right. This Lord Edmund probably had a secret network quietly preparing for the moment when their leader would emerge with the new champion, whereupon they were no doubt relying on the optimistic hope that all the malcontents in England would rally round and kick King William and the Normans back to Normandy.

I heard Rollo speaking in my head. *Does anybody truly want another battle like Hastings?* I thought of Granny Cordeilla, who still cannot speak of those terrible times without her voice breaking, for among those she had lost on that unforgettable day had been her best-loved brother Sigbehrt, known as the Mighty Oak, who fell defending his brother Sagar Sureshot, as well as his lord and, ultimately, his king. *Men fight battles*, Granny is wont to say. *Women break their hearts in the aftermath.* She is old and she has lost so many that she loved. But as I stood there beside Gewis, for a moment I was fired with the image of myself wielding a sword, shrieking my war cry as I galloped into the fray to fight for what I thought was right. The image faded, and my feet gently bumped back on to the solid ground.

Rollo was right. Twenty-four years ago the people of England had fought and lost, and since then there had been peace, give or take a rebellion or two. Even if a figurehead representing the great kings of the past were to materialize among us, did it honestly make sense to rise up and support him?

It just wasn't worth the price.

Gewis must have noticed I was no longer listening. 'Lassair!' he whispered. 'Are you all right?'

'Yes. Sorry, what were you saying?'

'I said he'll have gone inside the abbey. The monks knew I was there so obviously Lord Edmund has support among them, and I know the prior is in league with him.'

I felt a chill around my heart. The abbey was a great deal more secure than this house, stout and well built though it was. Did that mean Lord Edmund knew he was in danger? Had his men informed him that a Norman spy was in the

319

town?

Rollo was in danger. I knew it. I felt it throughout my body.

'I know a way over the wall,' I said. Gewis looked surprised; perhaps he had expected I would try to talk him out of trying to get inside the abbey. 'You'll have to give me a leg-up, and I have no idea how we're going to get you over, but we'll just have to do our best.'

He stood there, slowly shaking his head. Then a grin broke out on his face and, grasping hands, we hurried away.

I found the place where Rollo and I had got out of the abbey. As I had thought, it was very difficult getting up the high wall on the outside, without the help of the compost heap; Gewis made a stirrup of his hands and, after a few fruitless efforts where he shot me up too fast and I lost my grip, falling quite heavily on the hard ground, eventually I was astride the wall. Then I reached down and, fighting to hold on with my right hand, held out my left and tried to haul him up. I couldn't have lifted his weight unaided, but he was agile and his toes found all but invisible spaces in the stones of the wall, so that he supported himself and all I had to do was provide a bit of lift.

All the same, we only just managed it.

I pointed out the compost heap, and we dropped down on top of it. It broke our fall but at a price: we stank.

We brushed ourselves down as best we could, and I stood getting my bearings. There was no hope that I would remember the tortuous route along which Rollo had guided us, but there was no need to. We could see the walls of the new cathedral rising up some distance before us to our left; all we had to do was head that way and we would be in the heart of the abbey. Without a word, we set off.

Rollo had been inside the abbey since early evening. He had slipped in as the tide of workmen constantly going in and out had begun to tail off and found a hiding place in a secluded corner of the new build. He was going to seek out Brother Mark; he waited until the last of the workforce finally left and then, slipping off the worn cloak with which he had covered his garments, returned to the gate house to ask for him.

He had come inside in the guise of a workman. Now he would present himself as he really was.

Brother Mark arrived quickly following the summons. He looked curiously at Rollo.

'Do I know you?' he asked, smiling.

Rollo took in the details of his appearance. Brother Mark was in early middle age, wiry and muscular with springy, dark hair curling around the shaved tonsure. He gave the impression of enthusiastic vigour, and Rollo's instinct was to both like and trust him. He was, however, too cautious and far too experienced to go with his instinct alone. 'I am Rollo Guiscard,' he said. The name might mean something to the master of novices; it might not. It depended on what the king had seen fit to do.

The spark of interest in Brother Mark's eyes gave the answer. 'I see,' he said quietly. 'Come with me.'

He led the way along a narrow, twisting succession of passages, stopping outside a low, wooden door set in a pointed arch, which he opened, ushering Rollo inside. When the door was closed, he said, 'I was told that you might come and why. It is because of the boy, Gewis, known as Brother Ailred.'

'Yes.' Rollo studied the monk, all his senses alert.

Brother Mark hesitated. Then he said, with quiet passion, 'We cannot have another rebellion. We have been made to suffer greatly because of the last one. Ely will not survive again.'

Rollo made no comment. 'The abbey is on the threshold of greatness,' Brother Mark added softly. 'Our new church will be the wonder of the age. Pilgrims and good Christians will flock to us, and our place in the history of the world will be assured.'

Still Rollo did not speak.

Brother Mark smiled. 'You think it worldly, for a monk to view this matter so, in terms of our abbey and its fortune? You believe I should decide according to my conscience instead?'

'I make no such judgement,' Rollo said quickly. 'I have come to my own decision after long and careful thought, and I see no reason to suppose you have done otherwise.'

Brother Mark nodded. 'Thank you. I wish—' He paused, then said quietly, 'Many of our older brethren have put their faith in the House of

Wessex and the blood kin of King Edward the Confessor, whom they view as little less than a saint. The decision is, of course, theirs to make, as you have just implied, but many of the younger monks grow impatient with them.'

Brother Mark, as master of novices, would have much to do with the younger monks, Rollo reflected. 'They do not oppose the Normans for the harshness of their rule?' he asked.

'No,' Brother Mark said shortly. 'They are monks, and they understand the need for firm discipline if the community is to thrive. The same applies to a country as to an abbey.'

It was enough. Rollo was satisfied. 'I know that Lord Edmund, known as the Exile, is within the abbey,' he said. 'He has four bodyguards and also, I would guess, the means to summon many more fighting men. The object of his search has evaded him, and now I must ensure that nothing comes of his presence here.'

Brother Mark nodded, apparently understanding much from Rollo's brief words. 'We will be behind you, Rollo Guiscard,' he said. 'I have trustworthy brethren whom I can summon.' He paused, and Rollo guessed from his expression that there was more he would say.

Rollo waited. Brother Mark edged closer and then, lowering his voice, he murmured, 'Should this business reach the desired conclusion, I trust that the one who sent you will learn of our help?'

Rollo hid a smile. People were so predictable. 'He will,' he replied. 'Among his many pressing concerns, this will not be forgotten. If I am able to return to him with the reassurance he requires, he will, I am sure, be grateful.'

Brother Mark nodded again. 'Then I am satisfied,' he said. 'What do you wish to do now? Am I to gather my brothers and come with you to challenge Lord Edmund? He is at present—'

'No,' Rollo interrupted. 'Forgive me, but I would prefer to avoid a confrontation if possible.'

'I understand,' murmured the monk. 'I have another suggestion.'

'Yes?'

'There is one place in the abbey that is uniquely special to the supporters of the House of Wessex, and my guess is that Lord Edmund will go there before the night is very old.'

Rollo had already surmised as much, but it was tactful to let Brother Mark believe it was his own contribution. 'Where is this place?' he asked. 'Why is it important?'

He listened as Brother Mark explained.

Rollo had been waiting for a long time. He was aware that Brother Mark was close by, regularly emerging from wherever he was passing the time to check whether Lord Edmund had arrived. Then the bell tolled to summon the monks to the last office of the day, and Rollo knew he was alone.

Lord Edmund had evidently been waiting for this moment. As Rollo watched, he materialized out of the gloom on the far side of the site of the new church and, slowly and unhurriedly as if he were in a procession, walked to the place where the ruins of the ancient wall marked where the Saxon church had once stood. He knelt before it, closed his eyes and began to pray.

Rollo watched him. He was reluctant to disturb a man at his devotions and, in any case, there appeared to be no urgency. The mutter of Lord Edmund's words rose and fell on the still air, forming a rhythm that was almost hypnotic. Rollo felt entranced, as if he were falling under some spell, and for a moment he thought he saw a white form emerge from the ancient wall. He rubbed his eyes and the illusion vanished.

Enough, he thought. He walked forward, steadily closing the gap between himself and Lord Edmund. When he was a couple of paces away, Lord Edmund looked up.

'The boy has gone,' Rollo said. 'He will not come back, nor will he suffer himself to be your figurehead, for he knows that you killed his mother.'

'I?' Lord Edmund feigned innocence.

'Men acting on your orders,' Rollo amended. 'It amounts to the same thing.'

Lord Edmund got up from his knees with a groan. 'I regret the necessity for her death,' he said. 'It was, however, unavoidable. You must know, Norman spy, how the success of a plan depends so often on not releasing information too soon, and, knowing that the healer girl was on her way to visit Gewis's mother, I feared that she would discover what must remain secret.'

The healer girl. Rollo felt fear clutch at his heart. 'She has gone,' he said dismissively. Desperate to turn Lord Edmund's attention from

Lassair, he went on quickly, 'You have lost your last throw of the die, my lord, and—'

But Lord Edmund was not to be distracted. 'She has gone on meddling,' he said, anger darkening his face. 'I should have disposed of her as soon as I knew of her existence and, by God, I wish I had. I am old enough and experienced enough to know that people are not always as they seem and even one such as she, small and insignificant, can bring the threat of ruin to a careful plan. She came here to this sacred spot in the guise of a nun, and she met Gewis. I am told they spoke together. I do not know what the lad told her but I feared the worst. Now he has gone, and it is in my mind that he did not escape alone. Friendless as he is but for her outside the abbey, it is, is it not, logical to suppose she is involved in his flight?'

Treating the question as rhetorical, Rollo did not answer. His fear increased. Lord Edmund knew so much. He had but to reach out his hand for Lassair, and if his clutching fingers found her he would not rest until he had found out what he wished so much to know...

Frantic now, it took all this strength to keep his face impassive. The stakes ran high. To break Lord Edmund's dangerous focus on Lassair, he must risk his most powerful gambit. 'Of course,' he said laconically, 'it is by no means certain that the boy Gewis is who you think he is. The fifteen years of his life have been spent in obscurity in a village on the fen edge. Where is the proof of his illustrious ancestry?'

Lord Edmund's face had gone purple. 'He was

kept in obscurity because that was where we wished him to be!' he snarled. 'Nothing happened in that place, *nothing*, that was not relayed to us. We have watched over him since his birth, and we know who he is!' His voice had risen to a shout, and he was panting from exertion.

Rollo raised an eyebrow. 'And your proof?' he persisted.

He thought Lord Edmund was going to puff up until he burst. He struggled for control, and then said in a strangled voice, 'We know who his father was, and who in turn fathered him. The family resemblance is unmistakable. There can be no doubt whatsoever.'

'Ah.' At last they were approaching the crucial point. Rollo had already been told of this by the king but he wanted to hear it from Lord Edmund. 'You speak of that pale hair, white skin and almost colourless eyes,' he mused.

'I do!' Lord Edmund cried. 'King Edward the Confessor had the look and so did his brother.'

The rumour that reached the king was right then, Rollo thought. No wonder William had not been able to put it from his mind. 'They say the brother died unmarried and childless,' he said. He was gratified to hear how calm he sounded, as if this vitally important matter were of only passing interest.

Clearly, it was far more than that to Lord Edmund. 'Do you not know the story?' he demanded, the light of fanaticism in is eyes.

'Remind me,' said Rollo.

Lord Edmund took several deep breaths, then he raised his eyes as if searching inspiration

327

from the heavens and began. 'Our great king, Aethelred, left many sons, but fate decreed that, out of those born to his first wife, only one followed him as king. His marriage to Emma of Normandy produced two sons, Edward, later King Edward the Confessor, and Alfred Aethling, and in early childhood the boys were educated here at Ely, where the monks grew to love and honour them. But later, for their own safety, the boys were sent as children to the land of their mother, for in England the House of Wessex was gravely threatened. For many years the Danish kings ruled, and they would have killed the young princes to remove the possibility that either would ever be proclaimed king. The Danes were ruthless rulers.'

He sighed. 'When Queen Emma was widowed, King Cnut took her as wife but, always aware of those who would take his throne from him, he ordered the deaths of the surviving sons of Aethelred; still Edward and Alfred could not return. After Cnut's death, his son Harold, known as Harefoot, became king and for the first time the sons of Aethelred and Emma saw the glimmer of a hope that England might once more welcome them.' He sighed again, this time putting up a hand to knead his brow as if remembering old pain.

'Edward, later crowned king, was wise and, sensing danger even before danger threatened, turned around and left the shores of England behind him, not to return for five years. Alfred Aethling was more trusting and, when the great Earl Godwin went to meet him and offered his hospitality in his fine house at Guildford, the young man accepted readily. Godwin gave every indication of being a good friend and a loyal supporter, offering to swear his allegiance to Alfred and the House of Wessex.' A sound broke from him that was almost a sob. 'Poor Alfred, our own prince! Godwin betrayed him, for he was in league with Harold Harefoot. Every last man in Alfred's entourage was savagely butchered, and, even as their blood ran in the streets, Godwin's men mutilated Alfred.'

The tale was abhorrent, Rollo thought. To take a man into your house, to have him sit at your table to eat your meat and drink your wine, to offer him your loyalty while all the time you plot his death; these actions went against a code so ancient and so venerated that it should be inviolate.

'He did not die there, our beloved Alfred.' Lord Edmund picked up the story. 'They had hacked into him and castrated him, for Godwin's orders were that he was not to be allowed the slimmest chance of fathering a son. Then they brought him here to Ely, and as they led him aboard the boat that was to ferry him across they put out his eyes. Blind and impotent, he was no longer a threat, and nobody cared any more what became of him.'

Castrated. Blinded. Rollo shuddered. It did not bear thinking about.

'The monks received him with love and tended him with care and skill,' Lord Edmund went on, 'for they had loved him and his brother Edward when they were boys and that love stayed true.

The healers did their best but it was to no avail, for quite soon Alfred died of his terrible wounds.'

There was a long silence. Then Lord Edmund looked up and, meeting Rollo's eyes, said, 'Alfred greatly resembled his brother Edward, as I have said. Edward left no son, for he was a chaste and holy man and his marriage to his queen, Edith, was one of the spirit and not the body. You ask yourself, I do not doubt, how then it is that we are so sure that in Gewis the true blood of the House of Wessex runs pure.'

'I do,' Rollo acknowledged.

'The nature of Alfred Aethling was not like his brother's, and when temptation came he did not resist,' Lord Edmund said. 'What would you have done, Norman spy? Far from friends and kin, perhaps afraid and already suspicious of the man who would soon take your manhood, your eyes and your life, would you in your loneliness have turned your back on love when it was offered?' Rollo made no answer. 'Alfred did not. He bedded Alma, the daughter of one of his trusted followers, who loved and pitied him, showing him kindness and tenderness. It is said that in secret they were wed. After Alfred had been torn away from her and suffered his terrible fate, Alma realized she was with child. In time she was delivered of a boy, who, for fear of Harold Harefoot and his brutal, ruthless followers, was taken and hidden in a remote village. He was taught a skill, for he would have to live his life not as a prince of the House of Wessex but as a carpenter. He grew to adulthood and married, and his wife bore a son.' Rollo felt the power of Lord Edmund's eyes and, reluctantly, turned to meet their gaze.

'That man was Edulf and that son is Gewis,' Lord Edmund said. 'He is the grandson of Alfred Aethling.'

TWENTY-THREE

I tried to prevent Gewis's great cry, but it was beyond my strength. I had to listen as it tore out of him, bouncing off the vast, soaring walls of the new cathedral and heading out into the night sky.

We had clutched at each other as Lord Edmund told his tale. We had heard them talking as we approached the site of the old Saxon church – my heart had bounced hard as I identified Rollo's voice – and I wanted to race over to them to let Rollo know we were there and we were with him. But Gewis had stopped me. He shot out an arm and grasped my wrist in a tight grip, pulling hard so that I lurched against him. 'No!' he hissed in my ear. 'Don't you see? I have to hear this!'

It was only then that I actually took in the words that were being spoken. Then I understood.

As the story went on, and Lord Edmund described what had happened to Alfred Aethling, I could have wept. To be betrayed like that, by a man he had trusted! Then when Lord Edmund spoke of the woman who had born the Aethling's child, instantly I put myself in her position and my eyes filled with tears. Supposing it had

332

been Rollo and me, I thought. To love someone and then lose them in that unimaginably awful way was bad enough. To discover subsequently that you carried his child – oh, poor, poor woman.

I should have been watching Gewis more closely, for if I had I would surely have noticed that his tension was screwing him up to breaking point, and perhaps I could have comforted him in some way so that he did not react as he did. I don't know why I was so certain, but as soon as he cried out I knew, sure as the sun rises in the morning, that it was the last thing he should have done.

It was. His great shout distracted Rollo, who spun round to see who had crept up behind him. Lord Edmund took his chance, leaping on Rollo and getting the point of his knife to his throat before I could even blink.

All four of us froze. It was my turn to grasp hold of Gewis. I grabbed his wrist and held on with both hands, for I was terrified that he would rush at Lord Edmund and that the lord would plunge his knife, accidentally or deliberately, into Rollo's neck.

Lord Edmund stared hungrily at Gewis over Rollo's shoulder. 'You have come back, Gewis,' he breathed. 'Are you ready now to assume the role to which you were born?'

'No,' Gewis said coldly. 'I don't believe your story, and, even if I did, I would have no truck with the man who ordered my mother's death.'

Lord Edmund sighed. 'Whether you choose to believe it or not, the story is true, Gewis. We who remember and honour the glory days of the House of Wessex preserve our memories closely, and it is well known among us that King Edward and his brother had the distinctive pale colouring that you too possess, as did your father before you.'

'Many men are fair!' Gewis protested. I thought he sounded less certain than before.

'Perhaps,' Lord Edmund acknowledged, 'but not to the degree shown by the Wessex men. You are the Aethling's grandson, Gewis. Believe me.'

Gewis's mouth opened and closed as if, just for an instant, he had lost the power of speech. Then all at once his eyes shot to the right, to where the last vestige of the ancient church wall still stood, and his whole body went rigid.

I craned round him to see what he was looking at. I saw – or I thought I saw – the shimmering outline of a figure. It was dressed in ragged, pale cloth and down the front, from the level of the crotch, there were rust-coloured stains. More stains discoloured the shoulder and the breast. The face was deathly white, the hair silver in the dim light. There were no eyes; where they should have been were deep, dark sockets.

It is a vision from out of my own imagination! I told myself as I fought panic. It was quite likely, after all, for hadn't I just heard a tale of horror describing such a figure as this?

It was likely, yes. I might have believed it, except that I had glimpsed it before. And if it existed only in my mind, why, then, could Gewis see it too?

He moaned in dread, and I knew I must act. I had to break the spell and remove us both from whatever enchantment held us in its grip. I took a step back and then launched myself on Gewis, knocking him sideways so that he stumbled and fell.

The apparition vanished. I spared one quick glance at the spot where it had been, and then my head spun round because I had heard Rollo cry out.

In the first dreadful instant I thought Lord Edmund had stabbed him. But immediately my eyes met his I realized it was a shout of warning. I whipped round to look behind me and saw the four burly guardians coming striding across the open ground towards us.

Even with Rollo fighting beside us, the odds against the three of us were tough. Without him, Gewis and I might as well have given up straight away. I launched myself at Lord Edmund, my mouth open in a snarl, and as I leapt at him my teeth closed on the hand that held the knife. I wish I could say that my carefully thought out strategy was a success, but for one thing it wasn't thought out and for another it wasn't all that successful. Rollo got away, yes, but not without a deep wound in his shoulder. Lord Edmund's knife also tore into my cheek, but I barely noticed.

I did not see what happened next but, suddenly, Lord Edmund was on the ground, and Rollo had a bloodstained knife in his hand.

Now the three of us, Rollo, Gewis and I, stood side by side. Rollo had a sword in his right hand

and his long knife in his left. Gewis and I both had knives. We backed away from the four guards who were swiftly advancing on us, heading for the maze of passageways that would lead us back to the place where we could climb the wall.

The first two guards came at us. They, too, were armed, and there was a succession of jarring clashes as Rollo's one sword met their two weapons. Rollo fought with the ferocity of a cornered bear. He was so fast that I had no idea how he did it. One guard fell; the other aimed his weapon at me, and without thinking I ducked the swinging sword and brought up my knife. I found flesh, for something gave under my blade and the guard gave a sort of grunt. He dropped to one knee, but I did not think he was badly wounded.

We were at the start of the first passage. Turning, Rollo sped off down it, Gewis and I flying along behind. From somewhere near I heard the sound of chanting. As a background to what was happening out here, it was so incongruous that I almost laughed.

The remaining two guards were after us. I could hear the thump of their boots, feel it like a percussion in my body. We ran faster, Rollo twisting and turning through the dim passages with such speed that it was all I could do to keep up. He must have doubled back for I was quite sure we passed one place where several cloisters intersected at least once.

Then we were out in the open, flying through the moonlit gardens and heading straight for the wall. Rollo leapt up the compost heap, turned, caught hold of me and threw me up on top of the wall. Gewis scrambled up beside me and, as Rollo followed, all three of us dropped down on the far side.

'We have to get off the island,' Rollo panted.

'The boat is holed!' wailed Gewis. 'What shall we do?'

We stood there, and nobody said a word. Then in my head I heard my aunt's voice: *Keep your eyes wide open for the chance that will present itself.* She wanted me to see if I could find the secret ways across the fens. I had forgotten all about it till this moment.

Had she known this would happen? *The chance that will present itself.* It sounded as if she had, for here we stood, desperate to get away from men who wanted to kill us, and with no boat, and the ferrymen long gone home for the night, what other choice was there?

But I was afraid! Just when the waters had begun to recede, it had rained again, and once more the sound of hungry lapping could be heard all around the island. And I was expected to find a safe way across the dark water and the deathly, sucking mud...

My aunt had added something else: she had said, *You will not fail.* I trusted her. If she said I could do a task, she was invariably right.

I squared my shoulders, took a deep breath and said, 'Come on. There's a safe way.'

I strode off down the track that led to the water, and, to my surprise, without a word they followed me.

Two things worried me as I hurried along. The first, naturally, was just how I was to go about finding these safe ways. The monks knew, or one or two of them did, for they had betrayed the secret to the Conqueror during the rebellion of 1071. Where did the ways begin though? How was I to find my starting point? In the absence of any other idea, I decided to pace slowly along the water's edge and, using my dowser's sensitivity, wait to see what called out to me. It sounded straightforward and, indeed, usually I had no trouble in putting myself into the light trance that allowed me to pick up the clear and unmistakable signs. But now three lives depended on me, one of them my own, and I was to say the least a little anxious.

Breathe deeply, I heard my aunt say. *Put aside everything else and concentrate. The ways are there and will reveal themselves to you. Be calm.*

Her voice soothed and comforted me as it always did, and I sent her my swift thanks. She was on my mind, in my mind, for the other thing that worried me was that she and Hrype were on the island. I thought – hoped – they were perfectly safe, for Lord Edmund did not know of their existence and had no reason to hunt them down or harm them. And, really, I had no choice. The two guards might have lost our trail for the moment, but I was in no doubt that Lord Edmund had already summoned more men and even now they were fanning out to begin the search. There was just no time to go back, explain to Edild and somehow get Hrype to his feet and fit for a perilous journey across dangerous ground and sinster, treacherous water.

They would understand. I prayed that they would.

Rollo must also have been thinking about Lord Edmund's pursuit. 'How long will this take?' he said, close beside me.

'I don't know.' I paused, not sure how to explain. 'I have to sense where the crossing begins,' I said.

I felt his astonishment flare briefly, but he controlled it. As if he understood that I did not want to be distracted, he simply nodded and fell back to walk beside Gewis.

We had been pacing along the water's edge for some time. Nothing had as yet touched against my mind or my outstretched hands, and I was starting to think that I hadn't been doing it right and would have to start again. I stopped, breathed deeply in and out and made myself relax, from my toes to the crown of my head. I closed my eyes and asked the spirit guardians for help. I summoned my animal guide, and in my mind I thought I saw Fox materialize beside me. His mouth was open, tongue flapping, and it looked as if he were grinning. Then I stretched out my hands, and almost straight away I felt the familiar tingle.

My eyes shot open. For an instant I saw the path over the water lit up by a purplish-blue light, snaking to and fro across the fen. I stared at it, trying to fix it in my mind. I took very careful note of where it began, then I hurried off to the place where we must set out.

Unless you were a dowser, you really wouldn't find it unless someone told you where it was for there was not a thing to mark it out. It was just a stretch of shore, with a meadow and some alders. The slope of the ground was quite gentle and a spit of land led out into the water. Just beyond, in the last place you would expect, the secret way began.

Without pausing I stepped out on to it. The water rose up to my ankles but the ground beneath my feet was firm. That was no surprise, for this part of the shore was normally above the water line. I knew that the going would get progressively more difficult, as indeed it did.

Quite soon we were up to our knees. The water was very cold, but fortunately there was no wind and so its surface was smooth. I paced on, growing familiar now with the sensations coursing up through the palms of my outstretched hands so that I made fewer mistakes. Mistakes were dangerous; the first time my foot had headed down into deep water, it had only been Rollo's quick reaction and his iron-hard hand on my arm that had saved me.

Sometimes I had to stop because I simply did not know which way the path went next. Then I would have to fight my terror and swiftly turn my thoughts from the image of the three of us lost in the middle of the fen, unable to go forward or back, standing there until weakness and cold made us collapse into the dark water and drown.

No. It really was best not to think of that.

It seemed to take hours. My two companions

could not actively help me for only I could find the way, but they did not complain once, and I was strengthened by their obvious faith in me. Whether or not I deserved it remained to be seen.

Shortly before dawn, when the first pale glow was just beginning to appear in the east, I came to a complete halt. I tried to calm myself, closing my eyes and asking the spirits to guide me. Fox was puzzled – I had a glimpse of him casting this way and that. In my mind I saw the dark water before me. No helpful lights shone to show me the secret path. I did not know what to do.

We stood there for a long time.

Then I felt a light touch on my arm. Opening my eyes, I turned to see Rollo. He was smiling. Slowly he raised his hand and pointed.

I followed the direction of his arm and I understood. The light was waxing strongly now – it was going to be a lovely day – and I saw what he had seen.

The reason why I could no longer make out the path was because I didn't need to. Firm ground rose up before us.

We had made it.

I wish I'd had some warning. I wish I'd had the time, at some point in that extraordinary night, to think it through. As it was, he took me totally by surprise and the devastation hit me before I could get up the smallest, feeblest defence.

Gewis had thrown himself on his back on the damp grass, his arm over his eyes, and I could see that he was shaking. The crossing of the fens had cost him dear. I was about to go over to offer him comfort when Rollo caught my hand and led me a few paces away. Then he put his arms around me, pulled me against him and kissed me.

The kiss was hard and it went on for a long time. I had never before experienced the sensations that coursed through me, and all I could think as I melted into him was: so this is what it's like. I felt my heart leave me to join with his. I wanted to bed him there and then. I knew I loved him.

He broke away. He stood staring down at me, his dark eyes fierce, the pupils wide. I reached up my hand to trace the pale scar that ran through his eyebrow and, reminded, gasped as I recalled the wound on his neck.

He read my thought. 'It's all right, I've bandaged it,' he said shortly. I knew from his tone that he did not want me to look. Gently, he touched my cheek. 'You'll have a scar, Lassair,' he said softly.

I had forgotten my own wound. Now, reminded, it throbbed and I gasped at the pain. I would have to get Edild to stitch it, and that would make it hurt even more than it did now.

I managed a smile. 'We'll both be scarred then.'

He held my shoulders. He was staring at me with such intensity that I was afraid. I opened my mind to his, and what I read made me gasp in pain. *'No,'* I whispered.

'Yes,' he said gently.

'But—' I did not know how to deal with it. He

342

was going, he was leaving me, with no promise of a return. I did not need to ask why. He had come on a mission, and the man who had sent him wanted to know the outcome. Rollo had no choice. I realized that I did not know what that outcome was. I thought back to the moment when Lord Edmund had slumped to the ground.

'Is he dead?' I said, my words barely audible.

'Yes.'

Of course he was. Rollo was a professional. He would not have left his enemy alive to threaten the king again.

I stared at the man I loved and who I was about to lose. I held my head high and swallowed the sob that rose in my throat. I looked straight into his eyes, and he looked back into mine. I saw then that he loved me too.

Then he turned and, falling quickly into an efficient, ground-covering lope, set off across the grass. Soon he was out of sight.

I went about the many tasks I had to achieve in the next few days with quiet efficiency. It was good to have things to do.

Gewis and I made our way back to Aelf Fen. The crossing of the fens had landed us some eight miles north-west of the village, and as soon as I had worked out where we were it was relatively easy to trudge on home. We were welcomed with anxious solicitude by my family, and it was good to be in dry clothes that were not caked with black mud. Gewis ate as if he was half-starving. I had no appetite.

Gewis did not seem to know what to do. He

343

was still afraid that the Wessex faction would come for him and force him into the role they had planned for him, and even when I revealed to him that Lord Edmund was dead he was not reassured.

'Give him time,' my father said wisely. I had told him the whole story, although I had mentioned Rollo only briefly. 'He's suffered several shocks in a short time, and he's lost his mother. He can stay with us for a while – our own village carpenter can find jobs for him – and, when he's ready, he can think about his future.'

So that was Gewis dealt with.

I was about to return to Ely to find Edild and Hrype when they turned up in Aelf Fen. Edild had hired a boatman, who had brought them almost all the way, and a farmer had carried Hrype the last few miles on his cart. Now Hrype was safely at home with Froya tending him.

I did not like to dwell on how Edild felt about that. Her feelings for Hrype were her secret, hers and his. If they could manage to conceal their true feelings and smile about it, I had no business interfering.

Sibert came home.

I don't know what he and Hrype said to each other. Again, that is between them. I am almost certain that they did not tell Froya that Sibert now knew the truth about his parents. Knowing her as I do – and I admit I don't know her all that well – I don't think she is the sort of woman who could receive a blow like that and not show it in her demeanour. She's a nervy type and life's